Disclaimer

This is piece of fiction, all events are fictitious. Whilst real names have been used in parts of the novel, this is only to add an aspect of realism for the reader. People named are in no way associated with the events written about in the novel these are figments of the author.

This novel contains subjects of an Adult nature and graphic scenes of violence.

Copyright 2015 David Bewley ©

The Diamond Seat. By David Bewley.

The year is 1998, and John Bennet is the principle behind a company that is dedicated to the sport of motor racing.

John started his racing career as a sixteen year old in the amateur sport of Karting in the late sixties. During this time he found that he had flair, in both racing the machines and building them. Following a successful year when he was eighteen, he moved out of Karts, and into single seater racing cars. From there he moved through the various Formula, from Formula Ford, Formula Three, and then Formula 3000. However he was destined never to make it to Formula One as a driver.

It was whilst driving in Formula 3000 that he suffered a serious road accident, in a motorway accident. In the accident he almost lost his left hand, it was only through the very skilled work of the surgeons at St James Hospital in Leeds, that they managed to save the hand It did however bring an early end to his career as a racing driver. For a while he went back to his routes in Karting. He developed and built chassis for the sport. He wasn't however satisfied with just building and selling the equipment. So he started up a team, this allowed him to develop a flair for management.

As success came he moved the team on through into cars. Eventually the team was running cars across the entire single seater car racing classes, in the UK championships. They eventually branched out further into the international world of Formula 3000. This satisfied his desires for a while, but he still had the dream of joining the elite Formula One.

Gerry Watts met John by chance at one of the Formula 3000 races at Dijon in France. At the time John was forming his plans for the future. Gerry had never driven a racing car on a circuit. Though he had competed in hill climbing.

His interest in the sport was more from a design and conceptual angle. He had an Engineering Degree gained at Aston University in the mid seventies. On graduation he had joined the design team at British Leyland. During this time he discovered motor sport, but not relishing the cut and thrust of circuit racing he moved into hill climbing. Using his contacts through Leyland he built a number of cars over the next few years. The cars were successful, but he soon discovered that his skills lay not in the driving but in design and building. He took up an opportunity to work for Reynard who is a British company supplying chassis into many of the worlds racing teams.

It was during one of the races that he happened upon John Bennet, who Gerry had known as a customer. They had discussed John's plans, and between them had developed their plans to convert Westfield Engineering into a Formula One team.

Vanessa Plat was in many ways an enigma. She came from a very wealthy background her father had been *a* high ranking officer in the Army, and was now in his retirement a land owner, and country gent. She had studied at the LSE gaining an honors degree in Economics. However following her graduation she decided to follow the family tradition, and joined the army. It was in the army that she discovered her flair for covert work. For a while she was seconded to the Special Branch, but after a year she suddenly seemed to leave the service. The reason for this was never disclosed. However there were a number of rumors flying around, to do with sexual matters, but non were ever proved

For a while it seemed as if she had gone off at a tangent to the world she had just left, and spent about six months working as a stripper, and dancer, working around some of the seedier clubs of London. This she enjoyed, she got a kick out of exhibitionism. However she said to friends that it didn't satisfy her intellectual needs. Following her quitting the circuit a number of drug busts were successfully made around those same clubs.

She then formed her own advertising and public relations company using contacts through the country set. It was through this company that she met John Bennet. It didn't take long for John to entice Vanessa into Westfield. She said she was intrigued by the world he described to her. Once John Bennet and Gerry Watts had made their decision to move into Formula one, and John had created the new arm of his racing empire Vanessa joined the team as Marketing and PR Director. It wasn't until the team had been running for some months that she actually, joined them at the Wakefield site. She managed to fulfill all of her duties to the team through her own company.

Prologue.

Melbome Park had fallen silent following the cacophony of noise from that afternoons Grand Prix. The race had contained all the usual excitement, and drama of such an event. McLaren had come out the victors. For Ferrari it had been a mixed race. Their number one driver and car had failed after only a few laps, whilst their number two driver had finished behind their main rivals.

The spectator areas had an air of desolation, the light breeze blowing the left over remnants of litter about the stands. There was more activity in the paddock areas behind the pits. Mechanics and transport drivers were finishing packing the tones of equipment used during the last three days of the Grand Prix weekend.

As darkness fell a shadowy figure moved between the two large transporters belonging to the Ferrari team. He approached the middle of one of the trailers and slid underneath. Behind one of the many boxes slung underneath the trailer there was a compartment that couldn't be seen from the side of the trailer. It measured only one cubic foot. He dropped the lid down and removing a package from underneath his outer jacket he slipped into the compartment. The package only weighed a few kilos, but was probably worth as much as one of the cars that was inside the trailer above his head. Very carefully he made sure that the lid was secured, and the opening smeared with the road dirt and grease from the area around the hidden compartment. Later that evening along with a convoy of all the other twenty two team's transporters it left the paddock on the start of its long journey home.

Four days after leaving Australia the transporters arrived back at their base in Italy. Once again after darkness had fallen the package was retrieved from its hiding place ready for the next part of its continuing journey to Amsterdam where the goods could be sold.

Chapter 1.

There was the sound of escaping air as the seal was broken around the door of the pressure chamber. The heavy door was slowly opened to revel to the waiting group of engineers and technicians for the very first time the results of over 2000 hours of slow, detailed work. Time seemed to be standing still whilst the door was fully opened and secured into place. Great care was being taken, neither of them wanted the door to swing back and damage their master piece.

The two technicians who had secured the door into place stepped cautiously into the chamber towards the dark shape, which was to become the next contender into the high powered world of Formula One. This the first chassis from the small but highly skilled and motivated work force at Westfield Engineering Chris Watts and Dave Brian were the pressure chamber technicians with whom the responsibility lay for the loading and monitoring of the process to cure and harden the carbon fibre structure which had the simple name of WE001. As the two of them wheeled the two metre black chassis out into the world for the first time the group burst into spontaneous applause.

John Bennet the founder and driving force of Westfield Engineering walked forward and stood next to the chassis, with one hand resting on the top of the tub almost caressing the object as though it was a soft silky breast, he started to speak to the gathering. His voice was soft and almost emotional. "This is a day I have dreamed of; it has taken two long and hard years to change what was a dream into reality! Can only marvel at the time and effort that has been spent by each and every person stood here. We have all experienced highs and lows during that time. At some tunes it seemed that we had stepped into a never ending spiral of despondency, but behind it all we had the driving force of the sweat smell of success and the desire to feel that intoxicating atmosphere of noise, and smells of the pit lanes around this world. This is the first milestone of many to get us to that position".

What wasn't said by John at that stage was the amount of work still to be completed, not only by his team at headquarters, but also by himself. The task that they had set themselves was not only to build and contest an F 1 car in the 1999 season, but to also emulate Ferrari to also build their own engines. The design that they had chosen was also radical in that they had decided to use a flat horizontal opposed ten cylinder unit with an integral seven speed gearbox. In order to first of all achieve their first objective to just build the cars for the season he had to raise twenty five million dollars. It would then take at least a further twelve and a half million dollars in the first season to run the team. He had yet to finish raising the initial sponsorship to build the cars although he was getting closer to the goal he only required five million dollars more. The team had also decided to do this the hard way by not using tobacco sponsorship.

If the five million dollars wasn't forthcoming initially he knew that they could continue but they would have to cut back on some areas of design and testing, but would mean that qualification would be difficult in the early races. None of his team wanted start the season with all the long hall costs and then to have the pressures from their sponsors for not qualifying. Still this problem was 9 months away. He put those thoughts to the back of his mind.

Over at the other side of Westfield's 250000 square foot engineering and design facility, which is based on the Junction 62 development between Leeds and Wakefield, was the engine build and test area. This was housed in a secure, soundproofed and atmospherically controlled area. This was not only for the comfort of the rest of the work force to protect them from the noise generated by a screaming 3000 litre 800 bhp running at 18000 rpm, but also to ensure that there was little chance of any dirt or dust finding its way into the assembly.

The whole of the assembly area looked like an operating theatre. The area was split up into 4 bays, in the centre of the bay stood a fixture upon which an engine block could be mounted. Surrounding that fixture there were stands that could hold all the individual assemblies awaiting the final assembly into the engine block Currently only one of the bays had any work in progress, an engine stood on its own with all its bottom end i.e. the crank shaft and con rods and pistons in place but both head assemblies were missing. This was due problems that had been encountered in earlier testing programs, all work had ceased on build-up's until a successful test had been carried out.

To anyone looking around the assembly area they would have thought that nothing happened or was happening, the place was deserted. It appeared to be left in a time warp. There were however 15 Engineers involved in the engine program, four were at home resting following an all night rebuild of the one and only working engine, and the other nine were currently crowding around the telemetry from the engine to be tested.

The engines chief designer Gerry Watts and the electronics designer Ian Smith were at the front of the crowd. They were not having a good test session. The engine on test or that should have been on test was flatly refusing to start. Both were aware that John would be calling by once he had finished his troops rallying speech with the first chassis tub completion. He would also be accompanied by their PR director Vanessa Plat. Whilst Vanessa had been with the team for a almost six months she had spent most of her time away from base, arranging sponsorships and funding for the seasons ahead. She wasn't a 'racing person' but was from a society background with the figure and personal touches to match it was hoped that she could twist the rich and famous to part with their cash. It was critical to make a good impression on her at this test. Both wanted her to be able go away with a simple message that all was well on track, and that the car would be powered by the best engine money could provide. The fact was that at this stage of its development things were not going well. This wasn't to be unexpected all the other engines used within Fl were well proven and had had many years of development Westfield's engine had only been in existence for 2 months in a form that could be run.

"How's it going?" said John from the back of the group.
"Problems" Said Gerry.

"The bastard wont fire at all" was Ian's response. "It looks like the management system has blown a chip again. I'll have to get the other unit from my bench. I've spent all bleeding night repairing it from yesterday's failure."

Vanessa looked at John with a worried look in her deep green eyes and said "I thought you reported the engine problems were behind us now. I've told Microsoft the cars will be in a run able position by the launch date."

"Well yes I may have said that but you must understand that we are pushing the internal combustion engines technology forward with this unit. There is no way can you expect a perfect run each time. That's why we must run a comprehensive test program. Please excuse me I must speak with Ian and Gerry." With that John left Vanessa standing at the back of the group of technicians, and walked over towards the electronics assembly bench at the back of the workshop.

"Shit" said Ian he was busy running a test on the failed box of tricks.

"Have you found a problem" asked Gerry,

"I think it's because I've had to jury rig the box, we haven't yet got the go ahead for the rest of the controls that this thing has been designed to take, because of that I think the chips are being overloaded."

John came up to the pair and said "I thought you had found the problems from yesterdays failure, we cannot continue like this, Vanessa is important to us, if she gets the wrong impression of the work situation and the development stage then we can kiss good buy to any future funding from her set."

"Look John we know that" replied Gerry 'but until you decide how you want to play the driver aids thing than Ian cannot complete the engine management package, and since you wont allocate any more funding we cannot build a stop gap system. That's where the problems are occurring."

"Well what else can you two do your supposed to be the best in the business, so fix the problem, anyway what is wrong." Said John as he started to calm down.

"Its simple either we have duff set of chips, or the power supply isn't adjusting it's self to the actual requirement and is burning the chips out. Without the engine management in place then I cannot get the bleeder to even fire." Was Ian's simple reply.

"John can we talk." Said Gerry pointing towards his office. "Ok." Was Johns reply, already walking towards the door.

There was a lighter side to the test area or that's what it seemed judging by the laughter corning from the group of engineers stood around Vanessa. Bees around a honey pot came to mind. She was obviously enjoying the attention. Vanessa was well known in the circle that she mixed with for being rather a soft touch, and a bit of a flirt. Although that was only within her own circle. She would never entertain any of those gathered around her at present, but she didn't mind the attention. Hence her general choice of clothing, very flouncy and sheer. Today she had chosen a pale green blouse with a matching short tight skirt. She had done her usual and not worn a bra under the blouse. In the cooled atmosphere of the assembly area her nipples were pressing hard against the soft material, and her breasts were moving gently under the cloth with each turn of her body.

The engineers grouped around her were making her move frequently to further enhance their own enjoyment to her closeness to them.

Just before John entered Gerry's office he looked back at the group and shouted, "come on you lot there must be work to be done elsewhere. Vee come and join us." There was a general air of jovial discontent as the group broke up.

The Side of Gerry's office was not quite what would have been expected of a chief designer. It had an air of disarray about it. Simple line sketches scattered about the desk and chairs, broken parts of engines seamed to be scattered all around. Each one however was labeled with its failure time run time and which version of that design, also why the failure had occurred.

Vanessa entered the office with her normal air of utter self confidence that all males wanted her and she knew it.

Vee I wish you would wear something less revealing when

you're in the workshops. These guys are feed on red meat each morning."

"They were only looking at my tits", said Vee "what's wrong with that."

"All I'll get from for the rest of the day is comments about them. We need them concentrating on their work not your body. Anyway I'm sorry for the set back I had hoped that the test would have been more representative of where we are currently with the development program."

"Are these problems normal ?" asked Vanessa

"Well" said Gerry" we have been experiencing some of late. In the earlier days of engine testing we had some good results. The Dyno tests were very promising, we made changes and some big leaps forward. You know" said Gerry with a very thoughtful look in his eyes, "its not easy developing an engine that uses ceramics and carbon fibre in place of metals, for pistons valves and rods. We feel that in order to compete with the big boys we must push the barriers forward."

"Why do you need this management system that Ian's working on ?" Said Vanessa, then quickly "Please forgive my lack of understanding."

"Well an engine that powers your car in the days of carburetors just had a simple timing device to create a spark at the right time to ignite the fuel mixture. Once engines moved forward to injection systems then we needed to tell the engine when to squirt the fuel in for ignition. That was originally done mechanically, but then to enhance the properties of the engine if it was done electronically you could both improve the performance and the efficiency of the same unit, also by using electronics you could constantly monitor any number of aspects of what was been asked of the engine at any one time and therefore constantly adjust the mixture, the amount of fuel, the timing of the spark. This will then improve the overall performance of the engine for a given engine capacity."

"H'm I didn't want a thesis on the internal combustion engine, but that does help I think." Said Vanessa still looking puzzled. "So Ian's unit will just improve the performance."

"No it's required to run the engine fully. We cannot even get it to fire without that or some form of management system. During the startup we input a different requirement map to allow the engine to rev up to about 4000 RPM at that point the map will change to allow the engine to go up to its full RPM limit of 18000. The map change is required due in the main to its low reciprocating mass. Without it the engine will not continue running."

"Ok I give in ." she said "I'll stick to what I know best and leave you to all the technical stuff. I must go and make some calls. It looks like you need me to raise the funds anyway." With that Vanessa left leaving Gerry and John to gaze at her neat behind as she left the office.

"Phew" said Gerry "I don't know where you found her, but she's worth a million bucks just being here."

"Yes well I hope she does it I'm not the bothered how either at this stage."

"I'll bet you a tenner that she's not wearing knickers either" said Gerry laughing.

"Ok you're on, but you find out not me Fran would kill me for even thinking that. She's peed of enough with me for taking her on. I'm sure she thinks she screwed me to get the job".

Chapter 2

In a hotel in the centre of Paris a group of powerful team owners were having a secret meeting. The meeting was revolving around the fact that in their opinion the world of F 1 was becoming far too crowded, 2 new teams had declared their intention of joining the ranks of the current 11 teams for the next season. This would once again put pressure on the now crowded qualifying sessions, and create the need for even more technology advances. Whilst nobody would admit to the outside world that there was a form a cartel in operation within the current strong teams of Fl. This group was it. More importantly they were worried about money, or more to the point the lack of it. With tobacco sponsorship being withdrawn the teams were fighting to find fresh industries to enter the game. Another two teams in the game wouldn't help this situation. It had already being announced to the world that Microsoft would be backing the Westfield bid as principle sponsor. Microsoft had being on the short list of a number of current teams. This being one of the world's strongest and most financially secure companies who hadn't up until now ventured into the game.

"We must find away of slowing down the development phase of Westfield and Conoco (a Canadian team). If both don't show to the world that they can deliver their sponsors will pull out. More importantly we must ensure Westfield fail. That will release Microsoft, we can then agree to give Microsoft overall sponsorship of F1 So that we all take a share." Said the Fabrice Bleriot the Renault boss. He seemed to be taking the lead of the group of four.

Hisho Takkagi who was representing Honda said" I agree they must be slowed down, but it is doubtful this late in the run up that we will be able to make any financial changes for next year. I thought Westfield's bid had been faltered by us not all not agreeing to supply customer engines to them. None of us dreamed that they would decide to build their own."

"OK how will we do it." Said Kurt Langer of BMW, " Whatever is done must never be traceable back to us. Bernie would ensure that none of could ever enter into Fl again. Not only that but the world would turn against our products, it would be ruin."

Only Gianni Lorenzo remained quiet out of the group, he was quietly smiling to himself and thinking that he had already won the first battle with his contemporaries. Through his connections with the Italian Mafia he had managed to side line an order for components destined for Westfield and replace then with his own faulty batches.

Fabrice asked Kurt "How do you propose to stop the bid?"

"Well" said Kurt "We first of all must ensure that between us and the other teams that we control, sign up all the promising drivers as either Fl drivers or test drivers, with clauses within their contracts that prevents them driving for either Westfield or Conoco."

"That isn't as easy as you may think" said Giaimi "There are at least 200 drivers in the world capable of driving, and with the required license. The salary cost alone is probative. The only way is to prevent them from testing early enough. That way Bernie himself will call a halt to their bids, he will not allow any team into F1 that he believes will not make a good enough show of themselves. He will not allow F 1 to be ridiculed."

"Yes I agree" said Hisho "the easiest way is to tie up the major suppliers. We can do that by ensuring that they are too busy with our orders to take on further work from the other two."

"I don't mean like that" said Gianni "let them place the orders and be invoiced for the goods. They will then be committed to payment. We then either delay that delivery or exchange it for something that doesn't quite meet the standard."

"How" said Kurt

"Leave that to me and my contacts" replied Gianni "In fact we have already started" he said with a grin. "The first load of power supplies delivered to Westfield have the wrong output rating. All will seem to be OK until they are built up in the systems. The effect will then be to burn out the more expensive chips. A simple but both costly and time consuming problem whilst they conduct test and reorder the items. Good eh."

"Yes very good Gianni. Can this be traced to us asked Fabrice.

"No way" was Gianni's reply.

Chapter 3

"Bollocks" was the shout that came from the electronics bench. Everyone who was still in the workshop at the late hour looked towards Ian. The time was 10 past midnight.

Eric one of the mechanics walked over to Ian and asked him "Wats up mate you balls up anover box of tricks. The Boss ain't goin to be happy wiv you." He said without waiting for a reply.

"I've found the problem. Its not the bleeding chips its the power supplies. The stupid chinks have put the wrong bleeding labels on. The output ratings are double what was ordered. That's why we keep blowing chips." He said angrily. "Wait until I get that pilock of a rep tomorrow. Infact I should ring him now. That would spoil his legover." Said Ian reaching for the phone.

Eric laughed as he walked back towards his work area. At least young Ian's getting a sense of humor at last he thought. (Ian Smith had only graduated from Leeds University last year with an Honors Degree in Advanced Electronics and Telemetry controls.) Therefore he was seen to be a bit green around the collar by the more hardened Fl Engineers and mechanics with whom he was now working with.

Eric said to Jim another mechanic working with Eric on the test engine "listen to this, young Ian's going to upset a rep's night in."

Ian tried the reps home number but fortunately for him there was no reply. "Ha well" said Ian "perhaps it's for the best I'll try him in the morning. Well guys I'm calling it a night, see you two tomorrow."

"Not if we see you first" shouted Jim.

At that moment Vanessa was just finishing her Brandy following a meal with a potential sponsor. She had known the CEO of IDEK a games software publisher for a number of years, James Goodwin. He had married into one of the biggest Land-owning families in the country. Vanessa had been his wife's bridesmaid at their wedding. Although she wouldn't let such a small matter like that get in her way when she could smell success. Or at least she hopped that that was the smell of success. If not she may not be able to carry on with the night. She thought as once again an odor of male pheromones wafted towards her.

"Have you finished the hard sell yet" asked James "or are you going to keep this going all night."

"I may" replied Vanessa "should we continue in the lounge, or should we retire to my room for a night cap."

"You never did waste time did you Vee." Said James with a smile.

"I don't know what you mean." Vee replied innocently getting up and walking to the exit. She thought to herself if Jim follows I've got him. If not Oh well back to the drawing board I suppose. Vanessa was trying to sell space on the front wing and dashboard top of the Westfield cars. The dashboard whilst small was a highly prized position, this was due to the in car camera mounting. Any in car footage would put IDEK into Millions of homes. IDEK were also due to launch a new racing game at the start of the next seasons racing and therefore they were seen as an ideal candidate for sponsorship money. She was hoping to get James to agree to $ 500000 per season with a 2 year minimum deal.

As she neared the door James left his seat and followed her towards the stairs. Good she thought things are starting to look up. At least she thought with a twinkle in her eyes I hope he's looking up when I reach the spiral on the staircase. About half way up the first landing the stairs spiraled round to the left, anybody standing at the bottom of the elegant staircase could get a bit more of a view than they bargained for tonight. As she neared to spiral she checked behind her to make sure he was in the correct position, she adjusted her ascent slightly, then called to him "Jim have you made your mind up." This was only to attract his attention. As he looked up Vanessa spun and slightly leaped up two steps. The result of this was to fuck her dress up, and to make it billow away from her body. James looked up as she called and got a view of her panty less bottom, and into towards her pleasure zone. This made him breakout into and immediate sweat. "Yes" he croaked "I'm coming Vee." More to the point he thought I think I'm too late.

With her display she thought right you bastard I've got you right where I want you. She wasn't looking forward to having him between her legs, but she did want him to sign on the contract. Her only problem was when, he most certainly wouldn't sign tonight and therefore she would end up sleeping with him. That at least would give her some leverage in the morning, and more importantly in the future. She wasn't adverse to using such things as blackmail in any negotiations that may well crop up.

Vee stood at the door to her room, she had made sure that the hotel had placed her in a room closer to the stairs than James. This was one of the reasons she had been picked for the job. She was an excellent negotiator, she was a brilliant planner, and she had fantastic looks go with it.

As James approached her she said "OK what's it to be another Brandy or something else."

At that James grinned and said "thanks Vee but I think I'll turn in on my own tonight. I've got lots to think about. Thanks for a great evening I'll remember it for along time." With that he continued on down the corridor to his own suit.

Shit thought Vee as she entered into her room. She had both a relived look in her eyes, and also a puzzled look. Where did I go wrong? Have I gone wrong? Could we still land this, I thought I had him. Well at least I don't have to be screwed by him tonight.

She slipped the shoulder straps off her dress and let it fall to the floor, and walked naked to the window to draw the curtains. In the gardens below there was a couple walking around the fountain. They caught site of Vanessa standing naked in the backlit window looking out. She stood poised looking out allowing the couple to get a good view of her body, she enjoyed showing off her body to others. She had done a stint on the strip stages around the country for six months before becoming bored. She wanted to put all her talents to better use. She then turned leaving the curtains open and walked to the shower to wash away the evening before climbing into her four poster bed.

James opened the door of his room and stepped inside. A feminine voice said" I'm pleased you escaped that temptress." His wife Angela was lying reading in bed.

"It was a close run thing" said James "She was wearing next to nothing. In fact she gave me a view of her bum and no knickers coming up the stairs."

"The Sex craved minx, and you resisted sweety. Come to bed I'll help you relax."

When Vanessa awoke the next morning she thought OK I'll get him at breakfast, I must pin him down to sign today. She again showered and dressed in a simple pair of tight black riding Jodhpurs and a jumper, again no underwear. She didn't see the point in spending on such things since it only made washing for someone.

She walked into the dining room for breakfast expecting to see James already seated, he was well known for being a creature of habit. He would always eat breakfast at 8.0am and be finished by 8.30am every day. She took *a* table for two in a position where she could see everybody who entered the room. By 8.45 it was clear that he wasn't going to show. She stood up and went to the reception to call his room. The desk clerk said "Miss Plat I've got a message for you from Mr. Goodwin" he reached behind him and took down a large envelope with a message attached. Vanessa said "Thanks" in a disappointed air. She took the envelope from the clerk and glanced at the words. "Thanks for the show last night I hope that you will forgive me for leaving early. I hope that the attached will compensate you.'

With that Vanessa ripped open the envelope and quickly looked at the signature on the bottom of the contact. She whooped with joy. This made the desk clerk jump and look at her startled. "Good news I take it" he said.

"The best" replied Vanessa hurrying away to her room, "Please have my bill ready I'm checking out" she called over her shoulder as she neared the staircase.

Chapter 4

John arrived at the factory early the next morning to be greeted by his engine designer Gerry. "Hi what's up" Said John.

"I got a call from Ian last night. He's found what's been causing the management system failures First I owe you an apology. It wasn't the fact that the system isn't complete. The problem was faulty power supplies. They had the wrong output ratings. Even if we could have completed the whole box we would still have burned the box out."

"So" said John "is it the suppliers that's at fault or did Ian order the wrong ratings."

"The orders were correct I checked them, and I cannot believe that the suppliers got it wrong, Ian will speak to them today. I hope he's calmed down though from last night. It was 1.00am when he rang me. He was boiling at that time."

"OK now we know that it is the power supplies can we work around it."

"Yes even though Ian was throwing the teddy out last night he had already re-jigged the design, in fact he thinks that they may have done us a favor. We have more power to play with on the boards, therefore he believes he can monitor more elements, and speed up the control responses. We will be able to give the driver more aids than before."

"Let me stop you there" Said John quickly "we cannot talk about driver aids they are banned."

"Yes OK let's call them power control systems. They still help the driver to control 500kg of raw power. Without them the thing would be un-drivable."

"We'll agree to disagree on that subject for now, but at no time must you or Ian mention the phrase driver aids to anyone, not even me, understood."

"Fine" agreed Gerry. "Here comes Ian." He said looking round on hearing a car door slam shut.

"Hi genius calmed down a bit I see" said Gerry. "I've been filling John in on your discovery."

"Which one" Said Ian "I'm full of them I must come across 10 a day, Shit what's that," exclaimed Ian jumping at the sound of tyres screaming tortuously as a car sped into the car park at a terrific speed. The car braked to a halt perfectly positioned into one of the marked parking slots, the front bumper inches away from the side of the building.

"I think we have found one of our drivers for next season." Remarked Gerry as Vanessa stepped out of the car. "Can you imagine the racing suit though. Semi see through and cut to kill. Come on young Ian we have work to do she'll only put you off for the day Grit" He laughed walking into the building dragging Ian with him.

"What's the panic Vee?" asked John as she hurried up to him.

"I've got it I've got it," she shouted

"I don't think we all want to know that" said John with a hint of sarcasm.

"Pillock" she said "I don't mean the clap or anything. I've got James Goodwin's signature on the contract. He's going to pay us $750000 for the 1st two seasons, with an option on the 3rd depending on success. That's more than we bargained for."

"Bloody fantastic" said John grasping Vanessa around the waist and giving her a kiss full on the mouth.

"I hope you don't reward all your execs in the same way" she said.

"Come on up to my office we'll contact our legal agents and then have a drink to celebrate".

They both walked through reception saying good morning to Anne the receptionist. Who said "I take you've brought good news Vanessa." She gave Vanessa a slightly disapproving look once she had passed from her field of view. Anne didn't think Vanessa was the right type of person who should be working for Westfield. Her flamboyance and her passed history as a stripper alone should have ruled her out.

"Well" said Vanessa once inside John's office "Miss iron knickers was as warm as ever."

"Ignore her, she's a good receptionist she manages to keep all the unwanted away from us." Said John. "Right what about that drink."

"No I think I'll pass this time I want to check the contract fully and take to our solicitors." Said Vanessa leaving Johns office for her own.

John left on his own decided that he would have a drink to celebrate. Just as he finished pouring the whisky into his glass Gerry burst into his office.

"Where's the fire" asked John

"We've been broken into" gasped Gerry "my office has been ransacked."

"How can you tell" joked John not allowing Gerry's mood to destroy his good feeling so early in the day.

"Its no joke" said Gerry "the place has been turned over. I've asked Anne to call the Police and to pull last night's security tapes."

"Right is anything missing. Who was the last to leave last night?"

"I cannot see anything missing but somebody's been through my desk, and there are signs of an entry through the rear store area."

"I want a list of who was working late last night. Also a list of what was in or on your desk. We must try to establish what anybody could have been looking for."

"None of the engine designs are in my office. There's lots of bits lying around, all failures. I suppose someone could piece bits together, all the secret stuff is locked well out of the way. I've already checked the security vault that hasn't been touched. We only had three working late last night. Ian, Eric James and Jim Gilbrate. Ian said he left before Eric and Jim. Neither of them have arrived in yet."

"Go work on that list they must have been after something. What's more worrying is that they must have found it in your office." "Why ?"

"Because nowhere else seems to have been touched."

"True, I'll go and have a think."

John picked up the phone "Anne will you call Eric James and Jim Gilbrate, tell them I want to see them both in my office in half an hour. Oh and if the Police arrive before they do don't say anything to them."

John then dialed Vanessa's number "Can you come back in please Vee."

"Sure one minute." Was the reply.

John then started to try to think what could have been the motive. Why didn't the alarm system go off. Could it have been an inside job, although he couldn't believe Eric or Jim would have got caught up in anything to spoil Westfield's plans. He had known both for years.

"Vee" John said as Vanessa opened his office door, "We were broken into last night,.."
"Shit" she uttered "Why ?" was her next comment.

"Will you check that none of your files are missing. Would you know if any have been tampered with or disturbed. I can only think they were after information. Somebody is worried about us."

Vanessa left immediately and returned to her office.

John checked around his desk, he had a policy of not leaving anything out, he ensured that the last job of his on a night was to completely clear his desk and ensure that all sensitive documents were locked into the safe . The safe hadn't been touched. He then left his office and walked down to Ian's work area, he must forget the break in for now, he had about 20 minutes before Eric and Jim arrived.

"Ian how long will it take you to rebuild the control systems."

"I should be complete by late this afternoon, now that I know what was wrong. I'm more annoyed with myself for not figuring it out quicker."

"Don't worry about that son, just get it working. By the way what time did you leave last night ?"

"About 12.30 I think. Eric and Jim were just finishing off the engine recheck. They were going to lockup I think."

"You aren't sure then."

"Well no as I said they were just finishing when I left."

"OK I'll let you get on."

Blast John thought I bet they didn't set the alarm system. Or was the intruder already in the building before they left. Yes John thought that could be it. Anybody spying on us would not be expecting us to be working late 2 nights on the trot not so far away from the start of the season.

Just then Vanessa came down and said "I think somebody has been through my desk. The file where I keep the potential sponsors records in was upside down. The only information that could be got from that file is that we were considering them however. I don't even put a status report in there. More worrying is that the launch file has also being tampered with. That has all our plans for the Silverstone launch.

"Fine at least we know that whoever it was is aware of our approach and who we may be considering for sponsorship. The launch we'll just have to be on our guard."

Anne called John to say that both Eric and Jim were just leaving their cars in the car park, and that the Police hadn't yet arrived.

At the same time as Anne called John a swarthy looking man was seated in his top floor office above a Pizza restaurant in the centre of Wakefield he had just finished putting together his report of his late night excursion into Westfield's building. Whilst he hadn't taken anything from the building he had copied a number of documents. In the main he was looking for supplier lists and contacts. He had been lucky enough to find a number of order confirmations which again he had copied. All of this was in his report which he was now busy faxing to his associate in Milan. The people he dealt with in Milan had contacts all over the world most were not set up as this one was from Italian restaurants. Their specialty was industrial espionage. They would normally sell their findings to the highest bidder, but in this case they had been commissioned by Gianni Lorenzo of Ferrari. Any tifosi would work for free for that organisation. He had just seen Schumacher win for his beloved team in Canada. He had also just completed some work at the McLaren factory in Woking. Again his secret work within the factory had gone well. He hoped that his contribution would help the beloved red cars to beat the silver and black menace powered by the Teutonic goose stepping maniacs from Germany. Or at least that was how Alfons saw them. He had bad memories from his childhood in northern Italy following the Second World War. He didn't blame the Allies for his family's hardship but the fascists from both his own country but more so from the north in Germany. He did however ignore the fact that Schumacher was German. He drove for an Italian team, the only team, and therefore was Italian.

"Wats all the bloody panic for ?" Asked Eric as he walked into John's office with Jim.

"When you left last night what did you do ?" John Asked. "I took Jim home," said Eric innocently.

"No what did you do when leaving the building pratt,"

Jim said "I went to set the alarm and lock up whilst Eric went for his car. He brought it to the door to pick me up."

"So your sure you set the alarm." Asked John.

"Yeh" was Jim's response "Why ?"

"Never mind just yet, did you see anything unusual ?" asked John.

"Nah," answered Eric "I Don't fink so We just left quickly didn't fink to look around."

"Why do you say that" asked John furrowing his brow.

"Wat do you mean John, we just left the building. It's obvious that somots up or yer woodn't be askin us questions."

"Yes OK I'm sorry if it sounds as if I'm accusing you, I'm not it's just that we had a breakin last night."

"Owt gone ?" asked Jim,

"Not that we can find, will both of you please check around your work station, I want to make absolutely sure that we haven't had anything nicked for when the Police finally arrive."

"Yep OK come on Eric before he accuses us of nicking the crown jewels."

John decided to continue his tour around the factory for the rest of the morning. He hoped that later in the day he would be able to witness a successful test of their engine. In the morning he had a meeting with their principle sponsors Microsoft and Hitachi, this wasn't contractual but a meeting to discuss a new telemetry system they were jointly working on. He would need Ian at that meeting, and he desperately wanted to give them both good news on the power plant.

As John walked around the factory, there was an air of activity. In the lamination shop 2 more tubs were nearing completion and a fourth was about halfway there. Side pods and engine covers were all being laid up in the moulds, along with hundreds of small covers and panels, all form carbon fibre. The first nose cone was nearing completion, some work still needed to be completed in the wind tunnel to finalise the initial launch design. John new that the design used at the launch would not be the design that would be on the car at the end of the season. In fact they would more than likely have a different one for each venue. The more he toured and spoke to his engineers and mechanics the more John forgot about the problems at the start of the day.

By the end of the morning Tub WE002 was ready for the chamber, Chris and Dave were loading the mould onto its mounting, they were also keen to ensure that the engine cover and both side pods were in place before closure. It would take 24 hours under 4 atmospheres and 200 degrees heat to cure the components. Westfield had two chambers the main one for all the large items and a much smaller one for the hundreds of much smaller pieces required to build a Formula One racing car.

Chapter 5

It was late in the afternoon before Ian was finally happy with the electronics module. He had run a full power diagnostics check on the module. All the chips and eproms had stood up. All that he needed to do was to down load the engine test map form his lap top once the module had been connected to the engine.

The engine was already installed in the test house the cooling system was rigged and bled. The exhaust extraction was in place and fuel lines primed ready.

"At last said" Eric "The bloody Genius has arrived. I wanted an early finish today."

"Well get on with it," replied Ian as he handed the module over to Eric. "Stop moaning and install the dam thing."

Eric took the module and placed into its mounting on the test control panel and simply clipped in the special 50 station plug. Ian had powered up his lap top and plugged it into the input socket on the module, he selected the test program and said "Gentlemen start your engines."

"Haven't we got a comedian," said John as he walked up.

Eric pressed the starter button on the console. The air starter engaged in to back of the dynamometer and whined has it spun the engine up to its starting RPM. The electronic module triggered the fuel injection system and the ignition system simultaneously. There was a sudden increase in the noise level coming from the sound enclosure. Even though the engine was separated from the factory the noise could be heard throughout. All work stopped to listen.

The test parameters set were to take the engine up to fifty percent of its intended rev limit under load from the dyno. They would run the test for only 20 minutes today allow the engine to stand overnight and strip her down tomorrow.

"I'm still worried about the cooling and the lubrication." Said Gerry to John. "Nobody yet knows how either will react to the Carbon fibre casing under heat."

"When are you discussing the lubrication with Q8." Asked John.

Q8 were the fuel and lubrication suppliers, whilst they had been involved with Fl in previous years they hadn't come across any team trying what Westfield are doing. This was a big unknown for both of them.

"They are coming next week, by then I will have the results of this series of tests." Replied Gerry.

Vanessa walked up to the group and said "Wow what a wonderful sound, why are the exhaust glowing ?" she asked. Both banks of five pipes were starting to glow a deep red.

"That's nothing yet love" said Eric "when she's up to full throttle they'll be glowing bright red to yellow."

"A bye product of all the power that's being generated is noise and heat." Explained Gerry. "Most of the heat is being absorbed by the water and the oil. The noise is muffled by the exhaust, but we don't cool the exhaust pipes and therefore you can see the heat that's been generated. We've only been running her for 10 Minutes."

At the end of the 20 minute test the engine was slowed and then the ignition was turned off. The engine stopped instantly.

"Is that right" asked Vanessa worried.

"Yes it's ok" replied John. "With no fly wheel on these engines they don't store up power like an ordinary car engine, so they just stop."

"Good test guys and gal let's call it a day in here. You can get of home Eric I'll shut up shop." Said Gerry.

"Ian are you ready for tomorrow ?" asked John.

"As good as ever boss." Replied Ian "I'll do a bit more at home tonight then hopefully they will be able to give me enough information to allow me to complete the proposed telemetry package. Goodnight all." He said leaving to clear away his station before heading home.

John, Vanessa and Gerry headed off towards Johns office, when Anne called John on his cordless phone. "Police have arrived where do you want to see them," asked Anne.

"Show them to my office we'll meet them there," replied John.

Come on you two you may as well join me."

Outside Johns office stood a Police constable, he was looking at a number of prints of racing shots over the history of the sport.

"How do you do constable I'm John Bennet the Chief Executive, This is Vanessa Plat Pr and Marketing and Gerry Watts our Designer and Technical Director. Come on in to my office." He said walking through the door. "Do you want a drink or anything, take a seat." John continued hurriedly.

"No thank you Sir I'm Constable Smith, I understand you've reported a break in."

"We did at 8.0am this morning Constable." Said Gerry he was pissed off that it had taken all day for somebody to arrive.

"Sorry about that Sir but unfortunately we prioritise calls, industrial calls take a low priority I'm afraid. So What's gone missing." "Nothing that we can find Constable." Said John.

"So what makes you think you've had a break in Sir."

"My office had been disturbed, some of the papers on my desk were not where they should have been." Replied Gerry.

"Also my files were disturbed in my office." Said Vanessa.

"We are having our security contractors check the security tapes. They were collected this morning. I've been promised the results by this evening." Said John.

"OK Sir, I'll file a report on the matter but don't hold your breath. It looks as if it's just somebody looking around. If nothings been stolen then we can't do much."

"If we find a good image of who ever came in do you want that?" asked Gerry looking for some help.

"I'll attach it to the file but that's all I can do" Said the constable.

"Don't you want to see the point of the break in ?" asked Vanessa.

"No thanks it won't be of any help. Do you want the crime prevention officer to call, he may be able to give you some advice. Although you do seem to have good security here."

"No," said John "it won't be of any help." He continued with some sarcasm. This was lost on the Constable. "Let me show you out."

John got up and escorted the Constable down stairs to reception. He said his good byes and returned to his office.

"Bloody waste of time." Retorted Gerry as John re-entered.

"Is that what we pay our rates for, some dam help." Vanessa said angrily "I think I'll talk to Bobby and see what he can do. The Bobby she meant was a nickname she had for the Chief Constable of Yorkshire.

"No leave it for now Vee. It looks like no harms been done. We've had a good test today." Said John. "OK what's on your schedule for racking in more cash."

Vee replied "Well as you know Microsoft and IDEK are on board. Microsoft are not wanting us to put unrelated names on the car, they also would like the cars to be in their colours with the Windows Logo. We have a number of non cash generating sponsors who will supply goods and equipment, such as Q8, Koni, Bridgestone and Bosch. Whilst your speaking to Hitachi technical people tomorrow I'm seeing their Marketing Director Europe. I think I can squeeze some money out of him. Also I've managed to get a number of donations from some of the landed gentry, for services rendered so they say." Vanessa finished with a twinkle.

"How far short are we John." Asked Gerry.

"With the IDEK deal in the bag still about 4 Million I'm hoping that with a good day tomorrow, and with the fact that Microsoft have expressed a desire to not only principle but the Team to be Westfield Microsoft then I can twist them into coughing up more cash. Vee's talents are less likely to work on any of the Microsoft boys. Bill Gates will see to that."

"What if they're not forthcoming though ?" asked Gerry.

"We cut some of the development program." Was John's simple response. "Still we have plenty of time. The major spends are now well covered, providing the sponsors actually fulfill their agreements. It's when we get closer to completion that we will need to revisit the program costs."

"Next we need to look at signing two drivers, are you still fixed on having paid drivers and not going for a driver who will bring his own budget."

"Gerry we need to have drivers who are capable. Most of the buy in drivers only pay for their seats because they don't have the required talent to be given a contract of their own. If we are to become successful then we must have the right to choose our own man."

"There's no way we can entice any of the current Fl drivers to leave their own seats. We are complete beginners in their eyes, that means we have to look at other formula."

"F3 is my choice I have my eye on three or four guys and one female driver. Janice Higgins has done very well so far this season. Vee will you open up conversation with her. I would like to sign her up for early testing, we can then make a judgment on her abilities to handle Fl then."

"I'll go to the next meeting, no doubt she has a manager who'll need buttering up." Vee responded

"No I don't think she has yet." Said Gerry "I agree she may be a good match. It will help with our image as a new breath of air entering into Fl, but what about our principles."

"No problem." Said Vee "they know less about the sport than I do they only want in for further exposure."

"Just like you then." Laughed Gerry

"Swivel," responded Vanessa.

"OK guys let's quit while we're still friends." Said John. "I'll lock up" said Gerry leaving the office.

When Gerry had left the office Vanessa said to John Come over on Saturday afternoon with Fran, its time I got to know her better, it may ease your problems."

"Yes we've nothing planned on Saturday, are you going to Silverstone on Sunday ? I may as well come with you, we may as well try to sign Janice up there and then."

"I hadn't realised the next meeting was so close but yes why not. See you tomorrow" said Vanessa getting up to leave. "I'll give Janice Higgins a call."

Chapter 6

The meeting the next day with the Microsoft technicians and Hitachi was very heavy going for John. He understood very little of what was being talked about. Ian was handling himself well, but John decided that Gerry must also attend. Once Gerry arrived John said to the group, "If you don't mind I'll leave you to continue, please use my office for as long as you want. If you need me later ask Anne to locate me." John then got up and left.

Outside he bumped into Vanessa who was just taking a natural break from the meeting with the Hitachi Marketing Director Torra Toranago. "How are you going." Asked John.

"Quite good so far." Replied Vanessa "I'm not sure that he likes dealing with me. He keeps looking down my dress each time I lean over for something I'm not sure whether its lust or whether he just wants to have a good look. If it wasn't so important I may have got them out for him to look at in the flesh so to speak."

"Bloody don't." was John's reply. "Do you want me to come in and help."

"Not yet, it may be better in about an hour we should be getting to the short strokes by then, I hope I've got him by the short hairs by then. You can rescue him and let him sign his life over to you." She said with a smile.

"He's typical Japanese, women are not for business in his eyes, also he won't have had to deal with anybody like you before. God it took me long enough to get used to working so close to you before."

"Your making me out to be some sort of harlot."

"No way, but you do like showing yourself off. I heard about the night at Oulton Hall flashing to James Goodwin, then standing in the window naked. Word got around you know, your name wasn't mentioned but I could guess."

"They shouldn't have been out looking up at that time, I could have been having a bonk in the window for all they were to know. They must have enjoyed the view, there was little else to see at that time of night." She said smiling again. "Its nice to know my reputation spreads."

At that Vanessa re-entered her office to continue with the negotiations.

By the end of the day between Vanessa and John they had

managed to agree terms with Hitachi, John had spoken to Microsoft who had promised to have a look at the funding program. They had also agreed that Hitachi would be allowed to be co.-sponsors of the team. But the team would still be principally Microsoft. Both John and Vanessa felt good. They decided to leave early and have a small celebration drink.

Gerry and Ian were still hard at work with the Microsoft and Hitachi contingent, but the work was progressing. It was hoped that when complete they would be able not only to have a continuous telemetry back from the car, but to be able to re-program the on board computer from the pits. This would mean that the driver could get on with the job of driving, and the technicians could make adjustments to compensate for fuel weight reductions, fuel flow, atmospheric changes. This was critical with the design and materials used in the engine Gerry felt that the ability to compensate was required to ensure that the units would last the duration of the race.

Both John and Vanessa called into the Coach and Horses pub in Lofthouse a small non-descript village a few miles from the factory. John ordered a large Coke for himself and a Gin and Tonic for Vanessa. John didn't drink at all these days, a few years back he had been bordering on alcoholism following his accident. He had realised it in himself and quit drink over night He didn't have any problems with others drinking he was strong willed enough to avoid slipping back.

They moved into one of the small rooms away from the bar. This pub had a number of small private rooms dotted around a large central bar Room.

"Well here's to another successful day at the office." Said John.

Vanessa who sat opposite to John looked on smiling. She said "You should have seen Torra's face when he first met me. In a way I wish I hadn't worn this dress."

"Yes so do I" Said John looking towards her small cleavage. Vanessa picked up her drink and said "Never mind its all over." On picking up her drink the mat had attached its self to the bottom. It then fell away to the floor. She bent down to pick it up. In doing so her dress fell away from her breast's giving John a full view top down.

"Opps." Said Vanessa picking the mat up, then holding the top of her dress in with her hand. "Sorry."

"Don't worry." Said John "You've been threatening that all day. By the way" John said starting to redden "Don't take this the wrong way but were you wearing anything under your skirt on Wednesday."

"What do you mean." Said Vanessa in mock alarm.

"Well" John started with an embarrassed look wishing he'd never started "Gerry bet me ten Pounds that you weren't wear anything underneath, you know panties."

"Oh John", Laughed Vanessa. "I was wearing the same then as now." She said standing and moving towards John. She then took his hand and guided it under her dress and onto her tight bottom. John could only feel bare flesh. He pulled his hand away quickly and said flustered" Jeez nothing Vee."

"Nope" she said "I never wear them their bad for my circulation. Hope you didn't take him up on the bet, because you've lost."

Both John and Vanessa drank up slowly John settled back down after his shock, although he knew it was only her way. She was famous for such tricks. Vanessa had been brought up not to be ashamed of her body. After all she had been blessed with an absolute fantastic figure. She also seemed to have the ability to eat and drink large amounts with no effect.

As they both left to get into their own cars Vanessa said "Don't forget tomorrow. And don't worry I won't tell Fran you had a feel of my bum."

With that she shot off in her car, heading towards York.

John looked worried, what I am I going to do with her, she's good for us at the moment, but when we start to get more exposure its the amount of exposure Vee will give that worries me. John got into his car and headed to his home in Otley to the north west of Leeds.

He was met at his door by his wife Fran. "Hi lover" she called as he got out of his car. "How's the high octane business today."

"Fine, I think the money side is OK, worried about the break in though."
"Still no news." She asked

"No never will be from our Police, I think we will have to investigate ourselves."

Stepping through the door John said, "By the way Vanessa would like both of us to visit her tomorrow afternoon. I said it would be fine, that's OK with you isn't it ?"

"Why what does she want ?"

"Nothing she'd just like you and her to become friends."

"Why should I become friends with that woman. You know I don't approve of her in your face body tactics, I'm no prude but I don't believe in letting it all hang out in public."

"Apart from on holiday dear. Topless in France, Greece, and the Maldives well !" exclaimed John.

"Yes all right, that's on holiday, not every day." Fran said irritated.

"Oh before I forget I'm going to Silverstone with Vanessa on Sunday, we want to discuss a driving contract with Janice Higgins."

"Can you be trusted with two women I ask myself." Fran remarked disappearing into the kitchen.

The next afternoon John and Fran arrived in Acaster Malbis a small village on the outskirts of York shortly before 1.0pm. The day was hot which was unusual for this year, most of the summer days had been cold and wet so far, "Could this be the final break," said Fran as they drove into the village.

Vanessa lived in a large house built at the turn of the century. It stood well back from the road surrounded by a high brick built wall with tall trees behind it. The house wasn't the type you would expect a woman like Vanessa to own, she would have been more likely the type who
would have lived in an apartment in the centre of a city.

John parked his car by the garages and they walked over to the front door of the house. There wasn't a bell push but a brass knocker on the door. John knocked and stood back, there was no reply. He then tried the door handle, the door was locked. "Well I suppose she's around the back." Said John.

They walked back towards the garages and down a passage to the rear of the house. The garden at the back was huge, in keeping with the rest of the property. It again was well secluded with high walls and trees. On the back of the building there was a large conservatory with a stone patio leading off towards a screened area of lawn. As they walked towards the screened area Fran could see a swimming pool surrounded by stone edging. On a lounger on the lawned area lay the naked form of Vanessa. As John and Fran walked around the screen Vanessa stood up and said "Sorry I forgot the time I was just taking advantage of the sun. we've not had that much this year." Her body looked fantastic she was evenly tanned all over to a healthy looking light bronze. "I'll just go and slip something on." She said disappearing into the conservatory. "Pull up some chairs she shouted.

"Just what I expected another show," said Fran

"Oh it was in innocence I'm sure," replied John feeling annoyed with Vanessa "She didn't intend to be caught like that."
Said John but that wasn't what he was thinking. The bitch he thought she did it on purpose.

Vanessa returned wearing a casual neatly fitting mid length Cashmere and silk dress, it hugged her figure, showing off her well proportioned breasts and erect nipples the dress hugged and curved around her neat bottom.

"Look I am sorry about that" said Vanessa showing some sign of embarrassment, although it wasn't from the fact that she had been caught sun bathing in the nude, it was more for John She knew Fran didn't approve of her. She also knew that Fran thought John was having an affair with her. This was far from the truth whilst she liked John she had no intention of bedding him. "I simply lost the track of time no watch on you see" showing her arms. "Please help yourselves to drinks." She said pointing towards the trolley.

The general conversation drifted about holidays, where they'd been where they were going. What Fran liked doing, what she thought of motor racing. As the afternoon wore on and the chit chat died down Vanessa and John turned more to work matters. Fran listened to the two of them talking about different aspects of the car project, she was getting bored.

Fran then said "Would you mind if I go for a swim Vanessa."
"No not at all feel free."
"But you haven't brought your costume love." Said John.

"No I haven't have I." Returned Fran slightly irritated, getting up and walking to the pool. At the pool side she stripped, and naked dived into the pool.

"Well I didn't expect that," John said surprised.

"You never know," said Vanessa smiling, h'mm thought Vanessa she's got quite a nice body pity she keeps it locked away so much.

"Look John now that we are alone I wanted to tell you a friend of mine has connections around the circuits, she phoned me from Canada last night, she has heard a rumor around the pits that somebody has been spying on McLaren. Also that the same group is gathering information about other F 1 teams. She didn't have any other information but will keep listening."

John looking towards the pool where his wife was still enjoying her swim, turned towards Vanessa "You don't think that they are the ones responsible for our problem the other day ?"

"Look it could be" said Vanessa "We must be careful, after we've finished at Silverstone tomorrow I would like to take some time out from work at the factory to investigate this further, you don't need me there every day now in any case."

"Look I don't want this to sound wrong, but are you capable of that ?" questioned John.

"More than sweety." Replied Vanessa "I'll bum around Europe for a while, that's where the information will be going, I'll keep in touch, and hopefully we can turn events around."

"OK I'll talk to Gerry, we could put some misinformation out as well."

"Good I'm going for *a* swim." Said Vanessa jumping up, pulling her dress over her head dropping it onto the grass, and trotting naked to the pool. She joined Fran in the water.

Fran was enjoying herself it had been quite some time since she had swum naked, and had forgotten how free she felt in doing so . She looked round as she saw Vanessa dive in the pool to join her. Vanessa swam over to Fran and said "You gave John a quite a surprise doing that,"

"We're all full of them Vanessa." Said Fran

"Please call me Vee all my friends do."

"Am I a friend ?" asked Fran.

"Yes off course." Vanessa looked up as John stood at the pool side looking in. "I won't join you, in fact Fran do you mind if I leave you here for a while. I must go to see Gerry we've matters to discuss. I'll come back later for you."

"Nonsense," said Vanessa "Fran can stay as long as she wants, I'll lend her a car to go home later, I have three in the garage she can choose one of them."

At that John said "Well see you later have fun Girls. I'll see you in the paddock at Silverstone tomorrow." And walked out to his car. Vanessa's conversation earlier was worrying him. He needed to go through the list of documents Gerry had identified, he also needed to further discuss the work the Gerry and Ian had undertaken yesterday morning with Microsoft.

For about an hour the two women played around in the pool. Diving in and out swimming closer and closer. During this time Fran was becoming more and more relaxed with Vanessa. Fran said "I think I may go and have a sun bath to warm up again." With that she got out of the pool and walked across the lawn to the lounger. As she was about to lay down Vanessa said " Wait, dry off and I will put some sun block on, your skin isn't used to being exposed."

Fran picked up a towel and started to dry herself; Vanessa ran across the lawn and disappeared into the house, she returned a minute later with the block. She poured some onto her hands and started to massage it into Fran's back. Fran felt a little uncomfortable at first, but as Vanessa worked down her back and across her buttocks, then round her body and up onto her breasts she started to relax again. In fact she enjoyed the gentle touch of Vanessa's hands massaging her breasts and round her nipples, they began to harden under Vanessa's hands. Vanessa's hands moved gently down Fran's body and into her pubic area, as Vee's fingers touched between her legs she gave a gentle moan of pleasure. She allowed herself to relax even more under Vee's gentle touch. The two women sank down to the ground and very tenderly kissed.

Fran allowed her hands to start to explore Vee's body, she found to her surprise that she enjoyed the experience. Running her hands firstly over Vee's breast's and then slowly allowing her fingers to explore Vee's pubic area and between her legs. Vee continued to kiss Fran, and then slowly moved to play with Fran's breasts with her tongue. She then turned and explored between Fran's legs with her tongue. They both made love in the garden as only two women can.

"Vee I don't know what came over me," said Fran afterwards slightly shocked "That's the first time ever. I never dreamed I could do such a thing with another woman."

"You see," said Vee "I am not the man eater you thought I was. I would much rather make love with another woman than a man. Although I'will go to bed with men when I need to feel filled."

That was the reason why John was quite safe and that there was no way Vee would have had an affair with him. She would rather have it with Fran.

They both lay in each other's arms enjoying the closeness, and the late afternoon sun on their naked bodies.

Chapter 7

John was driving quickly along the A 64 towards Leeds, his thoughts were on the break in. One of the items that Gerry had listed was some confirmations of orders placed. He also thought about the problems they had already experienced with faulty parts. Could they be related ? he asked himself.

He was approaching an area of road works connected with the upgrade of the Al. He started to slow as the traffic ahead started to brake to merge into single file. John was at that point still in the outside lane, the inside lane was clear so he moved across, the car in front of him was about a fifty metres away, it suddenly braked to a halt. John applied his brakes, at first they bit, but then his foot went flat to the floor, he was covering the ground rapidly. The car in front was stationary by now, it was only a matter of ten metres away, John was pumping the brake pedal rapidly, but it had no effect. John still travelling at 60 miles per hour, each second he covered 8 metres, John pulled the wheel hard over to the right, his Jaguars 10 inch wide tyres squealed in protest as they struggled to respond to the command. The initial understeer lost him about another metre before forward inertia gave up to the friction generated between tyre and road. The big car swung away from the stationary Renault, the front of John's car missed the rear bumper of the Renault by millimeters. John was then heading diagonally across the carriageway towards the marker cones. He had to pull the wheel in the opposite direction to swing the car straight. Again the car slid on the dusty unused section of the carriageway. As the car hurtled through the cones scattering them in either direction, some flying into the cars stood on the inside lane, John fought to first bring the car under control and then to allow it to slow itself down to a halt.

Drivers of cars that had been hit by the cones leaped out of their cars shouting at the Jaguar as it careered down the closed off lane. They ran down following the car until it ground to a halt a further one hundred and fifty metres away.

John sat at the wheel of his cars sweating, and slightly shacking. The first driver to arrive pulled open Johns door and pulled John slightly out of the car, "You fucking idiot," the man yelled "Are you trying to kill us or what."

John just looked at the man not really hearing him, he just said handing over his mobile phone "Look call the police please, my car's brakes failed."

"Never mind the fucking police what about my car, look the bleeding doors hanging off " This was of course an exaggeration, the door did have a small dent in it where the heavy base of the cone had hit, but then it only complemented the rest of the car which to say the least looked as if it were on its last journey to meet its maker.

Another driver took the phone away from the angry motorist and started to call the police, when a patrol car pulled up on the opposite carriageway.

"Is anybody hurt," was the policeman's first question.

"No" said John, "My brakes failed, I managed to avoid the standing traffic."

"Like hell you did, look at my bleeding car, its wrecked," said the angry motorist.

"Belt up creep, your wreck was like that before," said one of the other drivers. "Look constable this guy," pointing to John "Missed everyone of us. The traffic in front stopped quickly, he says his brakes failed, and reacted quickly to miss us."

The police took details from the other motorists, their first move was to clear up the main carriageway. "Please just sit in your car for now Sir." Said one of the officers, "We'll take a quick statement whilst we wait for the recovery truck. Are you covered by any breakdown insurance?"

"Yes Green Flag I think." Replied John looking in his wallet for his membership card.

The police set about clearing the carriageway of cones, and re-setting them. "I think we'll leave your car where it is for now, but will you please step over to the outside of the road, just in case Sir."

It took about half an hour for the recovery vehicle to arrive, John said to the driver "The brake pedal just went to the floor, there's no pressure in system. Look my names John Bennet from Westfield Engineering, will you please take the car back there. Here's the address."

Back in Vanessa's garden the two women were still enjoying each other's company Fran was now giving Vanessa a massage with sun block. The phone on the drinks table rang, Vanessa got up and walked to the table, "Its John," said Vanessa holding the phone out for Fran.

"What's up," said Fran.

"Nothing serious, but the cars broken down. I'm on my way to the factory in a tow truck. Just wanted you to know. Will you ask Vee to come and pick me up in the morning." Replied John "How's things with Vee ?"

"Oh fine," said Fran feeling somewhat guilty "We're just relaxing in the garden, see you later tonight."

At that she put the phone down.

"Anything wrong," asked Vanessa, as she stood behind Fran and rubbed her neck and shoulders.

"No, he said his car broke down going to Gerry's."

"So he hasn't made it then yet "Asked Vanessa.

"No he's going to the factory. I suppose he'll see Gerry there. He wants you to pick him up tomorrow." Said Fran, then she remarked "Its started to cool off now could I go for a shower."

"Come with me, I've something you'll like better."

They both walked into the house, and up to the main bath room. The bathroom was large decorated in rich marble, it had a large sunken bath and a Jacuzzi, which Vanessa bent down to fill with steaming hot water.

Once filled she turned on the water jets, and they both stepped in to the steaming bubbling water laughing and giggling girlishly. In the water Vee said to Fran "Since I'm picking John up in the morning why don't you stay the night with me, I'll take you home tomorrow."

Fran asked huskily "In the same bed?"

"If you want Fran its up to you." Replied Vanessa

"I think I would like that" said Fran sheepishly leaning over and giving Vanessa a kiss full on the lips.

Chapter 8

At the factory John called Gerry, he asked him to come out and look the car over. There was very little external damage. The front lower valance had a few marks where the cones had been brushed away, but that was all. John couldn't help but think that the failure was connected to the break in, in some way, but he couldn't see how, he had driven miles in the last two days.

Whilst he waited for Gerry to arrive John decided to look over the security tapes again He fast forwarded to around midnight. At 12.30am he saw Ian leaving the factory by the front entrance and walking over to the car park, he was then picked up again by the car park camera. Then about 15 minutes later he saw Eric leave, and pick up his car, he drove it round to the front of the building,. Jim then walked out got in the car and it drove away. Nothing thought John, we should have had cameras at the rear as well. Then at I.15am John saw a shadow of a car pulling away from the top part of the screen which corresponded with the tap comer of the building, the car moved down towards the exit of the car park, it then once reaching the exit sped away, in doing so the driver turned on his light's. John thought that car must have arrived at sometime, and since he hadn't seen it arrive after midnight, then it must have been some time earlier. John rewound the tape to 11.0 pm. Just then Gerry arrived. "Lets look at the damage then." Said Gerry "What happened."

"I pressed on the brake pedal, at first the car started to slow, then my foot went to the floor, no pressure at all."

"Well that rules out pipe failure, unless two pipes failed at the same time. The dual braking system would still have given sufficient pressure to stop the car."

"So could two pipes fail ?" asked John.

"Highly unlikely," replied Gerry

"They could have been cut." Said John.

"Yes, but you were at Vee's just before."

"Yes true."

Gerry looked under the car, "There's no sign of any leakage under here." He said after giving the car a good inspection.

He then looked under the bonnet, "Here's the problem" he said pointing to the master cylinder, "The seal between the reservoir and the manifold has blown. That's allowed the brake fluid to bypass the seal's, giving you no braking pressure. A simple fault".

John and Gerry moved back inside. "Why the theory about cut pipes." Asked Gerry.

John told Gerry about the conversation he had, had with Vee earlier that afternoon, and that he had left early to come over to speak to him about a number of issues relating to the break in.

"We still haven't established what the intruder was looking for." Said John. "Was just going over the tapes again when you arrived, lets continue." John told Gerry what he had seen so far, and that he had just rewound the tape to an earlier sequence.

John started the player, at 11.12 pm they both saw a car slow, turn off its lights and pull into the car park, it drove through and round to the top of the screen out of view from the camera. Unfortunately the image from this view was no clearer than the later image. Due to the glare from lights they couldn't make out the type of car used.

"I think we can get that image enhanced." Said Gerry "there's a small company I know that will digitally enhance video, the problem is that the images then cannot be used as evidence for any prosecution."

"We're not going to be prosecuting anybody, the police aren't interested."

"OK I'll take the tape in on Monday, we'll see what we get."
John's mobile rang, "Hi John Bennet"

"Its Vee, Fran wanted me to ring to say she's decided to stay over here with me tonight, I'll bring her home when I collect you in the morning."

"Oh err fine," replied John shrugging his shoulders to Gerry, "Have fun then. Where's Fran ?"

"Oh I think we will, Fran's just finishing in the Jacu77i." She wasn't really. In fact she was stood next to Vanessa, Fran couldn't trust herself to ring just yet. She didn't feel that she was cheating on John in anyway, but didn't feel quite comfortable with herself. "See you in the morning." Finished Vanessa.

"Well its guys night tonight, the girls are staying together." Said John to Gerry.

"Sorry I can't tonight I have other things on." said Gerry. "I need to leave now I'm late already she'll think I've stood her up." "She

?" questioned John, Gerry was the last of the true bachelors.

"Yes she." Replied Gerry leaving quickly. "I'll tell you later, bye."

Gerry actually ran to his car which was parked just outside reception.

John decided to walk around the back of the building, he thought to himself they hadn't carried out a thorough search of the outside. He now knew that the intruder had been waiting around for sometime before making his entry. He hadn't banked on there still being somebody in the building at that time of night.

Meanwhile over at Vanessa's, Vee and Fran had agreed to go into York to eat that evening.

"Fran come and look through this wardrobe, we're similar in sizes, you should find something suitable." There was about 10 years age gap between the two women Vanessa was in her mid thirties and Fran was just forty three. Fran had kept her figure, and still managed to fit into size 10's. Vanessa in truth should wear 8's, but she did prefer to wear a looser fitting. "I'm afraid you won't find any underwear though, you could always wear the stuff you left by the pool."

"No thanks." Replied Fran "Your teaching a number of new tricks today, I suppose it will be fun to go without."

The two women spent the next hour trying on different outfits, until they both found a style they both felt comfortable with.

Fran decided on a soft and flowing off white trouser suit designed by Christian Dior, whilst Vee stayed with an above the' knee black dress form Gucci, which was low cut around the neck. Fran just couldn't see her being comfortable wearing such a dress without any underwear. Vee of course wasn't bothered by it she was totally confident in herself and her body.

They left Vee's house in her Porsche 911 for the centre of York. Whilst searching through the shrubbery close to where the intruder had gained access to the factory, John found a corner of a screwed up napkin. He also found close to the napkin a couple of cigarette ends, and an empty small book of matches. The book of matches advertised a Restaurant in Wakefield. It looks as if I may be getting somewhere thought John putting the items into his pocket. It was now about 10.0

PM and starting to become dark, the security lights were on around the industrial estate. Well he thought I'm stuck now no car. He walked round to the front of the building, and entered through the reception. He crossed over to the alarm panel situated under the reception desk and bent down to turn the alarms off. As he did so a shadow passed across the front of the building, someone was again prowling around the site. John saw the shadow and stayed down low, waiting to see what would happen next. He could just make out the silhouette of man standing in front of the doors. The man looked to be about five foot six inch tall, with longish hair. He could see that the man was searching in his pockets for something. The figure pulled a set of keys out of his pockets, he then tried to insert the keys into the door.

    Outside Ian had returned to the factory, he had been working at home trying to finalise the meeting he and Gerry had attended with the Microsoft and Hitachi contingent. He had found that he had left some of his notes at work, and couldn't complete the without them. Shit he thought as the door moved when he fried to insert his keys. He looked around, he couldn't see any sign of anybody in the car park his was the only car around. Johns car had been pushed inside the factory for safe storage until Monday when it could be collected by Appleyards for repair. Ian stepped into the lobby very gingerly, he looked around the lobby area, one to see if he could see anybody lurking in the shadows, and secondly to see if he could find something to act as a weapon for his defense.

    From Johns hiding place as the figure moved slowly into the lobby area, very slowly it looked as if the person was trying to gain access without disturbing anybody who may have been working late in the building.

    As Ian moved further into the lobby the lights from a passing car shone onto his face. He leapt in shock as a voice said "Bloody Shit Ian, what the hell are you doing creeping about at this time." John said standing up from behind the reception desk.

    "I could ask the same of you boss, why are you hiding behind Anne's desk," Then Ian added "Anne's not down there with you is she?" "Get away Ian. Come on why are you here ?"

    "I came back for my notes John I wanted to finish up my report."
    "Well its a good job you've come, my cars broken down, its in

the delivery bay. Gerry's shot off on some secret meeting with an admirer, and Fran's out with Vee so I'm stuck."

"Let me get the papers I want then I'll drive you home boss."

"Tell you what Ian, we'll go into Wakefield first, I just want to check out an address first." John said pulling the book of matches out of his pocket. "I found these round the back of the building, where the intruder made his entry."

"Fine with me." Said Ian.

It didn't take Vanessa long to drive the short distance into York, she handled the Porsche expertly. Its engine growling like a pent up lion at the back. The car felt restrained whilst town driving, Fran could only imagine what it would feel like on the open road. In imagining that feeling she allowed her right hand to rest gently on Vanessa's leg, gently stroking her thigh.

She was amazed at herself, she had only really known Vanessa for a matter of a few weeks at a distance, and only hours with any closeness, and now she had allowed that friendship to become most intimate. When John had first introduced Vanessa, on her joining the team she had been highly suspicious of her. John she knew had known Vanessa for sometime through a marketing agency she had worked for, before he had approached her to join him. When a beautiful woman like Vanessa was suddenly brought in, well what was a wife to think.

Vanessa for once wasn't fully sure of herself, driving into York she had been not troubled by the way Fran was reacting, whilst she didn't mind the playing around, and the thigh stroking, in fact she enjoyed it, she had a damp feeling already between her legs. She had considered skipping dinner and driving home. She didn't want to get entangled in an affair with her boss's wife. It could prove to be messy not only at Westfield, but she did have more important matters to consider.

Vanessa pulled into the entrance to the Royal York Hotel. She drove up to the main entrance and parked her car close to the steps. As Fran and Vee walked up the steps and into the Hotel, they were admired by a number of men standing in the lobby. Fran felt excited by the gaze of the group, she without thinking undid the jacket top she was wearing to reveal the silky strapped top she was wearing underneath. She could feel her breasts moving in time with her walk. She thought to herself I bet they can tell I'm not wearing a bra. This impish thought excited her even more causing her nipples to stand to attention. Vee led Fran into the dining room. The Matre'd said "Good evening Miss Plat, are you ready to dine know or would you like a drink at the Bar.

"No thank you we'll dine now please Jon-Luc." Replied Vee. They were shown to their table.

"Gosh I never knew it could feel so good to be eyed up and down like that." Said Fran once they were alone.

"You should try taking your clothes off in front of an audience." Replied Vee.

"No I could never do that, I'm far too self conscious."

"Not from what I saw entering the lobby. I saw you undo your jacket to show off your fits. I'm sure one of the guys stood there and got a hard on at the sight of them bobbling around."

"Well so were yours."

"True but that's me."

Ian parked his car in the centre of Wakefield, then both Ian and John walked up Westgate passed the address on the matches book. From the outside the place looked, and was a run of the mill Pizza takeaway and restaurant. The restaurant occupied the ground floor of a three storey building. The first floor had an accountant occupying the office space, and the top floor had a small time employment agency.

"What did you expect to see boss," asked Ian "They wouldn't advertise themselves as Industrial Espionage Inc. would they."

"I wasn't sure Ian, its just a start. The guy could have been here first, then drove out to break into us."

John went over to look at the accountants brass plaque, which was fastened to the wall by a door leading to a set of stairs up to the office space. The name on the plaque was A Galli Accountant.

"Come on Ian take me home," said John this isn't helping you finish your report."

It took Ian an hour to drive John to his home in Otley, John offered Ian a drink, Ian declined the offer saying he would prefer just to go straight home.

John got himself a night cap and went upstairs to his bedroom, there he picked up some of his notes for the meeting tomorrow at Silverstone with Janice Higgins, got into bed to sip his drink and read through the notes. He thought to himself I'll bet those two, meaning Fran and Vee are causing mayhem in York tonight.

In York the meal had gone well, it was about 11.30 PM and Fran said to Vee "I'm sorry but can we miss the night club please."

"Sure," replied Vee "Nothing wrong is there." She added slightly worried.

"No I would just like you to take me to bed, please." Fran's voice had once again taken on a husky tone.

Vee drove home quickly using the power of the Porsche's engine to the full. She knew there would be few police cars out at that time of night. It wasn't late enough for the true drunks, and was about the time they changed shifts.

Once home Vee led Fran upstairs to her bedroom, in the room there was a large king sized bed with deep red silk covers. The room was very simply decorated in plain white, with a deep pile cream carpet. There were a number of prints and paintings around the walls of the room. Some of abstract figures in love making postures, others of colour collage's. Vee went to draw the curtains. Fran said "No leave them open please I don't normally make love with the curtains open."

"You don't normally have sex with a woman either."

"No, but you are teaching me another side to life."

Fran walked slowly over to Vee, she slid her hands down Vee's body over the silken material of her dress, feeling the firmness of her breasts, on down over her stomach, as she allowed her hands to slide down her stomach she could feel the slight roughness of Vee's neatly trimmed pubic hairs. When she reached the hem of the dress she slowly pulled the dress up and over Vee's head. Fran then started to caress Vee's face and neck, and down over her breasts. She allowed her fingers to play with Vee's nipples.

Vee unbuttoned Fran's top and she allowed it to fall to the floor, Vee continued to caress Fran's breasts through the silky blouse, her nipples were already erect, but Vee felt them harden even more under her touch.

Fran moved her hands down over Vee's firm stomach and gently caressed her pubic mound, letting her fingers play with Vee's short trimmed pubic hairs. She then moved her fingers in between Vee's legs to her moist pleasure zone, where she gently massaged, allowing her fingers to slip in and out of Vee's pleasure lips. Vee gave a shudder of pleasure, allowing a moan to escape from her lips.

Vee then unfastened the waist band of the trousers Fran had borrowed and slid them down over her hips. She kissed Fran's breasts, and played with her nipples. She then moved further down Fran's body kissing her rounded stomach, and allowing her tongue to play with her navel. Her fingers were gently teasing and smoothing Fran's untended pubic hairs. She kissed her mound, and allowed her tongue to dart between Fran's legs. Vee could taste the fluids escaping from between the full lips of Fran's sex. It was Fran's turn to moan and squirm with highly charged pleasure.

Fran stepped out of the trousers and lead Vee to the bed where they both collapsed. They kissed and caressed each other in a frenzy for two hours, after which they both fell exhausted asleep in each other's arms.

Chapter 9

Vee woke up early Sunday morning, which was a surprise following the antics of the night before. They were still laying naked uncovered on top of the bed. Vee went down stairs to make some breakfast, she didn't bother to cover herself up, there would be nobody about to see her.

She didn't see the dark figure lurking in the under growth on the inside of her wall.

Fran awoke a few minutes later missing the feeling of a body next to her. She grabbed a toweling robe from the door and wrapped it around herself, and followed Vee down stairs. In the kitchen she saw the naked rear of Vee standing by the big range waiting for the coffee maker to produce its black liquid. She walked over to Vee and let her hands cup Vee's breast's.

The figure in the garden could see this through the kitchen window, although it wasn't the clearest view, he didn't dare move closer. He raised his camera and took a number of shots. Well he thought these might come in handy, he wasn't sure who the other person was. She was clearly female though.

Fran asked "What time are you picking John up at."

"When we're ready." Responded Vee

"Fine I'll shower, to freshen up. Can I borrow another outfit for today."

"Yes help yourself, I'm just going to wear Jeans and a Tee Shirt today."

Fran found a simple plain dress that fit her well, "Vee you look fantastic in those" said Fran when she turned and saw Vee in simple Levi Jeans and a white Tee Shirt. They complemented her figure, the Tee shirt was tight enough to form around her breasts and holding them in position. "Thanks," said Vee "Look we have to talk."

"Don't worry," said Fran "I know its not a permanent thing. I still love John, I still want John, this is just a fun thing, you wanted to be friends and well lets be good friends."

"I'm pleased your thinking the same way," said Vee "We'll be very, very good friends. We can do this again sometime then."

Vee drove the Porsche quickly through to Otley to collect John. She handled the car through the twisting lanes from Acaster Malbis to the A64 with ease and total confidence. Her driving style was total relaxation, whilst cornering she had the opposite belief of many drivers. Most would think that there was an obstruction in the road when approaching a tight corner, she believed that any obstruction would have moved by the time she reached it. She also believed if it hadn't then she and her car had the ability to take avoiding action. Once reaching the A64 she sped through to Leeds, taking the outer ring road to miss the heavy city centre traffic.

"Missed you," said Fran stepping from the car and greeting John.

"You look well," said John "I haven't seen you looking so glowing for years."

It was true that Fran did have a glow about her, she also felt extremely happy with life at that moment.

"Go on get off I'll see you tonight John, about what time,"
"About nine I should think."

"Good I'll be waiting," Said Fran holding Johns hand to her breast.

As John and Vanessa set of he said "What's got into her she's never done that before."

"Full of surprises your wife." Replied Vanessa impishly.

The drive to Silverstone whilst fast was uneventful. John thought that Vanessa was unusually quiet, she may just have had a heavy night last night. John knew that when Fran got going she could be a hand full.

At Silverstone they bypassed the crowds queuing at the general spectator entrance. Since John was the Team principle of Westfield he was a member of the select band of the motorsport fraternity, and therefore was given privileged entry to the worlds racing venues.

Any motorsport event is a special place, when walking through the outer spectator areas, all the commercial stalls are set up, there is noise, colour, the smell is a mixture of Hot Dog stands, burnt rubber from the track, and the smell of high powered racing engines. All around the circuit there is the feeling that you have entered a special place. In some ways it feels like your stepping back in time, to a time of medieval days of jousting. This is noted even more when you enter the domain of the paddock.

The paddock is where all the cars to be used at the event are prepared, each is in its own covered bay or large tent, they all have their colours flying as if showing their allegiance to their own Lord. They have their fair maidens handing out the sponsors literature. The mechanics are like the squires of old, tending to the cars as if they were the steeds. The cars are dressed in the colours of their sponsor as are the drivers, all carrying helmets and tokens from their loved ones.

Prior to racing commencing a quiet seems to descend over the entire paddock, as if in preparation for the cacophony of noise that will erupt once that race starts.

John and Vanessa had arrived at one of the rounds for the British Formula Three series. This series of race's was well known throughout the world as being one of the best for training drivers in the art form of close high speed racing.

All the cars had the same chassis design, with front and rear wings, and slick tyres. The teams had the choice of either an engine produced by Renault or one from Honda. Both engines were very evenly matched for performance. It is a formula where it is down to the driver skill, to set his / her car up to perform the best on the day. Janice Higgins who John had come to see was currently lying fourth in this year's championship. The three drivers ahead of her all drove Renault powered cars, and had been signed up by Formula One teams using that suppliers engines. Janice had Honda power in her car, and so far had not been given a contract by any team for next year. In the history of motor racing only a couple of women drivers had ever made it to the top ranks of the sport.

The grid like most other forms of racing was decided by a timed qualification session. Unfortunately for Janice she had had some problems in her session, her Honda engine had been giving trouble. It had for some reason being miss firing at maximum revs. Therefore in this highly competitive form of racing she had only managed to qualify in the mid grid slots in tenth position, she would have a lot to do to make up positions to ensure she gained points towards the championship.

She was aware that John and Vanessa were coming to see her following the race, she was keen to make a good impression on them. Even though she knew it was her performance up to date that had brought them to see her.

It was mid day when John and Vanessa arrived at the circuit, the Formula Three race was due of at 3.0 PM, that was to be the feature race of the day. Prior to that there were a number of other races, sports cars, Formula Fords, and Saloon Cars. Some of the races contained hopefuls for the future, looking to make impressions on team owners of more powerful Formulas, others were drivers who would admit if pushed they were on the decline of their racing days. They though wanted to show the young stars that they weren't finished yet.

John and Vanessa walked around the public areas of the circuit, visiting the many stands, where a range of goods were on display, from racing memorabilia to cars both model and real. From in car entertainment systems to packets of crisps. On such a hot day the commercial area was full of scantily clad girls advertising the goods on sale or display on their relevant stands, or handing out free goods in bags. Vanessa was enjoying the atmosphere, and the general sights through the tour. For John, he had seen it so many times in the past that he didn't really take much notice.

"This fantastic," said Vanessa "I never thought it was so popular, this is a wonderful marketing tool," she said thinking how she could further package the goods of their sponsors. She also realised how easy it would be to pass on or bring in other goods of an illegal nature.

"This is nothing," replied John "wait until the British Grand Prix, come on I'll show you where the stand you've been working on will be located." With that John strode off in the direction of the bridge to take people over the circuit to the inner paddock.

"We have booked this area where Max power have their stand today." On the Max power stand Vee could see four girls in their late teens to early twenties dressed in one piece tight fitting black Lycra cat suits. Whilst they covered their bodies they left very little to the imagination hugging every curve and crease.

"Will we have them ?" teased Vanessa.
"Can you see Microsoft going for that style." Commented John.

They managed to pass a couple of hours walking around the various areas of the paddock. "Come on lets go join Janice's team. They will be going through the final preparations for the start of their race."

They walked up and over the bridge, they showed their special passes which allowed them to gain access to the inner paddock, where the F3 teams were situated.

They walked into the teams tent area, and sought out the team manager. "Hi Jason", said John "I see your not in your usual grid slot." Janice would have normally qualified in a much higher position.

"No, we just couldn't get the bloody engine working right. It's brand new from Honda, as are the electronics."

"Have you found the problem," asked Vanessa shaking Jason's hand.

"Yes funnily enough we have. It was simply the rev limiter had been set just 200 revs lower than normal by Honda. We couldn't pick that up on the track. The rev counters in these things always lag behind the true reading."

"So you should have a good race," commented Vanessa.

"We hope so, but it will be hard. These cars are so similar that it can take four or five laps to make up a second let alone pass another car."

"Good luck, we'll just stay at the back for now. I don't want to disturb any of you. We can see Janice after the race."

As the time for the start approached, the cars were called to the assembly area. The atmosphere changed the team members became more tense. They moved around the car with a quickened pace, checking and double checking everything. The mechanics wheeled the car to the dummy grid where the cars are assembled in their respective starting order. This is done prior to the start of the preceding race. Each of the drivers goes through their own individual ritual before stepping into the car. Some like to laugh and joke amongst other drivers, or their own team. Others will walk around the car touching it. Janice just liked to put her helmet on and sit in the car quietly, while her mechanics fastened the multi point seatbelt. She would then close her eyes and play through the start of the race in her mind. Concentrating one hundred percent on the job in hand.

John knew of Janice's way of working, there was no way would he interfere with her preparation time.

Once the Saloon car race had finished and the cars had cleared the circuit, the clerk of the course toured the circuit in his car to ensure that it was ready to accept the next grid. The cars on the dummy grid were given the sign to start their engines, and move onto the circuit in grid order. The cars proceeded round to the starting grid. Once all the cars had taken up their position on the start grid they were waved off on a green flag lap.

This was to enable the drivers to ensure that all was well with the cars at a higher speed, to ensure that the engines were up to temperature, and more importantly to ensure that the slick tyres were also up to operating temperature. At best the tyres would spin at the start, giving a poor get away. Or at worst they would not grip the track on the first corner causing the car to spin off and out of the race.

As the cars returned to the start line following the green flag lap the leaders slowed down causing the cars to bunch up. The car following Janice didn't slow quite quick enough. It hit her gently on one of her rear wheels. This didn't do any visual damage to Janice's car, it did slightly knock that wheel out of alignment, but only by a degree or so not enough to cause harm. He did however damage his own front wing. One side of the wing was knocked backwards and up. The driver James Haden cursed Janice for slowing down. "Bitch." He shouted into his helmet, "You shouldn't be allowed on the bloody track." Nobody could hear him it was only to relieve his own frustration. Even though the accident was his own mistake he would never admit to it. All racing drivers have a self belief in themselves, its always the other persons fault.

Janice's grid slot number ten was on the outside of the circuit, James Haden who was in eleventh place was one car length further back on the inside of the circuit. Even though his wing was damaged James couldn't do anything about it, so he just took up his position.

Once all the cars were in place the race starter turned on the lights starting sequence, the sequence was automatic from that stage. The starters responsibility was to ensure that nobody stalled their engines from that point up to the lights turning green. If they did he would immediately take control and abort the start. I would take about fifteen seconds from the start of the auto sequence to the start of the race.

Inside the cars the drivers saw the red light come on indicating that the auto system had been started. They all depressed their cars clutches and selected first gear. At the same time they had to keep their right foot on the brake and also with their right foot keep the revs up on their engines to prevent them stalling.

To start the cars in motion the engines would need to rev at around 6000 revs. Whilst sounding difficult all the drivers were well practiced in the art of starting their own cars. Sometimes however they did get it wrong and an engine could die.

Once the light was on all the drivers attention was on that light they were looking for it to go out and the green light to shine. As soon as the green light came on they would all release the clutch.

The noise from the grid increased as all the drivers allowed their engines to rev up. The light changed from red to green almost as one the cars moved forward as the drivers released their clutches. On some, the rear wheels spun before the tyres gripped on others the cars were catapulted forward.

Janice chose to short shift from first to second gear. That is that instead of allowing the engine to reach full revs in first gear she would change up into second at about three quarters of the maximum. This was because on the side of the track that she was starting from the track wasn't fully clean, if she maintained first gear up to the maximum revs she would have caused her rear wheels to spin. By moving into second gear earlier she could keep her engine in its power band and then hold second gear slightly longer by which time she would have been on the clean section of the track.

James one position behind her had a cleaner line, his slot was on the normal racing line close to the pit wall, he therefore used the full revs in first gear. This allowed him to make up a small amount of ground on Janice before the first corner. Janice moved towards the inside of the track to try to cover any overtaking move from behind, at the same time she was looking towards the car in front trying to see if he would make room for her to slip by. She was also aware of her position on the track, how far away the first corner was and where her braking point was. By the time she was approaching her braking point she was travelling at 100 mph in very close proximity to the car in front, James was still behind her, but very close to her right rear wheel.

The car in front of her reached its braking point, she suddenly lunged forward gaining ground before she braked herself. She braked and changed down to third gear simultaneously, within a split second of completing that manoeuvre she turned to the right to take a mid line around the corner, she was off the normal racing line, but all the cars at the start were. James also braked hard when he reached his normal braking point. He was on an even tighter line than Janice, and well away from the normal line. The track at this point was dusty from the earlier race. Also James had damaged his front wing on the green flag lap. The consequence of his miss judgment of his line, the track condition and the loss of down force from his wing was that his front wheels locked. This didn't allow his car to slow as quickly as Janice, also much more of a problem it didn't allow him to turn into the corner. At least he turned his wheel but the car didn't respond, he went straight on he caught Janice's car just forward of her rear wheels. The nose of James's car, first of dived under her car pitching it up into the air, this spun her round and onto the car on her outside. Her rear wheels landed on the rear wing of that car breaking it off. James car continued sliding forward and he then hit the front of Janice's car his left-hand front wheel suspension arms folded back pushing his wheel into the side of his cockpit. The impact broke the lower front arm on Janice's car. The tangled mess of the three cars continued to slide off the circuit and into the gravel trap on the outside of the corner. All three were out.

    James jumped out of his car and gesticulated his annoyance to Janice as if it had been her fault. He again didn't consider that he was to blame for taking the three of them out of the race.

    The marshals ran forward from their safety post to first of all ensure that none of the drivers had been injured in the incident, and then to try to clear the damaged cars away from the track side before the leaders came around on their next lap. This was a time of danger. All that would protect them was the racing code, a yellow flag would be waived by the flag marshal at their post. Further up the track the preceding post would show a stationary yellow flag. This was to warn the oncoming drivers that there was danger ahead. That they couldn't overtake the car in front, and that they should slow down and be prepared to stop. At least that is what the rule book says.

    None of the drivers were injured, Janice was slightly shaken after being launched into the air at around 100 mph, her car could have turned over, but that was all. All three of the drivers made their own separate way back to the pits area to report to their respective team.

    Janice was to say the least pissed off, James Haden had ruined her day. In her own mind John Bennet would leave without her signature on the testing contract. She walked dejected back over the bridge through the paddock to the pits. She walked straight through her pit to the motor home parked outside at the back. By this time the emotion of the event had taken over, she had started to cry. This was unusual for Janice, she would normally have been able to keep her emotions under control.

She stripped off her racing suit and fire proof underwear and got into the shower. She was just finishing redressing when John and Vanessa arrived.

By this time she had calmed down, and felt more resolved. Bloody James Haden she thought, he always was a pratt on the track.

John said "Hard luck Janice, it's always the same just when you want to make a good impression shit happens."

"Shit always happens when James Haden's about." Janice replied.

"Look we didn't come here today to make *a* decision, we came because we have already made a decision." Said John. Vanessa was just sitting listening.

"Yes," said Janice furrowing her eyebrows.

"Yes, what I would like to propose to you is that you sign to be a test driver for us."

"Oh," Said Janice slightly disappointed. "Not a full driver."

"No." said John simply, then he followed on "We're not ready to sign a full driver as yet, but if you become a test driver for us, well then that will give us and you the chance to decide further. I can't say more than that currently."

"When will the car be ready for testing."

"Well the first fully assembled tub has to go for crash testing first. That will be ready by the end of next week. It will only have a dummy engine in place. The second tub assuming that the crash tests go well will be ready for its engine 1 week later. We plan to carry out the first shake down trials therefore in two weeks time."

"What happens if the crash test don't go well."

"We will still continue with the shake down tests, we can do whatever is required for the crash test simultaneously."

"So why not start testing with the first tub."

"Can't no engine as yet. It's coming on though. We expect to be complete and bench tested next week with the oil people."

"OK if I say yes what's the contract worth."

Vanessa said "We will pay you £20000 for the remainder of this year for testing. With a written in option to retain you for next season." "What will I be doing next season."

"Can't say for certain. As John said may be racing, may be testing."

"If its only testing will you stop me signing to race with anybody else."

"Another Formula one team, yes, but no problem within any other form of racing."

"When do you want an answer ?"

"Now." Said Vanessa simply "We are very close to starting to test we need to know the shape of the bum that's going to sit in the seat to put it crudely."

"Is there room to negotiate on the retention fee ?"

"Not this years," said John "Look lets not get down to the money side now. We're interested in you I'm only being cautious because I don't know fully how things are going to go through the test's. we hope all will be well but up until the car turns a wheel who knows. You know that we are trying a different design of engine. It is also the lightest unit in Fl the materials we are using are space age. You can see the my reasons for caution."

"Yes but 20 grand isn't exactly the highest is it."

"No but I could go get a pay driver. I don't want to I would prefer you."

"I can see that," said Janice thoughtfully.

"Look if you agree to sign now, and the test's run well we'll have the chance then to re-look at the contract. You can write that in can't you Vee ?"

"Yes sure." Said Vee surprised.

"OK write it in I'll sign for you."

"Great you'll not regret it." Said John getting up to shake Janice's hand. Janice didn't give John her hand but leaned over and give him a kiss.

"I don't normally kiss my drivers, shake hands, pats on the back, but kisses well."

"You've never had a driver like me," said Janice happily.

"Right," said Vanessa "Come up to the factory tomorrow and I'll have the new contract ready for you."

"Fine, give me directions can you."

Vanessa give a quick sketch to show her how to find the place. "Bring your racing suit, boots and helmet along, we may as well do the seat fitting at the same time "Added John.

John and Vanessa left the motor home. They said good bye to the team outside and headed back to the car park. The F3 race was still in progress, but their business at Silverstone was complete for the day. They may as well leave early thus avoiding the crowds of spectators who would flood from the circuit once the racing had finished.

Once in the car Vanessa turned to John, "Why give in to her, is she that good. We can't afford to pay more this year."

"I know that, but yes she is good. Whilst on paper the Renault and the Honda engines are the same, its common knowledge that the Renault develops more power than the Honda. She has a natural ability to feel the cars responses. She can tell her engineers just what the car is doing at any stage of the track. That helps them to set the car up. Its a pity James got in her way today. We may well have been robbed of a good race."

"I thought James Haden is your other target ?"

"He is, but I can't and wouldn't sign him yet. We'll wait for the test results, then see how things lie."

"You could be in for some fireworks when that time comes."

"Yes but I'm sure that we can work it out, sometimes that's just what you need in a team. Two complete opposites to feed off each other."

"Just so long as its only feeding. You don't want fighting on the track."

Vanessa started the Porsche up and drove out of the car park towards Silverstone village, and onward to Otley to drop John off.

Chapter 10

When Vanessa pulled into Johns driveway Fran came out to greet them she was still wearing the dress she had borrowed from Vanessa.

"Your early." She said

"Yes we managed to complete our business quicker than planned." Replied John.

"OK John I'll see you tomorrow with the new contract for Janice we can talk then about our investigation plans."

"Yeh fine," said John thoughtfully. He still wasn't sure about Vanessa going off on her own trotting around Europe. There was no telling where she could end up, or what she may find.

There was a squeal of rubber on tarmac as Vanessa engaged reverse and shot down the drive, straight out onto the road, seamlessly engaged first gear and squealed and smoked her way to the main road and home.

Over their evening meal they talked about how things had gone for John that day. He asked Fran about the trip to York which John thought that Fran was being a bit evasive about. All Fran would say was that she and Vee had become friendly. Fran was not sure whether she wanted John to know just how friendly things had become between both herself and Vee. It had been very exciting, and she hopped that the opportunity would arise again. She however was looking forward to going to bed with John, whilst she enjoyed the sex with Vee, she was left feeling somewhat unfulfilled. She needed to feel John between her legs filling her inner cavity.

After the meal was over Fran sat with her arms resting on the table, She was looking directly at John.

"What"

"Nothing" Fran replied still looking directly into his eyes. John was starting to feel a little unnerved about the look in her eyes. Fran slowly got up from the table and walked around to where he was sat. She rubbed up against him asking if he had, had a very tiring day? John had placed an arm around Fran's waist whilst she was talking. This he did automatically. Slowly he rubbed his hand up and down towards her thigh. Then he noticed that there was no lump underneath the dress where the underwear would normally have been.

"What's this?" he questioned looking up into her eyes.

"What's what?" She asked instantly

"I am sure that I should be feeling something under this dress. Infact I don't recall seeing this dress before?"

"No you won't have done, it's Vee's I only had dirty clothes with me, and when borrowing an item of clothing from anyone you must do what that person does. In this case since the item is Vee's there is no underwear underneath." Fran explained sweetly

John could feel himself getting a little hot under the collar with the thought that Fran had nothing on under the dress. Fran took hold of his hand and brought it down to the right knee and slowly moved it up under the dress. Once she had started it on its way She no longer had to lead the way. He took over the rest of the movements.

His hand moved up towards the pubic area and continued up towards her breast. He loved the feel of the cashmere dress on Fran's silky soft skin, that plus the feel of it on his own hand from the inside. Fran turned slightly to make it easier for him to touch her body. She reached down with her mouth for his and began to kiss him slowly. John was very surprised at this movement it was so unlike Fran that he almost thought that she was somebody different.

John moved his chair back from the table to make it easier for Fran to reach him. She slowly lowered her body down and straddled him. This caused her dress to come right up way past her thighs. Giving John the bird's eye view of her pubic area.

John gave a little moan, she was really turning him on Fran once again started to kiss him. Forcing his mouth open to accept her tongue she plundered into his mouth and John could not do anything but to respond to her every wish.

Slowly ever so slowly she left his mouth and went around to his ear and slowly made her way down his neck to where he had his shirt. She undid all of the buttons and continued to plunder his body with her tongue and mouth. She played with his nipples making them stand out like toy soldiers. Not content with tormenting his nipples she moved herself of his knee and continued to move downwards on her decent. She reached the trouser waistband and quickly removed the obstacle out of her way. She continued down with her mouth. This totally took John by surprise as he could not remember her ever going down to his private area.

Fran continued down taking hold of John's throbbing penis and gently placing it into her mouth. He took a quick breath and made a strange noise. Fran stopped and looked up at him.

"Do you mind or would you rather I stop?" She enquired still holding onto the hard mass.

"No you just took me by surprise." John managed to splutter out.

Fran smiled at him and returned to what she was doing. John once again took a sharp intake of breath. But Fran carried on.

She almost took him to the point of no return but just stopped in the nick of time, then she once again climbed up him and re-straddled him. She repositioned herself onto of his throbbing organ, and allowed it to insert it's self inside her. She slowly moved her body up and down and occasionally from side to side. She continued to kiss him and fondle him. She brought his hands up to her breasts and moved them in a way to give her maximum pleasure. Slowly she became so aroused that she could not help the soft moans of pleasure that escaped her from time to time.

John was also giving of moans of delight and kissing her breasts when all at once Fran felt him explode inside of her, at the same time or just a fraction afterwards Fran also came. John let out a loud cry of pleasure and continued to kiss and suck at Fran's boobs. After a short time the hot explosion feeling subsided and they slowly started to relax into each other's body.

"Wow Fran who taught you that?"

"Now that would be really telling. Like I said when you borrow someone else's clothing you most do as that person does.

Chapter 11

The next morning when John arrived at Westfield Engineering the place was a hive of activity. Gerry was orchestrating the buildup of WE001. It seemed a shame that, that chassis would have to go through a series of crash tests, but the safety of the drivers in what is a highly dangerous sport had to come first. Is was a requirement of the FIA that all designs had to be both front and side impact tested on a special rig at the MIRA research facility.

At least the chassis didn't need to be a full working example, the new requirement was that it had all its front suspension in place and all the body work attached It didn't need to have its engine or rear suspension. The chassis would be fastened onto a rig, then heavy weights would be smashed into the nose cone and the side pods, the amount of deformation would be measured. Also the front suspension would be checked to ensure that when it broke away from the chassis, as it was designed to do in the event of an impact to dissipate he impact forces, that it didn't encroach onto the drivers head.

As John walked through the assembly area Gerry remarked "Geez John you look knackered, heavy day yesterday with Vee. You lucky dog."

"No not at all. Just had a late night at home." He lied. "We managed to sign up Janice yesterday, she's coming to the factory today to put pen to paper. I asked her to bring her gear for a seat fitting as well, can you spare someone."

"Yes sure." Then Gerry shouted "DAVE COME HERE." When Dave arrived Gerry said to him. "We've a driver coming today, I want you to do the seat fitting."

"Yes sure boss anybody I know."

"Shouldn't think." Said Gerry smiling.

When Dave went back to the chassis to continue fitting the body panels Gerry smiled at John and said "He will enjoy the surprise."

At that moment Vee walked through the door from Reception into the workshop area. She was wearing a very conservative grey pin stripped skirt and jacket. The skirt was about four inch above her knee. Under her jacket she wore a simple plain white blouse.

"Wow," said Gerry "Even in a bloody suit she looks absolutely fantastic. She just oozes sex."

"Well I did ask her to dress down slightly."

"Hi," said Vee "Has Janice arrived yet."

"No" replied John "Should be in about an hour I would think. Come up to my office would you."

"Yes two ticks." Said Vee walking back through the door into reception. She went to talk to Anne about some travel arrangements. "Gerry, when will the test tub be complete."

"In another two days, some of the suspension parts are just coming out of the machine shop we need to integrate the bushes in to the carbon fibre."

"Good, see you later." Said John leaving through the same door that Vee had left by.

In the reception Vee was sat on Anne's desk with a map of Europe. She was asking Anne to arrange flights, and a hire car. Her skirt had ridden up her thigh giving anybody in the reception a clear view of her upper leg. John thought back to the pub on Friday and feeling Vee's bottom. He also thought about last night at home with Fran, and her words of wear the cloths act like the person. Just what the hell did those two get up to on Saturday he wondered. He could feel a stirring in his loins.

He left the reception and entered his office to wait for Vanessa. Vanessa arrived a few minutes later, John was deep in thought when she opened his door.

"First I just wanted to give you these items I found around the break in site." Said John handing over the tissue and the matches book.

"Ian and I had a look at the Pizza restaurant, it did have a couple of offices above, but no other leads. He could have called in the restaurant before coming here I suppose. We did see the image of his car pulling up behind the building, but we couldn't make what type it was. Gerry said he will take the tape for some digital enhancement later this morning."

"Right its a start, I'll do some fishing around at the restaurant, but there's not a lot that can be done until we have either the car or his face." Replied Vanessa.

"No I know it's not a lot, but it's more than the police have come up with."

"Here's a copy of the contract for Janice" Said Vanessa

handing the document over to John.

"Thanks, by the way you look fantastic today," said John shakily, as if it that wasn't really what he wanted to say.

"Thanks." Said Vanessa, "You did ask me to wear something more suitable."

"Yes true, err,"

"What,"

"Well h' nun what did you and Fran get up to on Saturday."

"Why," asked Vanessa looking slightly guilty.

"Oh nothing really, but well when we got back from Silverstone she was still wearing that dress of yours, and well err she sort of attacked me after dinner."

"How do you mean attacked."

"Err in the dining room."

"Not where, how."

"Well err sexually," John said reddening "She was like a demon."

"It must have been the cloths," said Vanessa "Or the lack of them, she did seem to enjoy the freedom in the pool." She continued trying not to show any other emotion.

"It certainly made a difference, I've never known her to be the way she was before."

"Was it good for you," asked Vanessa

"Very." Said John going bright red.

Out in reception Janice Higgins arrived earlier than expected. "Hi," she said to Anne "Janice Higgins, I'm here to see Vanessa Plat."

"Oh your the driver aren't you," said Anne smiling pleasantly.

"Yes at the moment."

"I think Miss Plat is in with Mr. Bennet, please take seat, I'll let them know your here."

Anne rang through to Johns office. "There's a Miss Higgins to see Miss Plat." Said Anne formally to John when he answered the phone.

"You mean Janice is here to see Vanessa," John corrected. "Yes, if you say so." Replied Anne

"Ok send her in." Said John smiling and putting the phone down.

"Please come this way," said Anne showing the way. She knocked, and opened Johns door for Janice.

"Hi," said John, "Please come and sit here," He said pointing to a leather settee with a low table in front of it.

Both John and Vanessa sat down on the settee with Janice.

"Here's the contract for you," said Vanessa taking the contract out of a file. "Please read through it, you'll see that it allows you to continue driving Formula 3 to the end of the championship. It also has a clause for renegotiating the test fee, following successful test sessions and the car performance meeting certain criteria."

Janice took the contract and started to read through.

"There are also non disclosure clause's built in." Continued Vanessa. "Please make sure you understand them."

"Coffee ?" asked John walking to the coffee pot by his desk.

Both Janice and Vee said yes.

John brought the coffee's over for the two women, and returned for his own.

As he turned Vee moved the position of her legs, uncrossing them from right over left, in doing so John was sure that Vanessa had flashed her uncovered sexual area to him. He again felt a stirring in his loins.

Out in the factory word had reached Gerry that Janice had arrived. There were five engineers working on WE001. Two were working on the front suspension. The regulations allowed them to use dummy springs and dampers, but they must use the working arms, hubs and wheels. The dummy components must also ensure that the ride height and hub position is exactly as on the race car. The other three were busy working of the body panels. All the body panels require trimming, whilst a number of items had been laid up, non at this time had been trimmed to final shape. This was a lengthy and time consuming job.

It is planned to produce four tubs initially, although if any accidents happen during testing or the season of racing then more may well be produced. All the tubs come out of a single master, the tubs are laid up to very exacting standards ensuring that each one is exactly the same. Every mounting point on the tub is machined into position following the release of the tub from the mould, by jig mounting onto a machining centre. This then ensures that every hole or groove is positioned within one ten thousandth of a millimeter.

Therefore WE001 to WE004 will be fully interchangeable on parts assembled onto them. Body panels can be jig drilled and trimmed off the tub and fitted in seconds at the track, but the very first set had to be done singly, and by hand to ensure that the programming of the machines had been done correctly. Once proven then the parts could be finished in groups of ten.

"Dave," Gerry said "Get the seat moldings round, The drivers here."

Dave left the side pod cover he was working on and brought round the dummy cockpit and the equipment that would be used to mould the seat shell to the exact shape of the drivers back, bottom, crotch area, and upper legs. This is essential to ensure that the driver doesn't move around in the seat, or that the seat which doesn't have any form of cushioning is comfortable for the driver. After all the driver would could be sat in that seat from two and a half hours at a time.

In the office Janice had completed the signing of the contract. "Come on then bring your gear, we'll go and sort the seat out and you can get to know the guys." Said John.

They both left the office, Vanessa went to her own office to fax the contract through to the solicitors office.

"Gerry, here's Janice." "Janice, Gerry is the technical Director and Engine Designer."

"Hi seen quite a bit of you on the circuits, glad your here." Said Gerry.

Dave looked up when he saw John arrive.

"Well hello again." Dave said to Janice, "They didn't tell me it was going to be you." Dave had worked with Janice before in Formula Renault.

"Yep you've got me again." She said.

"Dave will do the seat fitting." Said Gerry. "I'll leave you in his hands."

"Thanks, I'll change into my suit."

"Yeh use the store to change if you want." Said Dave

"OK, back in two." Said Janice heading in the direction of the store.

Once Janice had changed the task was simple enough, all she

had to do was sit in the Dummy cockpit, in the same position she would normally adopt when driving, Dave would then pour a foam solution into a plastic bag on the main body of the seat. The pressure generated by the solution whilst it was setting would mould its self to the exact shape around Janice's form. This once removed from the bag could be trimmed to shape, and attached to the seat base. This would then be the seat Janice would use for the full season of racing. All drivers in every team need to do the same.

By the late morning Gerry left the building with the video tape of the break in. He had called a friend of his in Leeds who ran a small special effects company. They specialised in digitally re-recording video with either altered or enhanced images.

They could take an image that was unrecognisable on magnetic tape, and once run through his computers which contained digital filters to remove all sources of interference be re-recorded onto tape and play back an image that in most cases was instantly recognisable. The problem was that because the image had been altered by computer then that image was not admissible evidence in a court of law. Gerry had spoken and described the conditions to his friend Cliff Lawton. Cliff didn't see any problems at all in being able to at least say what the cars make and model was. If the angle was good enough he might even be able to see part if not all the number plate. Cliff promised Gerry that he would work on the tape urgently, it would take him until Wednesday though to get a result. He would call Gerry when ready to show him the results.

Chapter 12

The following day Gerry was in deep discussion with Q8, the Oil and fuel suppliers. He was having problems with the engine design, under the test programs they had carried out so far the pistons had shown signs of wear and stress. This wasn't unexpected since the material chosen for the pistons was a ceramic compound and not a metal running in a coated aluminium sleeve. This sleeve was encased in the Carbon Fibre engine block. Q8 were trying to formulate a suitable oil for use with that design of engine.

The problem was that the engine so far hadn't been run in anything approaching full power or full load, it also had only been run for short periods. John had asked Gerry to run the engine today with the Q8 people an attendance, up to full power. He also wanted the engine running for one hour under those conditions, not the twenty minute tests that had been completed so far. Johns reasoning was simple, now he had a test driver on the books he wanted to start the testing by the end of the next week. WE002 the test car was under build, and progress was going well, but the build was rapidly reaching the stage where an engine and gearbox was required to complete the assembly.

Microsoft were also pushing now, they wanted to launch the car to the worlds media. They were pushing a spectacular launch at the British Grand Prix with the cars fully operable. It was looking very doubtful however that the chassis would be available in a fully working form for that event, unless the engine tests were completed on schedule.

Down in the engine test bay Eric and Jim were hard at work re-filling the test engine with coolant and Oil, Q8 had brought another formulation for them to try. They had also brought a super grade of pump fuel. The regulations called for the cars to be run on 'Pump Fuel', whilst all the teams complied with that requirement, there were variations in the specification of pump fuel. Therefore all the companies produce a high grade fuel right up to the specification within their own formula, samples of this formulation would be supplied to the FIA as a master prior to the seasons start. The FIA would then check samples of the fuel to that specification during the following season.

Filling a Formula One engine with fluids isn't like filling your own road car. The coolant system must be filled in a manner that ensures that it doesn't contain any air at all. The engine is what is called a dry sump design. That means that the oil is actually held in a separate tank from the engine, and not in a sump under that engine as in your road car. This allows the engine to be much lower than a standard engine. The oil is then pumped at high pressure through the engine.

The oil also is pumped through radiators which on the car will be mounted in the side pods alongside the engine cooling radiators. This ensures that they get the maximum air flow to cool the liquids.

In the test house both the coolant and the oil radiators are mounted in front of a high speed fan unit which pushes cooled air at high speed through the units. It took about half an hour for the two mechanics to re-fill the engine with its liquids and to be sure that it was filled correctly.

Ian brought a proven electronics module through for them to connect once they were ready. The engine was then test fired to ensure that it would run. They didn't want the embarrassment of last week when it refused to fire.

The engine fired immediately it was run for only five minutes, this allowed them all to check that the telemetry readouts were all functioning. Once satisfied the power to the engine was shut off, the engine again stopped immediately. Eric went off the call Gerry to report that they were ready when they were.

In Gerry's office the group were examining the various samples that had been removed from earlier tests. Some showed signs of improvement, whilst others at best had shown none at all. Eric arrived to interrupt the gathering.

"We're ready." Said Eric simply "All primed with the wonder liquid."

"Thanks Eric we'll come right out." Replied Gerry.

With that the group finished their examinations and followed Gerry out to the test area.

They all gathered around the telemetry monitors which were position in front of the glass window, looking into the test bay.

Inside the test bay they could see the ten cylinder flat engine, mounted onto a frame at one end, which was secured to the floor by bolts that looked large enough to hold down a Jumbo Jet. The other end had the gearbox attached, this was then mounted onto the dynamometer. This would give readouts relating to the power output from the engine. Two large flexible tubes hung from the ceiling. They were attached to the ends of the exhaust system. They were to carry the huge amounts of carbon monoxide out through filters to the atmosphere outside the building.

"OK start her up Eric." Said Gerry.

Eric pressed the start button on his console, this triggered the air starter which was attached to the end of the gearbox. Ian pressed the enter button on his lap top computer, this was connected to the engine through a plug on Eric's console. The engine burst into life immediately.

The noise level increased immediately, even though the engine was in a sound enclosure. Once the revs had settled following its burst into life Ian unplugged the lap top. The engine was now running from its own management system. The lap top is required every time to start the engine.

Following the test parameters that had been laid down by Gerry, Eric took the engine up to half revs, this could be seen on the screens in the form of simple line on a graph. At the same time the power curve also increased, as did the coolant flow and oil flow. The temperatures of both the coolant and oil were also climbing. The coolant temperature increased steadily whilst the oil temperature seemed to increase rapidly.

Gerry turned to Aaron DeBeers one of the Q8 chemists and asked.

"Are you happy with that ?"

"So far." Was the curt response.

The engine was allowed to run at half revs for a further ten minutes. During this time the coolant temperature increased up to 105 degrees, this was the planned operating temperature for the special coolant being used. The oil meanwhile continued to rise in temperature it reached 180 degrees.

"What's the flash point ?" asked Gerry

"205 degrees." DeBeers replied. Whilst he was well renowned for his expertise in the lubrication field, conversation didn't come easily from him.

"Take her up again for 10 then start the running program." Gerry said to Eric.

The running program was a computer programmed test cycle, that would represent the running of the engine in a typical race scenario.

After nine minutes of the next phase the oil temperature had increased still further. It was now running at 200 degrees only 5 degrees away from the point where it would flash and possibly cause a fire to start if exposed to air. The readouts from the piston crown temperatures were also steadily climbing. At this point they had reached 800 degrees centigrade.

"Do you want me to start the next phase boss." Asked Eric
"Aaron are you happy?"
"Yes."
Gerry looked at Eric and said "Well do it."
"Aaron what do you expect to happen to the temperature."
"It should stabilise when the engine revs start oscillating. I think the temperature is rising because the revs are being held constant." "Fine." Replied Gerry.

Eric pressed another button on his console to start the program. The engine immediately cut its revs down from 15000 to 12000 then the revs increased up to 17500 for a few seconds. These oscillations continued for about 5 minutes, the oil temperature during this time didn't fall, it continued to rise when it reached 204 degrees Gerry looked worried at Aaron. The crown temperature was now reading 850 degrees, but they had stabilised and finished climbing.

"I'm going to abort."
"No I still think its OK." Replied Aaron

Then all at once there was a load explosion and then silence from within the test house, the glass separating the onlookers from the engine was peppered with particles from the exploding engine, just like shrapnel from an exploding bomb. The glass was then covered in a mixture of steaming hot coolant and oil, the oil then on contact with the air in the bay burst into flames. When the engine exploded the fuel line, which had an automatic cut off, was ruptured. This spilled about a litre of fuel into the flames causing an even bigger flash of flame to erupt. All the onlookers ducked down in an automatic response away from the devastation in the test room. The glass was buffeted by a shock wave from the explosion. Gerry was worried that it may not hold and the flames would be allowed to spread into the factory.

John felt the shock of the explosion in his office, he ran out and down into the factory, where he could see the glow of the flames through the glass.

Eric who was stood at the console pressed the extinguisher button on his console. This flooded the test room with, first an inert gas to reduce the amount of oxygen in the room, followed a few seconds later by a dry powder which would prevent any further oxygen reaching the mixture to ensure that it couldn't re-ignite. In total it took less than a minute from the explosion to the flames being extinguished. In this time most of the staff working on the cars had arrived in the engine test area. It would take a further five minutes for the fumes to die down for the onlookers to see the amount of devastation the had been caused.

"Quick turn on the room extraction." Shouted John as he ran to the console. "What the hell went wrong Gerry." He added

"Haven't a clue yet John. We had just started the simulation when it went up."

"What was the telemetry showing ?"

"I was worried about the oil temp, it was close to its flash point."

"Have you any ideas." Said John turning to the Q8 men.
DeBeers said defensively "Your cooling system didn't work so the oil wouldn't cool."

"Look I don't want a fucking witch hunt on who's to blame, I want to know what caused this." Shouted John waving at the room.

"This will set us back days, we needed that engine running up and installing in the chassis."

"John once the room has cleared, we can start the investigation, until then I can only pass theories not reasons." Gerry said trying to calm things down. Then he said to the crowd.

"OK funs over for know, lets get back to work. Eric you and Jim work with me to collect the samples, Ian down load the telemetry to PC we'll re-run it in my office later."

Once the fumes had cleared Eric opened up the room, the sight that lay before them looked as if a bomb had gone off. The three men looked as if they were about to step onto the moon. They were fully suited in disposable coveralls, including hoods, with boots and gloves. They also were wearing goggles to protect their eyes and Darth Vader style face masks. The reason behind all the protective gear was not only to save their clothing from the mess, but the Q8 men were concerned that the resultant mixture following the explosive forces could be highly corrosive or even toxic. There was a mixture of carbon fibre, ceramic, oil and coolant covering most of the room. On top of all this was the dry extinguisher powder. The first job was to look around the room to locate any large fragments that had been thrown out of the main engine block. It took about half an hour of detailed and very dirty searching to find only six items that were larger than a fifty pence piece. Once these had been recovered and labeled with the location of where they had been found, and the distance away from the engine. It was useless at that time to try to identify the item. Then Eric and Jim could start to remove the remains of the engine block from the room to the assembly area.

Once the engine was in place Gerry could start his investigation. He was like a coroner performing an autopsy on a dead person. First he examined the engine from the outside looking at all angles, and closely examining the exit point on the block where the failure had occurred. From his preliminary look he could tell that one of the connecting rods had failed in a catastrophic manner. Parts of it had blown holes in the left hand bank of cylinders on both the upper and lower surfaces. He could still see the parts of the piston in the cylinder. From this he surmised that the failure wasn't due to any failure in the cylinder heads, or the crown of the piston. He would need to fully strip the engine down to find the route cause.

He worked steadily throughout the day carefully removing sections of the engine, working first on the side that had failed, he worked his way down to the central crank shaft this took him a total of 4 hours of painstaking work. Once he had reached the crank he called over DeBeers, who was watching the examination.

"I think it was the oil that caused the problem."

"Why do you say that." Asked DeBeers "Surely it was the oil coolers that failed."

"It may well have been the oil coolers that couldn't cool the oil sufficiently, but I think that when the oil approaches its flash point it loses its lubricating properties, that in turn generates more heat due to friction, creating more problems for the cooling system. Look at the shells on a bearing that didn't fail."

The shell that Gerry passed over had lost all of its bearing surface, it was a blue colour, which had been caused by the heat generated whilst running. DeBeers studied the component for some time, ten finally.

"I agree," Said DeBeers "But why did the heat rise so quickly I the first instance."

"That could well be our problem, the ceramic pistons will absorb heat like a heat sink whilst they won't change shape or size due to the heat they will continue to absorb it. We could see that from the piston crown temperature readings. Your oil is going to have to cope with a much higher flash point, and also retain its lubrication properties right through the temperature range."

"But you need to solve the heat problems also."
"Yes true, but that won't be easy."
"Can't you resort to a more conventional material for your pistons."

"We chose ceramic to keep the reciprocating mass down. Using a metal will increase that, and thus reduce the engines ability quickly rev up the range."

It was clear to both the engineers that they wouldn't solve the problem standing throwing queries back and forth like two tennis stars at the practice net. They would both have to go back to the drawing boards and have a re-think.

"Well John isn't going to be happy." Gerry said resigned to getting a bollicking from John when he reported his findings.

It took almost five hours for Eric and Jim to restore the test room back to its normal state. Even then the glass between the room and the test console would have to be replaced. It had been peppered with particles from the engine, these were a mixture of carbon and metal. The carbon was harmless due to its low mass. The metal however had left chips in the glass, another failure could cause it to fracture and scatter debris across the assembly area. This would cause a major delay, the entire area would need decontamination and any work in progress would also need a full and detailed clean. On leaving the test room they sealed the door, and left the fans running. The place had a foul stench still lingering.

Chapter 13

In total the team lost five days from their planned schedule following the engine blow up. Attention had to be turned to redesign and re manufacture of parts, instead of continuing the buildup of the test chassis.

The crash test unit however was completed on time. It had been loaded into one of the large enclosed mobile workshop come car transporters, and driven down to the Mira test facility. Once there it would undergo the independent tests that were a requirement of the FIA. Under normal circumstances Gerry would have been at the test as a witness, but since he was required back at the factory John had to attend. For once luck was on theft side and the tests were carried out without a hitch. Gerry s chassis design passed the test with flying colours. This would now mean that they could concentrate all their efforts on rectifying the faults in the engine design. They had decided that the engine that would be run in initial test would not have the ceramic piston design but would be run with alloy pistons. Gerry predicted that Q8 could then run the last Oil batch through track testing which would be far more searching than the test house.

During this time the team or at least Gerry had, had another result. The security tape had come back from Cliff Lawton, he had not only managed to identify the car but he had been able to pick out most of the cars registration number. This was in the main thanks to the UK's style of front number plates. Black letters on a white reflective back ground had given him a wonderful contrast. The car turned out to be a Fiat Bravo. John had asked Vanessa to use her contacts with the Police to find out who the registered keeper of the vehicle was. She had discovered that the keeper was listed as A Galli of New Miller Dam.

When Vanessa had shown this to John he said I've seen that name somewhere else, but couldn't quite bring it to mind. He had left Vanessa to continue with her investigations, she now had something to work on.

Vanessa had located the same office as John a day after finding the name, she saw that he was listed as an accountant on the door, but couldn't find any reference to him in the Yellow pages or any other business directory. She decided that she would have to pay Mr. Galli a call. Her call on him would not be during normal business hours, but much the same as Mr. Galli's call on Westfield, late at night. The only problem was the location of his office. Being above a restaurant in the centre of Wakefield. The particular street was also well known throughout the area for being where most of the late night activity occurred. This would mean that her visit would have to be timed to the quiet period. She had asked Ian to assist her.

It was 2.0AM in the morning, when Vanessa and Ian met outside the factory. The weather had changed from being warm to cold and wet much colder and wetter than normal for this time of year even in England. Ian looked nervous already, Vanessa was still her usual calm self.

"Are you ready Ian." She asked

"No not really." He replied

"Come on I'll drive, at east with this weather it should be quiet now."

"Hope so." Said Ian getting into Vanessa's car.

She set off for the centre of Wakefield, it was only four miles from the factory.

Vanessa found a dark back street close to the office to park.

"Program my mobile number into your phone Ian. Then you keep watch on the front door, I'm going to after climb up onto that outbuilding and enter through that window." She said pointing to a small sash type window

"It looks like a toilet to me. So hopefully it won't be alarmed. If you see any sign of activity at the front ring and let me know."

"These aren't secure lines you know." Said Ian worried about using the cell phone network.

"I know but it's the best we have, nobody will be monitoring us anyway."

"What if the alarm goes off."

"Go back to the car and wait for me there."

"What if you don't show."

"I will, look don't worry I'll be fine."

With that Vanessa started to climb up onto the roof. Ian left her and went round the front of the building. He found a dark shop doorway with a good view up and down the precinct, and settled down to wait.

Vanessa made her way across the roof of the outbuilding to the window. She tried the window, it moved slightly upwards then stopped. Shit she thought it feels like its painted in with age. She put more pressure onto the glass, it gave a bit more and again stopped. This time however it had moved enough for her to get her fingers under the frame. She slid her fingers in and felt along the frame. Before she put any pressure on the window she looked across the top of the sash, but couldn't see any sign of alarm wiring. Well here goes she thought, and gave a heave on the bottom of the window. At first it resisted the pressure, then suddenly it gave and moved up freely. Well I've done him a favor she said to herself, and stepped into the room. The room was as she had thought, a small and dirty toilet. Vanessa checked around the window for any signs of alarms, there was none to be seen. She moved to the door and tried it, it opened easily Again she checked the frame for any alarms, and again the door was clear. She ducked down and peered into the room, looking up into the corners for any sign of a FIR detector. Using a small mirror she looked above the door frame. The room appeared not to have any form of alarm system. Looking across the room she could see the outer door of the office. That door had a simple glass upper half with the Name A Galli on it. So Mr. Galli's office consisted of the single room. He eyes were becoming accustomed to the gloom, she peered around the walls, there was none sign at all of any form of alarm control box. She steadily moved out of the toilet and into the main room. It was small and very dingy, not the sort of place to spend a frill day working, depression would soon set in. The only furniture in the office was a single battered desk and hard backed chair. On the desk there was just a single Fax and phone unit. She tried the desk draws, none of them were locked, and all were empty. In fact the entire room did not have the air of an office where any work was actually carried out.

She went to the outer door and tried it, it was locked. Vanessa took out a small tool from a small bum type bag she had around her waist, and expel/1y picked the old lock. The door opened out onto a simple plain access corridor. She returned to the room and re-locked the door. She looked at the fax unit on the desk, it looked to be totally out of place in this room. The room reminded of something out of a late thirties private eye movie, but the fax was one of the latest units. Most fax machines have a storage facility for numbers. They can also print a log of the numbers dialed out. She decided that, that was going to be her only source of information. She pressed a few buttons hoping that the recall wasn't protected by any pin numbers. Luckily Mr. Galli wasn't security conscious, and the machine started to print. Only a single page came out. Vanessa picked up the paper and folded it into her pouch. She than left the room by the same route she had taken to gain access.

Outside Ian was still keeping watch, five minutes had passed since taking up his lookout position. From round the corner he could make out a shadow approaching. Ian started to get worried, should he dial Vanessa he thought to himself. As the person casting the shadow came closer, Ian let out a breath of relief he could now see that it was Vanessa.

"That was quick." He said.

"Come on back to the car quick." Replied Vanessa. Once they were inside Ian asked "Did you get in."

"Of course I did. What a strange place. It had nothing of any value inside."

"Didn't you get anything then."

"Only this from the Fax machine." She showed Ian the listing she had run off.

"Well what know."

"Back to the office then home I think." Said Vanessa slightly disappointed with their nights work.

She drove quickly back to the factory to drop Ian off, then headed home. Once home Vanessa looked at the printout, the fax had only dialed one number. This number however had been dialed ten times. A fax had been sent to the number the day after the break in at Westfield. The number was to an international code. The country code was Italy, and the area code represented Milan.

The next day Vanessa made here findings known to John. She said that once the reveal had been completed of the car at Silverstone the following month then she would take some time out and track down the recipients of the fax.

John was still worried about allowing Vanessa to travel across Europe on her own.

"Vee I haven't discussed this with you, but I really don't like the idea of you travelling on your own."

"It's no problem, I've travelled thousands of miles on my own, I'm a big girl know." During those travels Vanessa had been through many scrapes. None that she would ever admit to though.

"Yes but this is different. You just don't know what's going to happen or what your going to find"

"True, but what harm can I come across."

"Look this is big business, the destination of the fax has certain suggestions attached."

"Mafia you mean." Laughed Vanessa.

"Could be, but I also doubt it. Look there are some powerful people involved in the game, they don't take kindly to me coming in and taking the Microsoft money."

"So what do you want me to do?" Take Ian with me. "He was hopeless last night."

"No that's not what I want. In any case Ian is going to have to go to the states to work with Microsoft and Hitachi. I don't know what I want, but I know I'm troubled by you going off on your own."

"Look I'll leave you to think about it."

"No I know, why not take Fran with you. The journey will do her good, and two women travelling together will not look out of place."

"Have you asked her."

"No, but I'm sure she'll agree. She does like you, and seems to enjoy your company."

"True." Said Vanessa smiling. "OK ask her, its fine by me if she say's yes. I'll make the arrangements once you confirm." Vanessa thought it would be hard being a nursemaid to Fran, but it would have some compensations.

Chapter 14

There was a frantic air of activity in the assembly area over the following days. The chassis WE002 had to be completed, and chassis WE001 which had been returned following the crash tests had to be stripped to its bare tub and fully assembled as a working chassis, although this tub would never be run. Two new tubs were in the laying up process. The two chassis on build were required for the launch at Silverstone. Microsoft along with Westfield had planned to use the British Grand Prix to announce to the world media their cars for the 1999 world championship. Not only did the cars require building but also they must also have the graphics package which would have the Microsoft cloud background for the full car colour scheme, and Microsoft across the engine cover and rear wing.

The Westfield design differed from all the cars that were featured on the grid for the 1998 season in that it didn't have an air box on top of the engine cover. Due to Gerry Watts choosing to produce a flat ten cylinder engine, he would use the side pods not only to house the radiators, but also to collect and feed the engine with air. Because of this the side pods were slightly larger than the ones on the other cars, but the overall frontal area had been reduced. It also reduced the side facing advertising space.

Along with the Microsoft logo's Westfield also needed to incorporate Hitachi, IDEK which had purchased particular positions, Q8, Koni, Bridgestone and Bosch onto the package. The positions of each of the sponsors needed to be agreed finally, all had in principle agreed at the art work stage, but none had actually seen it in the flesh. Once the first of the two launch cars had been completed with the base colour scheme all the representatives of the sponsoring companies had to be called together and shown the positions. This was a worrying time for Vanessa because if any of them disagreed then new transfers would have to be designed and produced. Westfield had agreed to use a small local sign firm to produce all the logos in a computer cut vinyl. To produce the new art work would cause further delays. They simply didn't have the time. They only had a matter of two more days to complete the build program, load the cars and transport them down to the stand that was being constructed for them already at the Silverstone circuit.

Gerry and his team on the engine side had managed to redesign the pistons from alloy, manufacture fifty examples, build one test engine and one engine for installation into WE001. The test engine had had one test run in the test house, just to prove that it would run, not that they intended running the cars at Silverstone. John had managed to convince Microsoft to scale down their plans for the launch. They had wanted Westfield to run the cars around the Grand Prix circuit before the start of the Grand Prix. They had wanted the cars to appear out of the back of the two transporters in a cloud of smoke and parade around the circuit. Even if the engine tests had gone well John had not being happy with such an event. He had been furious with Vanessa for agreeing to it. She had done it he knew because of her lack of understanding, and Microsoft's understanding of the complexity of Formula One Cars. Both of them were virgins in the game.

John had asked Vanessa to ensure that all the representatives of the sponsors were called together at the same time. They did a mini launch for them, he felt that if all were together and saw the car for the first time then the disagreements would be reduced on the positioning of their names. As it was that policy worked all agreed that the car looked fantastic, their names were all readily visible to both television viewers and track side spectators. It was of course the television viewers that were the targeted audience. The car had to be both visually pleasing and also eye catching. They all agreed that it did that.

"Well done Vanessa." Said John after everyone had left "That went down better than we could have planned."

"What a relief, I haven't slept for days worrying about today. I think this was more worrying than the press release on Sunday."

"True." Then turning to Gerry John said. "Get both cars completed tomorrow then load them onto the transporters. We need to arrive Thursday. The cars will stay locked up in the transporters. The drivers can stay with them."

Not only were the transporters use to move the cars around the world, but they had full sleeping and living areas built into them, and also a mobile work shop once the cars were moved out. Each car had its own transporter. In total four units would be taken to each Grand Prix, three would house the cars, two for racing and one spare. The other would contain all the spares and a further mobile hospitality unit. Only two of the vehicles would be used to take the cars to Silverstone. The colour schemes of the transporters also matched that of the cars with all the same logos in position along the flat side of the trucks.

The trucks carrying the cars arrived at the Northamptonshire circuit early on the Thursday morning. Once the transporters arrived at the circuit they had to very gently manoeuvre themselves into position immediately behind the stand. This wasn't going to be easy, the circuit was already packed with display stand and people working in those stands preparing them for the coming weekend. The crowds would start arriving on the Friday in small numbers, this would build through the Saturday, with over one hundred thousand spectators expected for the Sunday race day. The drivers ably demonstrated their individual driving skills to those working around them, not that any of them were looking, by ensuring that the long vehicles were reversed up to the back of the launch stand without knocking down any of the neighboring stands.

"I'm sure they think we have rotor blades on these things." Pete Jakes said to his buddy Terry Smith.

"Yeh I must have been touching the back of that stand getting this in here. How the hell do we get the bleeders back out on Sunday." Replied Terry.

"We don't we wait until Monday." Said Pete "We're here to stay, four bleeding nights I reckon."

Later that morning John and Vanessa arrived to inspect the stand and their cars.

"Leave both cars locked up in the trucks please." John said to the two drivers. "I'm afraid you'll have along few days, the cars mustn't be of loaded until Sunday. You'll have to stay with them until then. We cannot risk leaving them alone."

"Can't we even watch the racing." Commented Pete.

"Later today we'll have more arriving from base, we can arrange a shift pattern."

"Great." Said Terry.

Later that day once the rest of the engineers and mechanics had arrived from the factory, they were all busy making the finishing touches to the stand.

The lighting and effects were all going to pose problems, the launch had ,had to be scheduled for 11 am on the Sunday. This was a lull in the day's proceedings. The morning warm up of the competing F I cars would have been completed, there would be no other races starting at that time, the track would be in its last stages of preparation before the start of the Grand Prix. The Grand Prix drivers would all be busy with their own final preparations, so this type of event was seen by the organisers of the event to be a good filler.

The background of the stage area was all black, as was the roof over the top of the stage. The front of the stage had a heavy curtain in place blocking the view of any passerby. On the front of the curtain was an advertisement of the reveal time.

At the back of the stage a group of Mechanics were busy building screens to ensure that the trucks were completely blocked in. Nobody would be allowed to see the cars before the launch.

By night fall of the Thursday the stage and the barriers were all in place. Friday would be an easier day for all, John told all the guys that they could have the day off. He did however still require the trucks and cars guarding following a rotation that Vanessa had drawn up. Working closely with the men on the stand had started feelings within Vanessa. She hadn't slept with a man for months. The weather was atrocious all during the construction, but many of the men had stripped down to shorts and tee shirts. Seeing the wet clothing clinging to their muscular bodies and where they had naked skin the rain made them glisten this fired her more carnal urges.

As John drove out of the circuit with Vanessa he said, "Fran said she would love to travel with you."

"Oh I thought you'd forgotten, or didn't have the balls to ask her."

"Well there you are, have I proved to you that I'm a man, and therefore do have balls."

"No, not yet." Replied Vanessa smiling, "There's only one way of proving you have the balls."

"And how's that." Asked John.

Vanessa reached across and started to stroke Johns thigh, he could feel the stirring in his loins again.

"This helping." She asked throatily. She moved her hand further up his thigh into his groin.

"Its helping with something." Said John "Oh look here's the

hotel, lets get checked in."

This broke the spell of the moment. Few thought John that was a close run thing, I couldn't have kept control much longer.

They both checked in at reception and were shown to their rooms, by a tired looking clerk. The Grand Prix weekend was one of the busiest of the year for all the hotels in the Silverstone area.

Following a quick meal Vanessa who had changed into a more shear outfit found a quiet corner in the hotel lounge come bar. John had gone to the bar for some drinks, once served he turned looking for Vanessa. He saw her tucked away in a corner away from most of the other people in the bar.

"Why come over here." Asked John.

"I felt as if that lot were undressing me." She replied.

"Well if you insist on wearing things like this," he said fingering her blouse, "Then what do you expect." In fingering her blouse his fingers slipped in the gap between her buttons, one of his fingers brushed against her small breast. Vanessa brought her hand up to his, and gently guided inside her blouse and onto her breast. He could feel the softness of her flesh, she moved his hand down and across her nipple. This started to harden immediately with the movement.

"Does that feel nice," she asked.

"Very." Said John turning towards her so that his body masked her away from the others stood around the bar.

"Lets go up to my room." Said Vanessa "I could find out if you've got the balls then."

Vanessa moved Johns hand away and stood up, she walked to the door, placing her empty glass on the bar as she passed. John followed a minute later.

Vanessa was stood outside her door when John reached the landing, She had undone the buttons on her blouse so that her breasts could be seen as the fabric fell forward. She took his hand and lead him into her room. Once inside they kissed. Vee took Johns hand and again placed it onto her breasts, whilst he caressed them gently she unfastened his shirt, and started to undo the top of his trousers. He moved his other hand under Vee's skirt, he moved it gently up towards her groin. Vee said quietly "No not yet."

John moved his hand away quickly startled.

"Just caress my breast's I'll let you know when the times right." She said. Vee then continued to remove his trousers. She then started to caress around his groin, moving here hands around his testicles and penis, she looked up to him and said. "I can feel the balls, but can't see them yet." With that she slid his shorts down. "Yes your a man all right you've got the balls and prick to go with them, she said crudely. John slipped his trousers and shorts fully off, along with his shirt. Whist he did that Vee moved to the bed and lay back, she looked at John's naked form and started to massage herself between her legs with one hand whilst the other caressed her own breast. John could feel his heart pounding in his chest, and the blood pulsating in his engorged organ. He moved to the bed and joined Vee. She again took his hand, and guide this time between her legs. She withdrew her own and placed her sticky fingers into her mouth, "H'mm." She said "I love that taste. Try it John." John removed his fingers and tentatively place one into his mouth. Vee then continued to massage herself, leaning away from John so that he could get a good display. "Lay down on your back John. I can than give you the fuck of your life." She said.

John lay back Vee climbed across him and lowered herself down onto his erect organ. It felt good inside her. It wasn't making love it was pure sex.

Once they were both spent, Vee got up and showered. She returned to the bed where John had sat up and recovered somewhat. "Didn't you enjoy that." He asked worried.

"Don't worry John, it was wonderful, I tend to have sex with a man only when I really need to."

"What do you mean."

"I'm not like most women, I don't need to have a man inside me regularly, when I do it leaves me well satisfied for quite some time." "I'm still not with you."

"Look I take my pleasures with other women, I enjoy the caressing and tender feel of their bodies and touch. Sex with men is much more physical. I don't need that to feel fulfilled all the time."

"Are you a lesbian."

"No, I suppose you could say I swing both ways, but I can leave well alone when I need to."

"About the other weekend."

"Yes."

"Did you, err you know err do it with Fran."

"If you mean did I go to bed with your wife then yes we did it. Just like you did to me. It had the same amount of meaning to her as this did with us. It happened. Please John don't take it out on her."

"How can I, if I accuse her of screwing you, then you'll say that! screwed you this weekend."

"Yes I can be blamed for adultery with both partners." "That would make a juicy court case wouldn't it." Laughed John.

"Where does that leave me travelling with Fran."

"I don't know, it's not as if she was screwing around with another man."

"No, true but how do you feel about her being in bed with another woman, she's no longer exclusively yours is she."

"The way she screwed me the other week after she'd been to bed with you, then I would say she still prefers me."

"True, I think it's added a little spice to her sex life that's all."

"Do you mind that ?"

"Not at all, I know she's married to you, and therefore will always turn to you before me."

"What shall I say to her."

"Nothing, just leave things be. If the time presents its self then either you or I can talk to her, I think you should leave know." With that John left Vanessa for his own room.

He didn't sleep much that night, he not only had the problems of the car build on his mind, but now his wife and his Marketing Director had screwed each other, and now he had screwed his marketing Director also. Where would that lead them. The strangest thing was that he didn't resent the fact that his wife had been to bed with Vee, he actually found the thought very erotic. He decided that he would still allow Fran to go with Vee. It wasn't as if anything would ever come from it. It would help her to relax.

Saturday seemed to be a long day, there was plenty of track action, and work was still being carried out on the stand. Although most of it was checking the systems, and ensuring that nobody managed to sneak through. They wouldn't have seen anything the cars were still locked away in the transporters with a constant guard inside.

As darkness fell the four of the team were left at the track the others drifted away, either back to their hotel, or further afield to try to find some night action. Fran had arrived at the hotel, John took her Vanessa and Gerry out for a meal to pass the time on. They also needed to discuss the final formalities for the following day.

On Sunday morning the cars were removed from the back of the trucks behind screens, to ensure that no reporter got a sneak preview of the cars. The guards had reported that the night had passed without incident.

"It looks like our concerns were unfounded." John said to Gerry as the cars were positioned on the stand.

"Yes, it could have been the fact that the guards were here, or that nothing was ever going to happen."

"Luckily for us attention seems to have been turned towards McLaren, they've had bad luck at the last two races, Ferrari has suddenly got the upper hand."

"It makes you wonder if things are linked doesn't it."

"Certainly, but there is also the fact that the Ferraris engines seem to make strange noises when accelerating away from slow corners. Almost as if they are running fraction control to limit wheel spin."

Any form of traction control is not allowed under the FIA rules. It is however well known that when an engines throttle is controlled through a management system then it is possible to tie the throttle opening to speed sensors on both the front and rear wheels. The cars speed can also be detected by air speed. All of this when fed through the computer in the car can then limit the amount of throttle opening to ensure that only the correct amount of power is fed through to the rear wheels. Therefore preventing the wheels from spinning. Thus giving traction control by another means. All of the programming for this can be hidden so deep within the program for the computer, that when down loaded it cannot be detected.

"John are you saying that Ferrari are running an illegal system."

"No not at all, its not up to me to do that. I'm sure that I'm not the only one to hear the engines rev variations. Its up to the other teams competing against them. If that's taking some of the heat away from us then good. It allows us to get on with our jobs."

The Sunday morning action continued on the track to plan. Even though the bad weather had continued. It had rained almost solidly the whole morning. The time was rapidly approaching the time for the press launch.

By about 10.45 a crowd had started to gather in front of the stage. At the stroke of eleven the speakers around the stage burst into life, the show began. It took about an hour for the full show to be completed, at the end all agreed that the reception from the gathered press and public went down well. The cars looked absolutely fantastic, they were shaped like an up turned wing. The whole body shape had been designed to take effect of Bernoulli's principle. This principle says that the faster a gas moves, the lower its pressure. Therefore the top face of the cars body had been kept as flat as possible in the direction of the air flow, the underside of the car had a curvature. This ensured that air moving under the car had to travel faster than the air moving over the top surface. This means that the air pressure under the car is lower than the pressure on the top, the car is then sucked to the ground. To assist with this principle the car also had front and rear wings. Gerry hoped that the pressure differential he had designed into the car would enable him to reduce the size of the wings and therefore cut the drag factor, making the car slip through the air cleanly.

The rest of the events on the track again went against the form book. McLaren's recent run of bad luck again struck, Ferrari's luck continued, with Schumacher winning the Grand Prix. That win was again a sign that the establishment was against Ron Dennis and his team. The McLaren had actually crossed the finishing line on the track ahead of the Ferrari. Due to an infringement earlier in the race the leading Ferrari driven by Schumacher was given a ten second stop and go penalty. Ferrari pulled their car into the pits to serve the penalty on the final lap of the race. Their pit position was actually beyond the finishing line. Therefore in order to take the penalty Schumacher crossed the line, at that time he was ahead of the McLaren. The stewards of the meeting following protests by the McLaren team decided that the result should stand, and that because the pit lane during a race is an extension of the track the Ferrari was the winner. That debate would continue for many years to come.

      Gerry couldn't help but think back to the conversation with John earlier regarding the legality of the Ferrari. Gerry had seen John talking to Ron Dennis the boss of McLaren and Max Mosley the chairman of the FIA. He wondered whether John had been discussing the issue. Those two men wouldn't be just passing the time of day with John

      Following the launch the cars were removed from the stand and locked away safely in the back of the transporters. The stand had to be cleared of all Westfield's equipment, this also stored in the transporters. This would allow the stand to be dismantled and shipped off to wherever it was to be used. All this took the rest of the afternoon. There was no rush, the transporters wouldn't be allowed to leave the circuit until the following morning.

Chapter 15

Once the cars had been returned to the factory they were both removed from the transporter. WE001 was taken to the reception area where it was placed onto a stand for display purposes. It made quite an imposing feature of the entry into the building, the car was tilted into nose down position so that people could look into the cockpit and see most areas of the car. Only the underside wasn't visible.

The second chassis had now to be prepared for track testing with Janice. The Third and Forth Chassis were under build. Gerry was hard at work with Ian trying to understand the telemetry package. Ian had been burning the midnight oil on the specification. It would require Ian to spend four weeks away from the factory in Seattle, at the Microsoft headquarters to finalise the spec and to ensure that the build-up was completed on time for February testing, prior to the first Grand Prix of 1999 in Australia.

"Its a bad time for you to be away." Gerry said.

"I know but it cannot be helped, all the expertise is over there. The sort of technology we're talking about in programming the chips just isn't available over here."

"Why can't they come here."

"Microsoft and Hitachi are working with the US government on similar systems for the Air Force. The equipment that will be used by us is a form of that technology the US just won't allow it to be removed."

"Are you sure that what you require can be done."

"Yes fully."

"Just leave me with all the required algorithms for the basic management system before you go."

"Its all here Gerry." Said Ian passing over a booklet and disc.

The booklet contained flow diagrams explaining how to reprogram the on board computer from the lap top from start, and how to modify the program for over one hundred different variations.

When Vanessa arrived she went straight in to see John. "How are you today." She asked, looking for any sign that John may have been on a guilt trip after Saturday night.

"Fine, I talked to Fran, she's still looking forward to your trip tomorrow."

"Oh good, did you talk to her about the other night."

"No way." Replied John. "She hasn't talked to me about the two of you, so they way I see it we're equal."

"Anne has booked the flights and Hotel for the first couple of nights, I will take care after that, depending on what or if we find anything."

"How long are you planning to be away."

"May be a week, could be two if there's anything to find"

"OK, its just I was planning to have a holiday away from everything in three weeks."

"Fine if I'm not back Fran will be I'll see to that. We'll be in touch in any case. Where are you going."

"It's a surprise for Fran, so don't let on. I'm thinking of taking her back to the Maldives, she enjoyed it there a few years back."

"Marvelous, I'm jealous. " Vee said leaving the office.

Out in the assembly area Gerry looked on with a smile on his face, the second fully assembled chassis was nearing completion. The car needed to be ready for the following weeks track test program. Whilst they only had the one driver, he wanted to take both cars, the second had a slightly different design of undertray. This should give more down force, he wanted to run back to back trials. He did have results from the wind tunnel, and these would favor the second design. He knew in reality though that out on the track things could be different, and often were.

By the end of the day Gerry was confident that the cars would be completed ahead of schedule. This however wouldn't help bring the testing forward, Donington had, had to be booked well in advance. They wanted to use the circuit for closed testing over a two day period. Whilst Donington wasn't used for Grand Prix races, it was the closest to the factory, and had been used in the past. Gerry called John to give him the good news, he also called Janice so that she could come down for final fitting and familiarisation before the track work started. Most of the work load had now past over to Gerry away from John. John had been responsible for the formation of the team and funding, Gerry was the Engineering brains behind the outfit, and therefore it was his responsibility to ensure that the cars were ready for the following season. Johns work load would now be concentrated towards ensuring the necessary driver line up was in place, and that the logistics for the transportation of the team and all of its equipment would be set up in time for the first Grand Prix in Melbourne.

That night the factory had another visit paid upon it. This time the intruder didn't want to take anything he only wanted to discover how advanced the team was. He again managed to gain access to the factory unseen, he also managed to bypass all the alarm systems. After all that was how he made his living, entering offices and factories gathering intelligence. Once inside he took a number of photographs of the cars in various stages of assembly, he also took a number of shots of the components around the plant. He spent around an hour in the factory. He wasn't an engineer, but he hoped that the end results would be of some use to the recipients of his work. Before leaving the factory he had one further order to carry out. He moved to the rear of the fully completed car and bent down around the right rear suspension assembly. He only spent a few seconds bent down before standing to leave.

All the photographs were taken on a digital camera. The results would be down loaded onto his computer and emailed via the Internet to his employers in Italy. The computer wasn't at the small office he used in Wakefield, but at his home in New Miller Dam to the south of the city.

He left the factory leaving no trace of his visit, he took care this time ensuring that he avoided the external security camera's. He had discovered the intrusion into his office the day after Vanessa had paid him a visit, she hadn't been as careful as he. The window she had used to gain access had been purposely painted shut. It was also made very enticing for an intruder to use the as the entry point. It was of no benefit he only used the office as a front. It had been unfortunate that his computer had developed a fault when he had, had to send the last lot of information. So he had resorted to the fax machine on that occasion, but he hadn't left any trace in his office, or so he thought.

The following day John had to run Vanessa and Fran to Manchester. On the way to Johns Vanessa had made a detour to collect Ian. He was also scheduled to leave the country that morning to fly to Seattle. It was struggle to fit everything into Johns car, but somehow they managed it. Luckily Ian travelled light, even though he would be away a number of weeks. Vanessa's baggage outnumbered his four to one

Gerry was the first at the factory the next morning, he set to work on his tasks for the day totally unaware that at that moment not ten miles away a record of his work was being edited ready for sending to their competition. In his study Alfons had down loaded his nights work onto his computer, using a picture editor he selected fifty of the best shots out of the hundred he took the night before. These he saved onto his hard disk, and selected the email facility. He then looked up the email address of his employers and entered it into the required position on his screen. He attached the file containing the photos to the mail and pressed send. Within seconds the file containing Westfield's progress was on its way through the ether of the World Wide Web. He would wait until he received a positive response from the recipients before he transferred the information back off his hard disk and onto floppy disk for safe storage. Even though Alfons was in his mid sixties he had picked up the modern era of communications extremely well. He knew enough to ensure that he covered all his tracks, just as if he were out in the field avoiding being tracked by his enemies.

After seeing Fran and Vanessa through into the departure lounge John sat for a while with Ian discussing the work that needed to be carried out at Microsoft. When after a short time he heard Fran's and Vee's flight being called he said his goodbye's to Ian and left for the viewing area to see the flight to Linate airport on the eastern side of Milan take off.

An hour later john arrived back at the factory. Gerry asked him "What were you talking to Ron Dennis about the other day."

"I passed on some of my thoughts regarding the sudden improvement in Ferraris fortunes."

"You mean about traction control."

"That and the fact that we had been broken into, and we also suspected that the same person may also have visited Ron's place in Woking."

"You didn't tell about Vanessa going to Italy."

"No way my friend. I'm not putting Fran at risk or Vee for that matter."

"What are they going to do over there. It's all been a little sketchy to me."

"First they intend to trace the number from that Fax printout. See if it belongs to anybody connected with the sport. Then it depends on what they find from there as to their next moves."

"How will Vanessa find the numbers owners."

"She tells me she has some contacts in Italy. Not in Milan though, they will have to travel to Genoa first. Right back to business where are we with the program."

"Car number I is ready now. Car number 2 will be complete Thursday. I intend running a complete systems check on car 1 today, and car 2 Friday morning. I contacted Janice last night, she's coming to the factory on Thursday she'll stay for Friday, then if all's well she go home and join us at Donington on Monday morning."

"Fine nothing for me to do then, I'll go home and work from there. Let me know tonight how the systems check out. Bye."

With that John left for home. On the way home he wanted to make his final preparations for his break in the Maldives.

Chapter 16

The flight to Milan took just over two hours. On landing and clearing customs the two women walked to the car hire desk's and hired an Alfa 1SS for two weeks. Vee wasn't sure how long she would be away for but was determined to ensure that she returned Fran in time for her surprise holiday with John. Once they had located the car Vee drove out of the airport and headed for their hotel in the centre of Milan. They would be staying at the Hilton in that cosmopolitan city.

Once they had checked in they were shown to their rooms, they had booked adjoining rooms, and were located on the third floor. Fran wasn't sure how much use they would actually get from having two rooms, but it did look more respectable that way. She was looking forward to her time with Vee with excitement. She wasn't sure whether it was because she wanted the closeness, and the gentleness of Vee's love making. Or the excitement of the investigation and the unknown aspect of the adventure. It was more than likely a mixture of the two.

"OK." Said Vee "Let's act the tourist today, we need to explore the city. Tomorrow we start the real work."

"Good lets hit the shops." Replied Fran "Milan is renowned for fashion isn't it."

"There's more fashion house's here than you can visit in a month. What are you looking for."

"Anything, lingerie mainly."

"Fine, not my line, but lets go."

The two set of for what a lot of women would say was better than sex, shopping.

At the same time as the women set off on their shopping expedition an email arrived on a computer terminal in a room at the back of an old tenement block in Affori a northern suburb of Milan. The recipient down loaded the file and started to print the information contained in that file. The file contained the fifty photos taken by Alfons Galli last night. It took Luca Morbidelli almost an hour to complete the printing process. The results were excellent they not only gave an over view of the progress made so far in the build of the cars, but also Alfons had managed to take shots of the under tray. Whilst to the uninformed the undertray looked like a base plate. To those in the racing game it was a part that tended to be hidden from view. Many of the designers secrets in how he intended to create ground effect lay within the shape and form of the undertray. Alfons had managed to unlock some of those secrets. Once this was added to the upper body and the wings, he knew Ferrari would be able to gather almost all of Westfield's body design intentions. He was surprised by the picture of the completed car. It didn't have any sign of an air box on the top of the car. He could see that the side pods were larger than normal, and that the cars exhaust appeared to exit from the top of the engine cowl. Much like the latest design from Ferrari. Luca placed the prints into a large brown envelope, and placed them into his safe. He also down loaded the images onto floppy disk and placed this in his safe. He then erased the file from his computer. Ensuring that the recycle bin had also been emptied. He didn't want to leave any trace on the terminal. He then called Gianni Lorenzo.

> "We need to meet." Luca said simply.
> "When." Replied Gianni
> "Today, The café in Piacenza as usual, 3.30 PM."
> "OK."

Luca put the phone down and smiled, this will go down well at Ferrari, they should be worth 100 million lire at least he thought. Following the information he had passed to Ferrari regarding McLaren they would be aseptically pleased. That information had, had two effects. Initially Alfons had been able to substitute some components, these components had failed at the Canadian Grand Prix, allowing Ferrari to win. Secondly the information had allowed Ferrari to put into effect changes to their own car that had enabled them to improve and put the pressure back onto McLaren. They had also discovered that McLaren didn't have the control systems that Ferrari had been experimenting with. Gianni had decided that he would introduce them into his package in France. They helped there, but really can into effect at the British Grand Prix.

Thanks to the programming in the management system the drivers were able to drive the cars flat out without the risk of spinning or losing control of the cars under acceleration due to the system measuring the wheel speed and throttle opening asked for by the drivers. If the computer detected the rear wheels revolving quicker than the front or the air speed indicator reading slower than the rear wheels the computer would decide that the wheels were starting to spin, it would then reduce the amount of fuel being supplied to the engine, thus reducing the power. This was fraction control. This allowed the drivers to always drive with the throttle opening above the normal limit.

     A driver in a car without this device could never balance the feel of the car and the throttle opening quick enough to prevent the rear wheels spinning. The result of which may just cause the rear wheels of the car to step out of line, causing the driver to reduce power under the breakaway limit to bring the car back under control. Or to cause the car to spin out of control if the break was too severe, or the driver didn't respond quick enough. For this reason Traction control was banned by the FIA. Ferrari had introduced traction control by programming and not by having a device in the car called traction control. It was debatable whether this was against the rules or not.

     For this reason following the British Grand Prix Ron Dennis taking into account the conversation he had with John Bennet considered protesting to the FIA. However the damage had already been done the 1998 World Championship was starting to slip away from McLaren to Ferrari. Ron knew this his only hope was to put doubt into the minds of the worlds motoring press and fans, this alone wouldn't reverse the past but may help to take the pressure away from his team, and allow them to get back to the winning way. On reflection he decided not to lodge the protest just yet.

     Back in Wakefield Gerry had assembled his team of technicians around WE002. The car was ready to start its systems check. This was a non invasive test of the car. To anybody looking at the car nothing seemed to happen. For a change with an Fl car there was no noise, or vibration. In fact the test didn't involve any moving part. A computer was plugged into the entry port on the side of the car, this then ran through a program written by Ian. It went through each component on the car and simply spoke to it in an electronic sense. Once the program was happy that all the components were individually answering in the correct manner, it would then start grouping the components together into their family of corresponding components, and so on until the program got to the final stage where every component had to work as a fill system and would be bombarded with commands. Once the test was complete then the program would print out a full report of every stage, giving response's and response times. The report could then be analysed by Gerry. The test would take about an hour, it would then take Gerry a further two hours after to go through the report. Once the test was started there could be no other activity on or around the car. The car itself was packed with sensors measuring loads on suspension, wheel speeds, air speeds. Acceleration curves, deceleration curves. G forces on the driver. Fuel flow, air flow, oil temp and flow etc. the amount of information that could be got from the car was beyond most people's imagination. All of it was required to ensure that the best could be wrenched out of the car.

    The modern Formula one car is on the limit of technology, they help to push forward the frontier of car and systems design. This was the reason for Ian going to Seattle, he would return with a telemetry system that could take all of these feeds from the car, analyse them and give the engineers any proposed changes.

    The major difference to other systems is that in the current Fl car the on board computer can only be programmed by plugging in a lap top computer and down loading the new program. This must be done in the pits with the car stopped. Westfield would be able to do this on the move by using the telemetry in two directions, and allow it to reprogram the computer at racing speeds. This hadn't been thought of by any of the current competitors, more importantly it hadn't been thought of by the FIA. So the rule book didn't mention such a system as being illegal therefore Westfield determined that it could be used if it was possible. They were desperate to ensure that the system remained secret. If it got out then other teams could protest the system and get it banned, or they could adopt a similar system, and then Westfield's advantage would be lost. In the world of Formula one not only did the cars move quickly but also the technology behind them. If a team could find an advantage for one race then it was worth the effort.

    Outside the café in Piacenza Luca saw the usual bright red Ferrari 3SS of Gianni Lorenzo. The time was 3.25, he's early for a change thought Luca I do wish he would park away from the front of the café though. Like most Italians Gianni and Luca for that matter would have parked their cars on the top of the counter if they could.

    Luca entered the café and saw Gianni sat at a table in the far corner, he ordered an espresso as he passed the counter. The waiter behind started to charge the machine that would produce the thick black liquid that the Italians loved to call coffee Luca sat opposite Gianni and pulled out the envelope, he pulled out a single picture of the car sat in the workshop. The picture he chose could have been bought from any press photographer who had been at Silverstone the previous weekend, it didn't show any secrets or fine details of the car. It was the background to the car that was of more importance. It showed that the workshop and other parts of the assemblies in progress. The photograph proved that Luca or one of his associates had gained access to the factory and been able to take photographs.

"This is one of fifty, I can guarantee that the others are of more significance than this one."

"How much ? Luca."

"150 million Lire for them all."

"And the negatives."

"No negatives, they are digital, you can have the disk."

"I won't pay 150 Million without exclusivity. You could sell them on to another party."

"We wouldn't help any other team you know that Gianni." "No 150 million is too much. Its not that I cannot trust you, but you must have had help to get these. How can I trust them."

"They are in my employ they are trust worthy. 125 million." Luca said taking a quick drink of his espresso.

"100 million is all Twill pay, if I find copies of these else where I will send some of my people looking for you."

"OK 100 million it is, payment by cash tomorrow."

"Not possible if its to be cash then it will take me two days to collect it. The payment will be made on Thursday at the lookout post on Passo del Cerreto on the SS63 to La Spezia at 10.30am."

"Fine I'll leave you this." At that Luca stood up, he finish his drink and left the café. That was easy he thought, too easy in fact. Why had Gianni said up on that pass road. It would be quiet, can I trust him, I may have to arrange some insurance. At least he's given me plenty of warning of the location.

Gianni left the café a few minutes after Luca. He jumped into his Ferrari and headed out of Piacenza to the Autostrade Al which would take him back to the Ferrari headquarters in Maranello a small town to the south west of Modena. It took him about 45 minutes of steady driving to return to his offices. He didn't notice the small Fiat that had been following him since leaving the cafe.

Luca had decided to first see where Gianni would go with the print. Not that it would be conclusive that he wasn't involving another party even if he went straight back to his office. He would then pay a visit to the hand over site high up Passo del Cerreto. Indeed Gianni went straight back to the office complex. Luca then turned onto the SS467 and then onto the SS63 to head up the pass road. The road climbs steeply as it approaches the summit of the pass. The view point at the top of the pass is at 1261 metres. As Luca got out of his car he could feel the drop in temperature even at this time of year. Looking to the south he could make out the summit of Mount Cusna some 10 kilometres away. At 2121 Metres it was partially shrouded in the sort of haze that hangs around the Mediterranean high peaks, giving it a bluish tinge.

He was pleased to see that within his close surroundings there was very little cover, and provided that he made sure he was here well before Gianni then he could check out most of the places where an accomplice could hide. At the he departed and headed back to his home in Affori.

Back in Wakefield the systems test hadn't gone as well as Gerry had expected. Following the first run through the test had been aborted, the test computer had detected problems in the some of the sensors attached to the gearbox. These required changing, whilst it wasn't a major problem to change the sensors, all had been positioned in an easily accessible position. The problem was that the replacements all came up with the same fault. Gerry could only surmise that they were all faulty, and therefore would have to abort that days test. The sensors had all been supplied by the same company as the power supplies that had given them the same problems earlier in the program. He would have to resort to changing the sensors to an alternative type. These he hoped would be available over the counter at one of the local electronics suppliers like RS. He allowed the test engineers to leave for home and then rang John to give him the bad news.

John was extremely annoyed about the result. Not that the test had failed, but that the components from that one supplier had yet again shown problems. "How many other parts have been supplied by them." He asked.

"Virtually all the electronics in the current cars." Replied Gerry.

"ALL " Shouted John down the phone. This took Gerry slightly by surprise as John wasn't prone to shouting often.

"Yes all, but not all in the same supply batch. The items that have failed so far all came with the same delivery. I haven't found any problems with items that came in earlier deliveries."

"What's left of that delivery then."

"Nothing now, I've check the inventory against the delivery notes, we've cleared all the remaining stock out. RS will replace it all tomorrow."

"How do you know they can, it's critical that it's done tomorrow."

"I've checked their catalogue, they carry alternatives of everything I need."

"Good, see you in the morning then." John put the phone down worried, how can all of one delivery be defective he thought. Unless someone's deliberately exchanged or supplied defectives to throw us off. John fried to call Fran at her hotel in Milan, when the reception tried her room there was no reply. He asked the reception to leave a message for either Fran of Vanessa to call him back.

Gerry was having similar thoughts.

It was late in the evening when Fran and Vanessa returned to their rooms in the hotel. On returning they didn't call at reception since they had taken their keys out with them, therefore they didn't get any message to call John.

They had managed in that one afternoon to cover most of the fashion houses in the centre of Milan. Fran ordered a diner in Vanessa's room via room service, she was told that it would be delivered in one hour. That gave both of them time to bathe before it arrived. Fran returned to her room to inspect her goods from the afternoons trip. She had managed to buy a total of five different sets of underwear, all of it very sexy.

After they had finished their meal, they had eaten wearing only the bath robes supplied by the hotel. Fran turned to Vee and said "Would you like me to give you a show with my new collections."

"Very much." Responded Vee.

Fran went through the connecting door and brought her outfits through. She slipped off the robe and started to put on each of the outfits in turn. They both enjoyed the experience and the outfits gave pleasure to both women. Fran left her most revealing and sexiest purchase to the end, instead of parading in front of Vee with it on she slipped under the bed

cloths and invited Vee to join her. Vee responded by slipping her robe off and sliding in next to Fran. She kiss Fran all over her body caressing the silky underwear and teasing her pleasure zones through the material. Vee said "John will love this on you."

"I do hope so, it may soften the blow when he sees the bill." Fran said wickedly.

Gently Vee removed the bodysuit from Fran, they both continued to enjoy the sensuous contact with each other. They slowly made love together. Slipping into a very relaxed sleep in each other's arms.

Chapter 17

Early on the Wednesday morning found Gerry waiting outside the RS electronics outlet in Leeds. He had a long list of items that needed urgent replacement. He knew that even if they were all available over the counter it would take him and his technicians most of the day to replace
the defective items on the two cars, it would be late in the evening before he could again start the systems check.

John had woke early that morning, he hadn't received a call from Fran the night before, he was worried that they were both all right. He decided to call the hotel again. The reception tried Fran's room as requested by John, again there was no reply, he asked the reception to Try Vanessa's room.

In Vanessa's room the two women were both still lying in bed, Vee was laying wrapped around the back of Fran cradling one of her breast's in her hand, her other hand was lying across her own pubic area. The phone rang and woke her with a start. Sleepily she picked up the receiver and said "Hello."

"Vee is that you." Came the reply "Its John."

"Oh hi John, what's wrong."

"Nothing, but have you seen Fran, I rang yesterday, but there was no reply from either of your rooms. I asked the reception to leave a message to contact me."

"Yes I've seen Fran." Vee said looking at the stirring form of John's wife, "We didn't get any message yesterday."

"OK look we've found that a full delivery of electronics all faulty, I cannot believe that they were like that when they were dispatched from the factory. They could have been substituted somewhere on the way."

"Right OK I'll take note of it. Can't promise anything though."

"What's your plans today."

"We're heading to Genoa today to see a friend in the Police he will help me find the address of the fax number we have."

"Good, let me know what turns up to night. Give my love to Fran. Where is she by the way."

"Oh she's just walked in do you want *a* word."

Vanessa passed the phone over to Fran.

They passed a few pleasantries then Fran said Good bye and put the phone down.

"That was embarrassing." She said.

"Don't worry about it, John won't mind that you were in my room."

"No may be not in the room, but in bed, well."

At that she got up and headed for the shower, "Breakfast I think after this."

"Yes and then to business."

Whilst Fran had her shower Vee dialed the phone number of her friend. He also happened by chance to be an old friend of her fathers. He was now the equivalent of a Chief Inspector, and worked out of the Genoa central police department.

Anton Abonovicz was of mixed decadency his fore fathers had originated from Poland, they had started to make their way south before the 1st world war. By the late 1930's they had reached the south of France settling close to the city of Nice. There they stayed during the occupation by Germany during the 2^{1d} world war. They managed to escape internment by the Germans by hiding out in the mountains to the north of Nice. There Anton's father had been in command of a band of resistance fighters. It was through that resistance movement that the Abonovicz clan had befriended the Plat family. Vanessa's father had been command of a detachment of Guards stationed in Nice following the war. There he had come across the young Anton. Once the hostilities had ceased, and movement was again possible Anton's father moved the family out of France into Northern Italy. They settled down in the small town of Celle Lingure about 31 kilometres from Genoa. There his father opened a small Hotel and Restaurant. Anton didn't want to continue in the Hotel business and joined the local Police force.

Vanessa made arrangements to meet Anton, he had asked to go to the front desk at the central station, he would come down and take them both out for lunch.

Gerry was in luck RS managed to provide the items he required ex stock, when Ian had designed the systems he had tried not to use any special component just in case they had a failure whilst on one of the long haul Grand Prix's. In all it took the technicians until 3.0 PM that afternoon to replace all the components and get the car back onto test. This time the test ran through with no hitch.

    It took Vanessa about 2 hours to reach Genoa, once she had found her way out of Milan and picked up the Autostrade. On entering the city she headed for the central police station.

    When Anton saw Vanessa he was extremely pleased to see her again, it had been sometime since they had last seen each other. He gave her a the usual greeting of two kisses, she introduced Fran to him. He gave her the look of a typical Italian working close to the Riviera. He took her hand and said "Where shall we go to get away from her." He cranked his head in the direction of Vanessa.

    "Leave her, alone Anton. I'm looking after her for her husband."

    "Your never married my dear, are you."

    "I'm afraid so, but if I'd meet you first he wouldn't have had a look in." Fran teased.

    "Come we'll go to a little bar around the corner, we can catch up on the last couple of years."

    With that the three of them left the station. The desk sergeant looking on envious of the old detective with two gorgeous women, one on each arm.

    After a while in the bar Vanessa broached the reason for her visit. She knew Anton wouldn't be pleased about the information she was requesting, but hoped that he would agree to allow her to continue her investigation.

    He did agree, but requested that once Vanessa found the address, she didn't enter the property. She could only use the information to find the identity of the owner. He told them both to wait in the bar, he would go back to his office and use his computer to find the information.

    He returned in half an hour, he had a grave look in his eyes. He didn't like the address that had come up he recognised the district as being one of the least desirable in Milan. "I must insist that you keep in touch with me, please call before going to find the building, and again when you return." He said handing over the slip of paper. "What you are doing is most dangerous, there are people living in that district that are not the sort of person you would want to meet at anytime."

"I promise Anton I'll be careful. Fran and I can look after ourselves."

"Not against these people, we cannot control them."

Fran was looking on worried, she had never been in this type of situation. Anton's warnings were giving her the willie's.

Anton then said his good byes with further warnings and requests that they kept in touch with him Vanessa and Fran made their way back to their car. Anton's concern centered more for Fran than Vanessa.

"Anton look scared when he gave you that paper Vanessa."
"Yes he's not usually like that, come lets head back to the hotel. I'd like to find this place today if possible."

With that they left Genoa picking up the Autostrade back to Milan.

That evening Vanessa and Fran set out to find the address Anton had given them. They had asked basic direction from the Hotel Reception. The Receptionist had given them both a strange look when he had seen the district they were asking for.

It took about an hour of driving around the busy Milan streets to finally find their way into Affori. When they saw the building where the apartment was both looked at each other down hearted. Vanessa had hoped that they would have been able to park the car a block away, and Fran could have stayed in the car whilst she had found a spot from where she could have waited to see who can and went from the building. This particular tenement had just a single door leading to a central flight of stairs. All the apartments lead of that one staircase. In order to spot the owner of the apartment they would have to enter the building, one of them would then for safety would have to go past the apartment door they wanted to watch whilst the other stayed lower down. Fran could see the reason for Anton's concern. The building looked particularly run down, more so than it's neighbors'. The lighting in the stairway was very low, it looked as if each landing was only light by a single 25 Watt bulb. This would however help them to hide within the building, as the dismal light cast deep shadows down the corridor. As they entered the building Vanessa decided that it would be more dangerous if they split up. Therefore she said "We'll both go one flight up from the apartment we want, and find a suitable position. You keep a look out above us whilst I watch the door to the apartment."

"If your sure, I don't like this place one bit." Replied Fran "What if someone comes down the stairs."

"We'll have to act natural or something." Said Vanessa.

They found the door to the apartment they were looking for, they were in luck the door was just off the main landing, if they went up to the next landing Vee could still see the doorway.

They hung around the next landing for quite some time. The smells coming from the various apartments was quite overpowering standing around. "I don't want another Pizza or any garlic ever again." Whispered Fran to Vanessa.

"Shh," Vanessa replied,

Just then a door opened on the landing they were standing on, casting brighter light across them. Vanessa grabbed Fran and pulled her into an embrace. Fran didn't have time to even struggle before she felt Vee's lips on hers. When the door shut again the landing went into immediate darkness. However Fran didn't break the embrace, instead she continued the kiss with Vanessa.

"What was that for." Asked Vanessa when Fran finally broke the kiss.

"Just in case they came back out again." She replied cheekily.

The door from the apartment they were watching opened, and out stepped Luca. He turned, locked the door behind him, and went down the stairs.

The two women gave him time to get another flight of stairs in front of them before they moved to follow. As they approached the front entrance to the building Vanessa paused, putting her hand up to indicate to Fran to hold back from the doorway. "let me just check outside." She said, poking her head out of the door. She could just see the man getting into a car parked further down the road. It was a small Fiat.

"Well either we follow him know, or we come back in the morning."

"Best to follow know I suppose." Fran replied, not so sure of herself.

Once the car had pulled away and had gone past the door entrance they ran across the road to their own car, and jumped in.

Vanessa immediately pulled away from the kerb, luckily they were pointing in the right direction. She followed the car at what she thought was a safe distance until it pulled up outside a Banks automatic money dispenser. The man got out and proceeded to withdraw some cash from the machine. he then walked a short distance down the road and into a supermarket.

"He's doing his shopping." Fran said to Vee.

"Yes very disappointing, not much like a master criminal is he."

Shortly after the man came back out of the Supermarket carrying his purchases, he got back into his car and headed back to his apartment. Vee said "May as well leave him to it. We'll come back in the morning and wait outside for the day. At least we know what he looks like now." They quickly left the area and headed back to the Hotel.

On arriving back Vee reported into Anton, while Fran reported back to John on the day's work.

"Early night for us to night I think Fran." Said Vee "We need to be back out early tomorrow. Take plenty of reading it could be a long day."

"Fine see you in the morning then." Said Fran "I think I'll sleep on my own tonight." The call that morning from John had spooked Fran she didn't want to be caught like that again so quick.

Chapter 18

At five the next morning Vee opened the interconnecting door to wake Fran. She stood over her bed naked. Fran awoke with a start seeing only the silhouette of Vee's naked form leaning over her.

"It's only me." Said Vee "Time to go I'm afraid."

Fran slid gently out of the bed, herself naked and went slowly into her bath room. Once inside she had a quick shower to wake herself, she dressed quickly, and went into Vee's room to join her. They quietly headed down the corridor to the lift to take them to the car park. Once in their car Vee drove out to the tenement block, and parked up so that she could see the entrance. She was pleased to see that the old Fiat was still in its parking place.

"Looks as if he hasn't stirred yet."

"Yeh." Said Fran yawning, she was glad they had slept separate last night, she wouldn't have been able to wake up at all this morning if they had carried on like the night before.

They settled down for a what could be a long wait.

Back in Wakefield it was only just turning 4 AM, but it found Gerry leaving the home of his newly aquatinted girl friend. Newly aquatinted in the sense of courtship. He had know her for sometime know, but never really taken much notice. It was Anne Edwards Westfield's receptionist. Gerry and Anne had managed to keep the relationship quiet for the last month, since it had started to blossom. Gerry had been under pressure from John to divulge, the name of his new found love, but so far Gerry hadn't relented. Neither of them wanted it to get out yet until they were happy that the relationship was more stable. Last night was the first time they had actually gone to bed with each other, it had been quite some time for Anne since she had been to bed with a man.

She wasn't the luckiest woman around in holding down a relationship. She was in her late thirty's and had thought that the time for meeting a good man had passed her by. She had, had her eyes on Gerry since the formation of the new team, and Gerry had joined John's company. When she found out that Gerry was still a bachelor then Anne had been hoping to catch Gerry s eye or catch him to ask him out. Gerry didn't seem to be interested in the opposite sex, he was more engrossed in his work. The opportunity had arisen and Anne most out of character had pounced. They were both glad she had.

Gerry was leaving at that time, not due to him sneaking away, but because of the delays earlier he wanted to ensure the test's were all complete. He also had to finish the steering wheel connections on the second car, before Janice Higgins arrived. She would be wanting to start cockpit familiarisation today, before the tests on the track next week. Gerry found himself humming on his way to the factory.

The sex hadn't been fantastic, it had been like all first attempts a bit clumsy and hurried. Neither of them were the most confident love makers, it had been years since Gerry's last encounter. They were both very unsure of each other's bodies, but he knew in himself that it would improve the next time, and there would be a next time. Hopefully tonight.

When he arrived at the factory the work to be done that morning wasn't very glamorous, first of all he needed to sit down with his strong black coffee and pour over the printouts from yesterdays test session. They had done a quick scan last night, which hadn't shown anything major, it had shown however a couple of minor faults. These were more than likely connection problems rather any component fault. He need to trace back through the reams of paper to find where the connections had failed. He hoped that by around 7 AM when the technicians would start to arrive he would have traced the fault, and could direct one of them to the repair task.

Things were starting to move in Italy, Luca had just left his apartment and set off in his car. This time he was heading away from the city, he picked up the outer Autostrade which circles around Milan, he turned to the east and took the anti clockwise route, to pick up the main AI route south. Vanessa allowed him to get a safe distance in front of her before taking up the tail.

"This looks more promising than yesterday." Vee said turning to Fran. The starting up of the car had woken Fran up. She had dozed off while waiting.

"Where's he going." Asked Fran after a while.
"Don't know, but the route signs are for Modena."

"What's there." Asked Fran

"Nothing, but guess who's close to Modena."

"No idea."

"Ferrari have their base in a town called Maranello. It's only about 20 kilometres away from Modena."

They followed the Fiat for about an hour, when it suddenly turned off the Al onto the A15, where they travelled about 25 kilometres before turning onto the SS62. Vanessa had to take more care know, the Fiat had taken to provincial roads. They were starting to climb up and over a high pass, there was very little traffic on the road at that time of the morning. After descending from the summit of the pass they travelled for a further hour before the Fiat turned back east onto the SS63. They again had started to climb back into the mountains. This road was even quieter than the previous one. Vanessa dropped back about a kilometer from the Fiat. They could only just see the car ahead as it made its way slowly up the pass road. At the top the car pulled off into a parking area which served as a view point. Vanessa quickly found a place to pull her car off the road, she didn't dare to drive any further.

"It looks like we're walking from here." She said to Fran. The temperature was already starting to increase, it would be hot walk uphill.

"Afraid so." Said Vanessa taking a small camera out of the glove box.

Luca pulled to the far side of the parking area well away from the road. There was very little cover, but at this side he could half hide his car from immediate view of the road. He walked round to the back of his car and withdrew two throwing knives and a holster. The holster would hold the knives just behind his left and right shoulder out of sight of anybody approaching him from the front. Into his waist band in line with his spine he pushed a Semi automatic pistol. He couldn't afford to take any chances. He then set about checking out the area. He walked the entire summit of the pass, checking around all the outcrops of rock and ravines. Once he was satisfied that e was on his own he turned and walked back to his car. He took up a waiting position behind a rock close by his car. From there he could see down the pass in the Direction of Busana. This would have been the quickest route to the summit of the pass, but he had decided to take a more circular route, just in case he came across Gianni.

Vanessa and Fran were finding the climb to be difficult. The terrain was very rough with steep ravines flowing down from the summit. The ground on either side of the ravines was loose, and the ravine bottoms were boulder strewn. They were very carefully picking their way up. "I hope he didn't just pull off for a pee." Said Vanessa

"Oh shit why did you have to say that word."

"Why you don't need a pee do you. Would you have rather me say have a slash. It's more manly." Vee said in a deeper voice.

"Yes I do need one." Fran said undoing her trousers, and pulling them and her knickers down. She was so desperate to empty her bladder that she didn't even find a rock to go behind. She just had to squat where she was.

"Careful." Laughed Vee they'll think there's a flash flood on its way down.

"Oh to be a man, they can just whip their prick's out any where any time, not like us having to get undressed." Fran said standing up to pull her clothes back into position.

"So true." Vee said pointing the camera at Fran.

"Don't you dare." Fran said louder than she meant.

It was approaching 10.30 AM by this time. They still have a few hundred metres to climb before reaching the summit.

Luca had been watching the red Ferrari climbing the pass for about 10 minutes, before it pulled into the parking area. Gianni climbed out of the car and looked around him. He didn't see the car parked at the far side of the area at first. When he did he opened the door of his car and removed a brief case from the passenger seat.

He had had orders from his bosses at Ferrari that this would be the last payment they were prepared to make to the little crook Luca. They didn't like the game they had found themselves playing. Following the British Grand Prix, a protest had almost been levied against them for running illegal systems, they had been forced to down load their computer programs, so that the FIA could investigate the allegations.

They had also discovered that Gianni had employed through Luca, someone in the UK to break into McLaren s factory in Woking. Whilst they couldn't tell what the individual had done, what was clear was that McLaren had suffered from a number of sudden failures in the last three Grand Prix's. These had all been to Ferrari's advantage. If these failures had been as a direct result of the intrusion then Ferrari certainly didn't want anything to do with it. They wanted to divorce themselves from Giant and his associates as much as possible. The money provided was to be a pay off. Giant wasn't so sure that he would be able just to pay off Luca like that. For this reason he had also brought along a pistol of his own. He wasn't a good shot, and he hadn't ever had to shoot a man before, but the thought of 100 million Lire in the case would help. He planned to shoot Luca and take the money for himself.

Luca from his hiding place watched Giant step out of his car and look around for a short time. Them pull out the brief case and place on the front of his car. That meant Gianni was expecting Luca to walk over to him. This wasn't really what Luca had wanted, he had thought that the berk would have spotted his car hand driven over to him. Gianni wasn't known to enjoy walking far or dealing at a distance. Luca had no option but the step out of his hiding place.

"LUCA." Gianni called out. "COME."

Shit thought Luca they can hear us in Busana at this rate. He set off walking towards Gianni. He watched Gianni carefully he didn't know what to expect from him. He had known him for some time and had never known him to carry a weapon before, but one couldn't afford to be careless in his line. He approached to within about five metres of Gianni. "I've got the money, where's the photographs." Gianni asked.

"Here" Said Luca holding the envelope out.

"Throw it across there " Said Gianni pointing to a spot over to Luca's left.

It was at this point that Vanessa had finally made it to the top of the climb. She very slowly edged her way up. Across the open ground she could see the back of the man they had been following. He was standing in front of another man, she recognised him from her other work. She pulled her camera out and zoomed in on the two men, she quietly fire off a few shots.

Suddenly as Luca tossed the package over to the spot Gianni had indicated Gianni pulled a magnum 45 out from behind his back and fired. Luca was almost caught off guard due to him throwing the package to the side. He just caught sight of Gianni's movement. It registered in his brain that it was a hostile move, without thinking his right arm reached over his left shoulder for the throwing knife. In one fluid motion that would have put one of the wild west quick draw men to shame he grasped the knife and threw it at Gianni, at that moment Gianni fired, at the range the two men were standing Gianni couldn't miss, but he almost did. The bullet should have struck Luca in the centre of his chest, the 45 caliber snub nosed bullet would have tom his heart out as it passed through his body, instead the bullet hit Luca high on his right shoulder. He was thrown backwards by the force of the impact. The bullet, it's soft nose spreading on impact with his body took away most of his upper arm and bone leaving his right arm dangling by a small flap of skin from what was his arm pit. The artery feeding the blood supply to his arm pumped the life blood from him.

The final throw by Luca was a good one. The blade struck Gianni high in the throat. The blade penetrated deep enough into his throat as to reach the base of his brain severing the spinal cord as it leaves the brain stem. He died instantly. Luca meanwhile died a slower death, he watched his blood pumping from the shattered remains of his shoulder. He tried in vain to stem the flow with his left hand. He could feel himself growing weaker, he could feel the pain now from the terrible wound. He wanted to scream with the pain, but no sound came from his lips. His vision was becoming blurred, he thought he could see someone running towards him, but the vision was becoming darker, until blackness descended upon him, and he could feel no more.

Vanessa had been taking photographs when she saw the gun raise and fire. As if in slow motion she watched the events unfold before her eyes. All the time she had kept her finger on the shutter button on her camera. The power winder had ensured that she caught all of it on film.

Fran had only just reached the top of the climb when she saw Luca go down. His arm hang from his body as he fell. She had immediately ignored a shout from Vanessa to stay back. She continued to run towards the fallen man. As she approached she could see that the man who had fired the shot had a knife sticking out of the front of his throat. The impact of the knife had thrown him backwards. She could see blood at first spurting out of Luca's shoulder, then slowing to a dribble. Her first thought was to check for a pulse. Partially in shock she reached for his right wrist. Of course there was no pulse in that arm, she dropped it to the ground and sobbing went for his left wrist which was still holding onto the damaged shoulder. She hesitated not wanting to touch the blooded object. The ground all around him was now wet with blood. The human body holds eight pints of blood, most of this was now on the ground around the dead form that was once Luca. In her heart she knew he was now beyond help. She quickly came to her senses and checked for a pulse on his neck. Once satisfied she then checked the other man. She then turned and left the two corpses, returning to Vanessa who had continued photographing the scene. Vanessa was the first to speak. "I need to report this to Anton. There's a small town back down the mountain." Gianni had been under investigation by Anton for other reasons.

They both quickly turned to leave the area, when Vanessa said "The envelope, we'd better take that with us."

Fran quickly ran back to pick up the envelope, as she bent to pick it up she saw the brief case sitting on the front of the Ferrari. She decided to take that as well. Collecting both items she ran back to Vanessa, not looking at the two bodies lying in the muddy pool of blood surrounding them. They set off walking quickly back down the mountain to where they had parked their car.

In Busana two men sat in their car looking at a small screen, they were watching a small dot on the screen, "It's started to move." One of them remarked.

"Yes, but it's going the wrong way. It's heading West." The other said after a few minutes.

"Shit, lets get moving. It can't be Gianni, he would have come back this way."

They quickly started the car's engine and shot off to climb the pass. Busana is about 12 kilometres from the summit, it would take them about 10 minutes to reach the summit.

It was much easier going down the mountain than climbing, the women could follow the road. It took less than 5 minutes to reach the car. Once there Fran said, "Here's the envelope you check that whilst I look in this case." She passed the envelope over to Vanessa, looking inside she could see a pack of colour prints. When she pulled them out she could see that they were prints of the cars back in Wakefield under assembly. "Wow, she said, he was passing these over to that other guy, he was from Ferrari you know."

"LOOK AT THIS." Screamed Fran as she opened the case. It contained 100 Million Lire in neat packs of large denomination notes. "He must have been going to give this to the guy with the prints."

"What the fuck do we do know." Exclaimed Vanessa "Look I don't know why, but empty those notes into the boot of the car and throw that case away." She had a bad feeling about taking the money.

"Why."

"I don't fucking know why, but it could be bugged or something. They wouldn't just let the guy go off with all that money without tracing it."

Fran quickly emptied the case and threw it into the drainage ditch at the side of the road. They jumped into the car and sped off down the mountain. As they approached the small village of Fivizzano Vanessa turned off the main road to approach the village

"We must ring Anton and fill him in"

"What about the money." Asked Fran

"It's a major complication now, but I think we keep it." "Can we take it out of the country."

"Legally I think we can, but it will look very suspicious if stopped at customs with all those notes."

"Oh shit Vee I'm really out of my depth know. I don't think I could just walk through the customs and look calm. I'll fuck it up for us."

"I'll think of a way Fran. Don't worry. Look there's a café I'll call Anton from there, come on lets have some caffeine it'll help calm you down. You get them in while I call, but first put this coat on. Your cloths are covered in blood." In fact Fran's hands and face had tracings of blood on them. It didn't show up as much on her skin as it did on her light clothing.

The two men who had been watching out for the money had by now discovered the bodies of Luca and Gianni. "Quite a shoot out." One of them said

"Never mind that the money has stopped moving. It's just over the top of the pass."

They set off in their car to the place where Fran had thrown the case.

"Shit. There's nobody here." Said the one called Michali "Look around for the case, it's still showing to be here." The other who was called Stefan said.

"Here I've found it," called Michali "Balls it's empty." He said after picking it up out of the ditch.

"Oh shit, Mr. Bettoni isn't going to like this"

Mr. Bettoni fronted a security company, this company was employed by Gianni for Ferrari. Bettoni had a number of personnel around the world who amongst other activities were responsible for the safety and security of Ferrari. Stefan and Michali were two of those employees. It is fair to say that the company also was involved in activities outside of the law.

"Stefan, you'd better call in, tell him we have a problem. I'm going back up to clear that mess up there." Said Michali pointing towards he parking area. He set of quickly whilst Stefan called into his boss.

Once Michali had reached the two bodies he first of all removed all means of identification. He then looked around, spotting the old Fiat he felt in Luca's pockets, finding a set of keys he walked over to the car. He got in and drove the car over to the bodies. Michali then dragged each of the bodies into the Fiat. By this time his partner had arrived back up on the summit. Stefan said, "The boss wants' us to clear up, and then drive down the way the money must have left the area. Not that we'll find anything."

Together they pushed the Fiat towards the steepest ravine across the road. When it was close to the edge Stefan opened the door and ripped a section off Gianni's shirt, he opened the fuel filler and pushed one end of the shirt down into the petrol. He then lit the other end, the material soon caught fire, the petrol being wicked up out of the tank by the cloth. They then pushed the car hard into the ravine. As the car bounced its way down, one of the front wheels hit a rock and turned the car sideways on to the slope, it at first traversed across the fall line, before gravity once again took over. The car turned onto its side, it slid for a short while then started to somersault, as it did petrol sprayed out of the tank. This immediately hit the burning rag, with a sudden whoomf the old car burst into all consuming flames. The fire spread very rapidly through the small car turning it into a rolling inferno. The heat from the burning ball could be felt by the two men stood on the rim of the ravine. As the flame took hold the smoke turned thick black, and billowed up into the sky. "We'd better make ourselves scarce, that smoke will be seen down in the valley." Said Stefan.

Stefan then got into Gianni's Ferrari and followed Michali down the mountain towards Fivizzano.

By this time Vanessa had finished her call to Anton, he had arranged to meet her at the first service area on the Al2 towards Genoa. They finished their coffee's and set off.

"Anton thinks he can keep us out of this, I told him! had some photographic evidence for him to prove that only those two were involved." Vanessa said to Fran as they set off for the rendezvous with Anton.

"Did you say anything about the money."

"No, just keep quiet."

Fran and Vanessa were just leaving the village as Stefan and Michali entered it. They actually stopped at the same café, not surprising it was the only one in the village.

Whilst ordering a beer Stefan asked the waiter "Have you seen any strangers here about today."

"Yes, in fact you just missed two women, one made a phone call whilst the other ordered coffee. The one that made the call is quite a stunner. The other is a bit older, still very good looking. I could have given her a good time, no what I mean." The waiter replied gesticulating luridly.

At that both Michali and Stephan dashed out of the cafe and jumped into their cars. They estimated that the women had about five minutes head start on them. They wanted to catch them before Anita where they could join the Autostrade net work. Once there they would lose them for sure.

Vanessa on leaving Fivizzano looked back up the mountain, she could see a plume of smoke rising from what would have been close to the parking area. She didn't say anything to Fran, she knew Fran would have been even more worried than she currently was. Vanessa however knew that they could expect company at any time. Whilst she didn't know who had started the fire, or what had caused the fire she could guess that someone had come across the bodies. That someone must have set about clearing the mess up and dispatched the bodies into a funeral pyre. It was a good assumption that they knew about the money and would have been looking for it. They would soon find the empty case, they would then know that somebody else had been on the mountain that morning. Since Vanessa and Fran hadn't seen anybody come up the mountain from their side then these people must have been waiting somewhere over the far side. They would come to the same conclusion, and quickly follow her and Fran's tracks. She knew that once they reached the Autostrade then they would be in the clear. Vanessa drove the little Alfa like it had never been driven before.

By the time Vanessa had reached the Autostrade the two men chasing were only a matter of 500 metres behind, luckily for Vanessa though, the roads twist's and turn's had meant that they hadn't caught sight of the little Alfa. Vanessa and Fran managed to get clean away.

Stefan stopped the chase and got out of the Ferrari to wait for Michali to catch up."Shit missed them, no point in continuing now, they'll just mingle with all the traffic." Said Stefan leaning on the driver's door of Michali's Fiat Bravo.

"Best go back to the Café, and speak to the owner we need to get better description's of the women and the car they were driving." Michali said restarting his car. With that they set off back to the village.

Chapter 19

Janice Higgins spent the morning sitting in the cockpit of the Westfield car. At first she sat in without her helmet on, going through the controls with Dave Brian.

Dave had been appointed Janice's race engineer. He was well qualified for the post following his experiences in Formula Three and Formula 3000. He also had worked in other teams with Janice.

After about an hour she removed the steering wheel, and asked for some of the control buttons to be changed around. Unlike the steering wheel of a normal car the wheel of a Formula one car first of all isn't round, it has a flat top, and a flat bottom, it is only designed to turn to an angle of forty five degrees in either direction. Across the top of the wheel there are a series of lights, these indicate the current gear, and when the engine revs are approaching the correct point to change gear, on shifting up the gear box. The lights also show when the engine has reached its rev limiter. Across the spokes of the wheel there are buttons, these control things like the car to pits radio, the pit lane speed limiter, the start line clutch actuation. Janice can also control the brake balance and the anti roll bar balances from these buttons. At the back of the wheel on one side there were two paddle's the top one changed gear up the range, the bottom one down the range. When the driver actuated one of the paddles this disengaged the clutch, adjusted the engine throttle opening and changed gear automatically, leaving the driver to concentrate fully on the task of racing. On the other side there was another paddle this was the emergency clutch actuator. This was only designed to be used if the car spun or if the driver needed to disconnect the drive from the engine at any time.

It may seem strange for the driver to just sit and play with the controls in the car without the car actually moving. This was being done to allow Janice to become fully familiar with the layout and feel of the controls in the car. She needed to be able to operate them without thinking. When racing or simply driving the car to its limit, she must drive it without conscious thought, leaving her to concentrate fully on the race or track position.

After the controls had been adjusted to her preference on the wheel, she sat for a further hour, this time with her helmet on, getting used to the view forward and to the side of her. Once happy she then spent the rest of the day going through the car systems with Dave.

Vanessa met Anton on her own, she didn't want Fran to be seen outside the car in the state she was in. How the café owner hadn't spotted the amount of blood that covered Fran she didn't know. Fran could see from her position in the car Vanessa give the film canister to Anton. As far as Fran was concerned Vanessa had somehow convinced him that they hadn't been involved in the killing's, and that it would be best if neither of them were detained.

On the drive up the coast road Vanessa said to Fran "I'll pull off at the first secluded spot. You'd better strip off and go for a swim to wash all that blood off."

"Fine, that looks like a good spot up ahead." Fran said pointing to a small bay. The small beach looked to be empty. Vanessa pulled off the road, and they both walked down the small cliff path to the shore. There Fran did as directed and stripped naked. Whilst she waded into the sea Vanessa gathered up Fran's cloths and pilled them into a heap along with some drift wood. She then poured *a* small bottle of spirits onto the heap and set fire to it.

"What the fucking hell are you doing." Shouted Fran as she ran out of the sea towards Vanessa.

"I'm destroying the evidence that you were ever at the scene."

"Fine but now if you hadn't noticed I'm naked."

"So you are, very nice you look too. If we weren't in such a hurry I could screw you here on the beach fair maid." Laughed Vee

"Stop pissing around will you, what am I going to wear."

"You'll have to wear that coat again until we get to the hotel. Then I'll nip up and bring you something down from your room."

They set off back up the cliff path to the road. Fran, naked leading the way, muttering to herself. Vee kept slapping the cheeks of Fran's bottom. "Nice arse." Laughed Vee on the way up. Fran turned and stuck her middle finger in the air to Vee, meaning swivel on that.

"Later." Replied Vee still smiling. She had missed her fun with Fran last night and was determined to make it up tonight. Seeing the naked body of Fran only brought those desires closer. As they reached to top of the climb, Vee took pity on Fran and told her to wait behind a rock while she brought her top coat from the car.

Back at the cafe Michali was busy questioning the owner about the two women. He wanted to know about the car they were driving, and any other facts that may be relevant to them being able to find them, other than how sexy they were. After plying the owner with a bottle of his own brandy, they had found that the car was an Alfa, that it carried hire plates, and that it had been registered in the Milan district. That the women were English, and that he thought the one that had used the phone had been talking to the Polizie. From that information Michali thought they would by using contacts in and around Milan be able to trace who had rented the car. They with luck would also be able to trace the hotel they had registered in. this was looking good.

Stefan called Mr. Bettoni, he told him firstly that they had lost the women. Once his anger had died down sufficient for Stefan to continue, he then told him the other information. Bettoni told Stefan to wait at the café he would call him back with further instructions shortly. Bettoni would be passing the information that had been obtained by Michali on through his underworld contacts.

It took about an hour for the phone in the café to ring. Stefan picked it up immediately. He was told by Bettoni that the car had been rented from Linate Airport. That it was booked out to a Miss Plat. She was registered in the Hilton *in* Milan. Bettoni told Stefan that the money must be recovered without delay whatever force or tactics necessary should be used.

Late in the afternoon saw Vee and Fran well on their way back to Milan. They had stopped once for a quick lunch. Vee for a change had bought the lunch, which had been eaten in the car. Fran whilst she was becoming less worried about showing off bits of her body, she felt that showing all from below her hips a bit too much. Well away from the coast at least.

Vee was becoming very sexually aroused by Fran's sifting position. Fran had sat purposely in such a position to show off her full pubic region, not only to Vee but to almost any other vehicle that was tall enough for the driver to look in. To further excite Vee, Fran would occasionally look across at Vee and gently rub herself between her legs, blowing her a kiss at the same time. Vee couldn't wait to get back to the hotel room.

Michali and Stefan had left the Fiat at the café they took Ferrari and a quicker route back to Milan. At this time they were just entering the outskirts of the city, they headed straight for the Hilton. They took up position in the underground car park to watch for the Alfa to make its appearance.

Vee had reached the point where she couldn't contain herself any longer. "Well you dirty bitch." She said to Fran "I'm stopping at the next Motel, and once I've sorted a room out I'm going to screw the arse of you."

"What have I done." Said Fran innocently. "You took my cloths away."

"Yes but you didn't have to keep playing with yourself all the bloody way did you."

"Just passing the time on." Fran smiled back at Vee reaching over and inserting her hand onto Vee's crutch. "H'm you are a bit damp."

Vee nearly lost control of the car as she shuddered at the touch. She saw a sign for a motel a few Kilometres ahead. "That'll do" she said

When they reached the Motel Vee ran in to book a room for the night, Fran stayed in the car and smiled. She too was feeling very randy and looked forward to the evening of pleasure. Little did they know this saved their lives.

Michali and Stefan waited until after dark before they entered the Hotel. They went straight up to the room that had been assigned to Vee. Faking a lost key to a maid Michali gained access to the room leaving Stefan outside. He quickly, and without care searched the room. Finding nothing he tried the connecting door, this opened into Fran's room. He searched that room in the same way. It was obvious that the rooms had been searched. Clothing and bed covering's were scattered all around the room.

Chapter 20

The following morning after a long night of pure sex Fran awoke still feeling exhausted Vee had been true to her word, she had tried every position she knew and experimented with a few new ones. Vee was still asleep, when Fran thought, 'shit I bet John has been trying to get hold of us.' She decided to ring the Hotel to see if any messages had been left. "Hello this is Mrs. Bennet room 212."

"Mrs. Bennet, I'm glad you have called."

"Why, is there a message for me."

"No, but your room and the room of Miss Plat has been, err entered."

"What do you mean entered." Fran said Shaking Vee to wake her.

"It has been entered and disarranged."

"Disarranged." Fran asked quizzically.

"Yes it looks like someone has gained access to the room and searched it."

Vee by this time was sitting up on the bed, she snatched the phone away from Fran.

"This is Miss Plat, are you saying that the rooms have been searched."

"Yes that is what I'm saying. The Hotel didn't know of the search, and didn't help in it." The Receptionist replied apologetically.

"Ok look will you bill me for any damage, and pack our cloths. Send them to my home address in England. I'd like to check out now. Can you please debit my charge card for both mine and Mrs. Bennett's bills."

"Well it isn't normal practice to check someone out over the phone."

"Yes but it isn't normal practice to have a room broken into, is it."

"No, true. OK I'll work out the bill and debit the blank stub you left. I'll have to charge for the cleaning and delivery of your belongings."

"Fine, just don't rob me." Said Vanessa putting the phone down. Then she turned to Fran. "I think its a good job we stopped here last night. I think it will be best for us to leave Italy now today."

"I heard you tell them to send our things on, but have you forgotten, I'm starker's." Fran said standing and holding her arms out. "You burned my cloths yesterday."

"The next town we come to I'll nip into a shop and buy you something." Vee said smiling "Come here." She said grabbing Fran and kissing here nipple.

"Leave it off Vee. Didn't you get enough last night." Fran retorted. "God but my fanny is sore."

Vee laughed, "Put some cream on it lover." Vee got up to shower.

Michali had spent the night sitting in the Ferrari watching the car park. Whilst a 3SS is a marvelous car to drive, it isn't the most comfortable car to just sit in. his legs were cramping up. His backside was numb, and his neck was killing him. Furthermore he needed to pee, his bladder was at bursting point. Stefan had drawn the better straw, he had been sitting in the bar watching the reception area. It was surprising just how many people stayed up all night in these places. Whilst the bar wasn't busy, there had been sufficient customers coming and going, for him not to look conspicuous. Whilst neither of them had seen either of the women enter the Hotel, Stefan had been close to the reception at the time of the call from Fran. He realised that somehow they had guessed that the Hotel was been watched, he managed to here the receptionist agree to check them out over the phone. At this he ran down to the car park. He arrived in time to see Michali standing at the wall peeing up against it.

"Stop pissing and come on." Shouted Stefan

Michali turned hurriedly trying to stuff his penis back into his trousers. At the same time liquid was still spurting from the organ. He managed to splash down his trouser leg and onto his shoes. "Blast I can't even have a piss in bloody peace." He said shaking the droplets off his shoe. He jumped into the passenger seat of the Ferrari. "Where's the fucking fire anyway." He said.

"I don't know how, but the bitches didn't come back last night. I found out that they've asked to be checked out. God knows where they are now."

Vanessa had decided that they would leave Italy by driving over the Alps and into France. They were just entering into Alessandria so that Vanessa could buy Fran some cloths to make her more decent. She had been sitting in the passenger seat with the short coat on, covering her breasts, but failing to cover her pubic area. She had kept pulling the coat down, but her pubic hair seemed to have a mind of its own and kept poking out from under the coat.

"My bet is that they are still south of Milan." Michali said to Stefan. "Look at the map, they can either take the coast road, and into France that way, or my guess is that they were on the way back yesterday, but decided at the last minute to stop off on route, in that case they could stick to the Autostrade to Turin. They can then head over the Alps. They could then take two routes either through the Frejus Tunnel at Bardonecchia, or the route I would take if I was carrying money would be over the pass at Clavieries and Montgenevre. Stefan lets go my bet is there." Michali said pointing at the pass road on the map.

At Westfield it was to be another long day for Gerry, Dave and Janice. Janice had picked up the car systems well the day before, but she still needed to go through all the possible adjustments, and the theoretical changes that could be made to the car. Whilst it wasn't her job to recommend changes, she did need to be aware of them. During later test sessions when performance testing would be completed if she felt that the car was handling in a certain manner then she would have to radio back to the pits what the problem was, and if possible give a solution. This would be required more when there was time pressures, and the engineers resources were stretched. The time spent at base also allowed Janice being the newest member of the team to integrate with the rest of the bunch.

Vanessa had bought Fran a simple but stylish dress. It would at least cover up Fran's embarrassment. Fran quickly took of the coat and slipped the dress over her head whilst sitting in the car. She had to get out to pull it down over her bottom. As she got out of the car she saw a group of old Italian women staring at her. She then realised that they had seen her breasts through the cars window as she took the coat off, and then her bare bum as she got out of the car. Fran went red and smiled at them, she quickly got back in the car and said. "Fuck lets get out of her."

Vee laughed at her, started the car and drove out of the square where they had parked. "Don't worry about it dear, it'll keep them in gossip for the next ten years." Vanessa picked up the A21 Autostrade heading for Turin.

Stefan was at that time driving at about 150 kph on the A4 also heading towards Turin. They didn't have any idea whether they were on the right line of thought, or just where the women were. All they wanted to do was make as much ground as possible. Stefan had a saying he always liked to use. 'You never know your luck in a big city.'

By the time Vanessa reached Turin, Stefan was about 20 Kilometres behind them, and catching fast, but had Turin to negotiate. Vanessa had two choices she could join the A32 to head into the Alps via an Autostrade or she could go onto the SS25 then the SS24, in either case she planned to join the SS24 later to climb over the pass. She felt it would be too risky carrying the money through the customs at the Tunnel. She decide to use the district road and wind their way more slowly up into the mountains.

Late in the mid afternoon Vanessa was approaching the border town of Clavieres. First they had to negotiate the border crossing into France. "Just keep calm, with luck the guards will just wave us through." Vanessa said, pulling the blouse top tight so that the shape of her breasts showed through the material. She also rubbed her nipples to make then harden, this made the thin material bulge even more. "Pull the top of your dress down a bit, to show them a bit of tit."

"Why."

"To take their minds of what they're supposed to be doing, if they pull us over."

Fran pull the neck of her dress down so that her cleavage showed, she also pushed her breasts up and half supported them on her arm which she folded across her body.

"That's great." Smiled Vanessa "It'll be just our luck that the guy on duty's gay.

"Oh don't say that I'm nervous enough." Said Fran worried.

As Vanessa stopped the car at the check point the Italian

border guard walked up to the open window on the driver's side and looked in.

"Afternoon ladies." He said smiling, his smile widened as his eyes wandered to the sight of Vanessa's breast's beneath her blouse. "Afternoon." Vanessa smiled back.

"Err, carry on through." The guard stammered back.

"That was easy". Vanessa said to Fran as she drove out of Italy. When Vanessa looked in the rear view mirror she could just see the front of a red Ferrari approaching the border post. Shot she thought to herself, I'm sure that was the car that was on the pass yesterday.

The French guard didn't even bother to approach the car, they just drove through and into the small town.

"Right you can put them away." Vanessa said to Fran as she readjusted her own blouse. She accelerated down the road. Since crossing the French border Vanessa hadn't been able to see the Ferrari in her mirrors. She just wanted to get as much ground between them as possible. She knew that there was no chance of throwing them off her track, once through the single road ski town of Montgenevre.

The town of Montgenevre was basically a collection of ski Hotels and Apartments alongside a high pass road. There is a number of chalets leading of the main road up towards the ski slopes. None of these would give Vanessa sufficient cover. It was a straight decent down to Briancon from Montgenevre. There she did at least have some options. She drove the wheels off the Alfa on the decent, at times the car was almost out of control. Fran sitting in the passenger seat didn't dare even speak to Vanessa, in case here voice distracted Vanessa's concentration. Fran hadn't seen the car behind, but she could guess why Vanessa had suddenly increased her pace. In a straight race the Alfa would stand no chance what so ever against the Ferrari even with a moderate driver, Vanessa hopped that on these mountain roads, the Ferrari's driver wouldn't be able to use all of its potential. Once they reached Briancon she could drive into the town and hopefully find a place to hide the car from view, at the same time keep watch on the road from Montgenevre.

The Ferrari had just cleared Oulx and was approaching Cesana climbing towards the border when up in front Michali thought he caught sight of a lone car on the pass climbing to the border. "I think we're onto them." He said to Stefan who was driving. Stefan immediately increased the pace of the Ferrari, at times he struggled to hold the car. It's power on the type of roads they were driving on causing the rear to break away.

By the time the Alfa in front had cleared through the Italian border the Ferrari was a matter of five hundred metres behind. Stefan continued to accelerate towards the border post. He hoped that the guard on seeing the Ferrari would wave them through.

The guard was facing away from the oncoming Ferrari he was still looking at the Alfa disappearing through the French side almost as if he had x-ray sight, looking at the occupants of the car. Phew he thought to himself. The French will have fun with those two. As he turned he saw the Ferrari approaching his post rapidly. His first thought was to let them through. Anybody driving such a car was fine by him. Then he realised that the car wasn't following the normal driving pattern, when cars approached the crossing point they would slow down. The drivers would be looking towards the guard waiting for his signal to either pull over of the continue on through. This car's approach was very aggressive. The driver and the passenger also seemed intent on the car he had just allowed through. He made his decision, it was almost too late, the Ferrari was only a matter of thirty metres away. He put his right hand up in the international stop sign and pointed to the pull off area with his left arm.

"Shit." Shouted Stefan. At first he thought about driving straight through, but immediately dismissed the idea He braked hard and turned in towards the parking area. The car's front tyres squealed in protest with the demands being put through them by the driver.

The guards eyes opened wide at the sight of the oncoming car. He could almost feel a movement in his bowels, as the squealing noise intensified with the approaching car. He stood frozen to the spot. His hand still in the stop sign almost as if would give him protection.

The Ferrari gave up its protest and slowed sufficiently for the tyres to grip the loose surface and allow the car to turn. As the front turned then the rotational forces were transferred to the rear of the car. The rear tyres were already unloaded by the weight being transferred forward by the heavy braking. They lost the fight for grip. The rear of the car pirouetted round, just missing the frozen figure of the guard. If his bowels didn't move with his first sight of the oncoming car, they surely did now.

The sound of squealing tyres brought the guards colleagues miming out of the post. By this time the Ferrari had come to a halt facing the wrong direction. The two occupants were sat slumped in the car. The passenger his right hand gripping the handle above the door, his knuckles white. The drivers colour had drained away from his face, his eyes staring ahead, his knuckles also white from the strength of his grip on the steering wheel. A racing driver he was not.

They were hustled out of the car at gun point. The unfortunate border guard had waddled somewhat ungainly away from the scene to the latrine.

In Briancon Vanessa pulled off the main bypass road to enter the town, she found a good place to park the car where they could sit and watch the pass road from the border. "We'll wait her for a while."

"You think we were being followed don't you."

"Yes, I thought I saw the Ferrari from the shooting yesterday behind us at the border."

"How did they find us."

"No idea, it may not have been them. I just want to make sure. Once we're happy we can find somewhere to eat, and a bed for the night, I'm knackered ." Said Vanessa.

They stayed in the parking spot until darkness fell. No Ferrari was seen descending from the border road. Feeling happier Vanessa set off for the centre of Briancon, an old fortress town high in the French Alps, it is actually the highest market Town in France.

Back at Westfield the day had been long and tiring. The work wasn't yet complete. The transporters needed to be loaded with all the equipment and the cars for the testing session on Monday at the Donington circuit. The cars required an amount of disassembly prior to being loaded. The nose and rear wings had to be removed, and all the wheels changing for special narrow solid wheels to allow the cars to fit into their special transport positions. All the fluids also had to be drained from all the tanks in the cars. This is to ensure that if a leak occurred during any of the journey's then there was no risk of fire or explosion, thus destroying millions of pounds worth of equipment. For Gerry it would be a long night, but it would be worth it, for it meant he could have the weekend off with Anne.

Fran and Vanessa had managed to find a decent restaurant in Briancon and a hotel for the night.

Over dinner Vanessa told Fran of her plan to get back home. They would drive through France to St-Malo where they would buy return day tickets to Jersey. This would appear as if they were going on a simple day trip. This would be further reinforced by the lack of baggage, only the soft bag that had the money in. once in Jersey they would then buy a single to Guernsey, followed by a Ferry to Weymouth in Dorset. They would then hire a car for the journey home. The current hire car would be left in St-Malo. Once they had returned back to Westfield Vanessa would phone the hire company at Linate airport and make her peace with them. It was going to be a long day of travel. It is possible to almost reach St-Malo by the French Autoroute system, they would travel over the Col du Lautaret to Grenoble. There they would enter the Autoroute system travelling via Lyon, Dijon, Auxerre, Paris and Le Mans finally leaving the system close to Rennes about one hundred Kilometres from St-Malo.

Michali and Stefan were detained at the border post until the local Police arrived, when they were taken and detained at the local Police station. The problem was the Ferrari, it was registered to Gianni Lorenzo. When Anton and his detectives had finally managed to extract the bodies of Gianni and Luca for the burnt out car there was sufficient left of them to be identified. It had also been established from the blood mixed in the gravel on the car park where they had died. Vanessa's photographs also helped somewhat in that matter. Somebody had therefore moved them and tried to cover up the evidence, not very well. The breakthrough had come quickly, with the attempt to drive through the border crossing. Stefan wasn't aware that Anton had alerted all the borders and Police patrols to look out for Gianni's Ferrari. Again the photographs came in very handy

When Mr. Bettoni heard that his two men had been detained by the Police, to say that he was not amused was somewhat of an understatement. He fumed at anybody that came near. After a while once he had calmed down he thought, they were Westfield people, then they will be heading back home.

Chapter 21

The drive through France on the Saturday went well. By the time they reached St-Malo however it was too late to catch a suitable Ferry. For the rouse to work they would have to overnight again and catch the Sunday morning Ferry to Jersey. They managed to find a simple pay on entry Motel for the night. It was basically a room with a bed and shower room, no frills, but very cheap. "This isn't up to my normal style." Vanessa said looking around the space. The room was clean and air conditioned, and only cost One hundred and Fifty Francs Entry was simple, push your credit card in the slot, the machine gives you a pin number. This you key into the lock on the external door and your room door. They found a simple restaurant close by to spend the evening.

It was quite a surprise for John on Sunday evening when a car pulled up outside, and out stepped Vanessa and Fran. "What the hell." He said as he approached them.

"Boy have we got something to tell you." Said Fran hugging her husband and kissing him.

They went into the house to bring John up to date with events. Showing him the prints, and then the money.

"That will come in useful." John said "I've had a long day talking to Microsoft."

"Why." Asked Vanessa

"The interim payment didn't come through on Friday from them. Neither for that matter has any come through from IDEK. I've not had chance to talk to Goodwin yet. Since your home Vee you can do that."

"So." Asked Fran not fully understanding the impact of John's words.

"It means we are short of cash. Whilst on paper we are due the money and are solvent, *in* actuality without that payment we cannot continue." John explained.

"What did they say." Asked Vanessa.

"Nothing yet. The people I've managed to talk to are blaming technical problems with the transfer."

"So what's the worry."

"Ian phoned, he saw Kurt Langer from BMW out there this

week. Following that visit by him he said relations started to change. Up to then he had full co-operation from the programmers, then the following day they all had other work that needed their attention. He was told Bill Gates had taken them off the project. Ian is asking to come home. I told him to hang on a few days, and I would contact Bill."

"Have you managed to get him" Vee asked puzzled.

"No he's too busy to talk. He's an awkward son of a bitch to get at the best of times. I've sent E-Mails the lot, but no response so far."

"Look leave this with me I'll fly out on Monday if necessary, it must be something to with Langer."

"I know Microsoft were pissed off with us over not running the cars last week at Silverstone, but they just weren't ready. They are now. We'll be doing the shake down runs tomorrow and Tuesday."

"What if *I* schedule a press show at Donington on Tuesday, so that they can see the car on the track performing." Vanessa suggested.

"It may work, could you ensure that it was shown in Seattle."

"Don't know I could ask CNN."

"OK do it." John said

"What about Gerry, he won't be happy."

"Leave him to me, I'll sort him. I've been trying to get him all weekend as well, he's disappeared, and so as Anne by the way. I fried her to see if Gerry had left word *as* to his plans."

Fran said to Vanessa. "What are you going to do now."

"Go home."

"No Vee you stay here tonight there's no point in going back home then travelling over to Manchester tomorrow."

"I've no clothes with me."

"Don't worry we can sort that in the morning." Fran said.

"H'm Ok fine, I need to go to the office in the morning anyway to arrange the press for Tuesday."

Alfons had been sitting in the shrubbery all afternoon. He had received a call from Mr. Bettoni that morning warning him that the Plat woman had managed to leave France. Her hire car had been retrieved from St-Malo. The hire company had called Bettoni to inform him, at his request from one of his agents who worked for the company. Alfons not realizing that the other person seen with Vanessa Plat was Fran Bennet had staked out Vanessa's house.

Darkness had descended when Alfons decided to try entering the property. He managed to climb onto an outbuilding, there was an upstairs window that looked easy to open from the outside. It was a top hung UPVC style window. He inserted a small jemmy against the side of the window, and applied pressure, this moved the whole frame sideways springing the bottom of the window off its catches. He then simply stepped into the house. He had entered a small bed room, simply furnished with a neat single bed and wardrobe. He checked the window to make sure there wasn't any magnetic sensors attached, it was clear. Moving out of the bedroom onto the landing he carefully checked around the ceiling line looking for any infrared sensors. Not seeing any upstairs he moved from room to room, pausing only momentarily in each. At the front of the house he found the master bedroom. He spent longer in that room going through the draws and wardrobes. Funny he thought to himself, no underwear. Neither was there any sign of a man living in any of the rooms. Before he moved down stairs he bent down lowering his head below the floor line looking again for a sensor. As he turned his head he caught a flash red and then the alarm sounded. Shit, triggered the bastard, he thought getting up and quickly checking through the rest of the rooms. He found the study, he checked through the desk, satisfied that there was nothing to help him he ran back up the stairs and out of the same bedroom window. He had just made back to the shrubs when a Police car pulled up in the drive. The alarm had also sounded at the station. Alfons moved deeper into the shrubs until he was well hidden from view.

The Police made a quick tour of the property, they saw the window open above the outbuilding and made an attempt to make it secure. They radioed back to base before leaving the property.

Alfons waited for an hour before he decided to head home himself, there was no point in hanging around tonight.

In the early hours of Monday morning the phone rang next to Johns bed. It was Ian Smith ringing from Seattle.

"Yes," said John. "Oh hello Ian. Do you know what the bloody time is over here."

"Sorry John, but I've been talking to a friend I've made in the Microsoft development section."

"Oh good Ian I'm pleased your making friends." John said

sarcastically.

"No, listen John. Teresa has told me that Kurt Langer has told Bill Gates that Westfield are in deep trouble, and that whilst we have a chassis we don't have a power unit. He has said that the design that Gerry is working on has failed. In fact we have suffered a fire in the assembly area, and that has set us back so far that we won't have a complete and tested engine ready for the start of the next season. Also all the other engine suppliers have been warned off by Bernie Ecclestone. Microsoft should cut their losses and move their sponsorship to a BMW backed car."

"So that's the reason the installment hasn't come through." John said with a sigh.

"I think so, what should I do. I would like to come back home, you need me there anyway with the track test's due."

"No stay put. It's too late for you to come back for the first test's. Look we're planning to show the car running to the press on Tuesday. We'll use Monday as a shakedown session, only run the cars for a short period, that will allow us to give one of the cars a good run on Tuesday. Will you try to get a message to Bill Gates and those git's that are advising him that the car will be running on Tuesday in his bloody colours."

"I'll try, Teresa may help. Look tell Gerry to set the engine management to fifty percent for the Monday runs, and seventy Five Percent for Tuesday. That should ensure no problems. I wouldn't want the thing to go bang in front of the TV cameras."

"Will do Ian. Good luck."

John put the phone down and looked up. There was a slight knock on the bedroom door. Fran called "Its Ok Vee you can come in." Vanessa entered the room wearing a borrowed gown. "I heard the phone ring John. Bad news."

"Could be, it was Ian." John filled Vanessa in with Ian's report.
"Well it looks as if the inner circle are starting to show their colours." Vanessa said sitting down on the bed.

"Yes I think you should stay over here. You will be of more good at the track on Tuesday with the press."

"I agree." Vanessa said getting up to leave.

The following morning Gerry had already departed the factory for the test sessions when John and Vanessa arrived. Vanessa got straight onto the press agency they used, to arrange the coverage for Tuesday. Next she sent an E-Mail to Bill Gates, expressing her concern that he was listening to gossip and not fact. She informed him about the planned coverage for tomorrow and that he should either watch the CNN broadcast or visit the Westfield Web site. She didn't expect to get a reply from Bill, but she did tag the E-Mail so that she would know if it had been read.

Her next call was to James Goodwin. She could understand Bill Gates being cautious, but not Goodwin. He didn't have anything to lose by going in with Westfield. The amount he was paying was peanuts compared to the price the big teams would demand for the space he had bought. James didn't prove to be as difficult to locate as Bill Gates was, he picked up his phone at the first ring.

"James, darling." Vanessa started

"Oh hello Vee." James answered "Its nice to hear your voice."

"Same here James."

"You haven't just called to pass the time of day on have you Vee." James stated

"No James I haven't. Look according to our contract we should have received payment from you by now, and so far we haven't seen a penny."

"No I won't fob you of my dear, you haven't."

"Why not."

"Because I have been advised not to pay all up front."

"You can't just change your mind James, we have an agreement." Vanessa said hardening her voice.

"Yes I can when it's you who aren't going to deliver the goods Vanessa." James retorted back.

"What do you mean not deliver the goods." Vanessa asked angrily.

"The contract is that you will place my name in the positions agreed on your racing car."

"Yes that's true, and that's just what we have done. Didn't you see the launch at the Grand Prix last week."

"Yes I did, but I have been informed that you haven't got an engine. Without an engine you cannot race. Therefore you wont fulfill your end of the contract. I will have paid good money out for nothing, and won't get any return."

"I can see your point James, but the advice you have been given is wrong. We do have an engine, and further more it will run Tomorrow at Donington. Furthermore James unless you release seventy five percent of the agreed sum today, I will strike out your name from the car. You won't get any initial exposure. I will also sell that space to one of your competitors. The ball is in your court James."

"Don't be like that Vee." James said trying to cool the conversation.

"James never mind saying don't be like that. All I want from you is for you to abide by our agreement. As I have said we have an engine, and it will be a competitor."

"What guarantees do I have."

"I can guarantee that we have an engine James."

"I should hope so, but I mean guarantee that the car will be a winner."

"James I didn't say winner I said competitor. Nobody in the world of F I would ever say their car is guaranteed to be a winner." "Ok not a winner then competitor."

"What I can say James is that we will be at the first Grand Prix next March."

"Vee I will pay you twenty five percent now, and the rest when you reach the start line next year."

"No James that's not good enough, look fifty now and fifty in November this year. If you don't agree then your name is off the car that's my final position." Vanessa said sharply. Then more calmly "Look you don't want me to announce to the world that IDEK doesn't honor it's contracts do you. Just think what that will do to your share price, and standing in the commercial world."

James thought for a while, then said. "Ok Vee you win. Jeez you can fight dirty when you want. No wonder Bennet wanted you. The money will be transferred to your account be mid day today."

"Thank you James, and I will check you know."

"I know dear. Good bye." Goodwin put the phone down. He then called his bank to arrange the transfer. The last thing he needed know was an attack on his shares.

Chapter 22

By the time John Bennet and Vanessa arrived in the pits at Donington the cars had been off loaded from the Transporters along with all the equipment. The mechanics were busy, some were working in the garage setting up the telemetry equipment, others were busy on the cars reassembling ready for the fluids fill and then the engine test run ups. Janice Higgins hadn't arrived, but had called through on her mobile to say she was on her way the Monday traffic out of London had held her up, she was about half an hour away.

The day wasn't the best for shake down tests. It had been raining all weekend, and was still drizzling. The track had no chance of drying out. One problem the driver would have was the surface of the Donington circuit. It was very smooth, but the tarmac wasn't very grippy at the best of times. In the wet it was very slippy, part of the problem was its location. It was basically on the landing and takeoff flight path of the East Midlands airport. The fallout from the jet engines deposited a film of kerosene on the track. When wet this came to the surface thus reducing the grip level even further. Janice would have her hands full today. It was also critical that she didn't throw any of the cars into the Armco surrounding the track. The team didn't have sufficient spares with them to carry out chassis repairs.

John had told Gerry of the press coverage tomorrow, and the reason why. Gerry hadn't been too pleased to say the least with the plans. One the track conditions. Two Janice had never driven the cars. Three he wasn't sure about the engine under true load. All the engine tests had been carried out on the Dyno, whilst the results following the fire had been better there were still a few problems to iron out. Yes Ian's suggestion relative to the engine management system was good and would be done, but it was a risk. Gerry was an engineer and not a risk taker. John had however managed to calm him down in the end.

When all the fluid filling was complete Janice still hadn't arrived. Gerry decided that while they were waiting it would be a good opportunity to run the engines in both cars up to temperature. He had just started the first cars engine when *a* car pulled up at the back of the pits.

"Where the hell have you been." Gerry shouted.

"Sorry." Janice said apologetically. "Just after I called in there was a bloody accident. Then I couldn't get through on the mobile."

"Ok just get changed."

"Dave go with her and brief her whilst she's doing that."

There would be no privacy for Janice, she just had to accept that she was one of the boys. The bumps were just in different places that's all.

Janice was stood only in her bra and pants when Dave entered the trailer. "Sorry," he said "But I have to run through the program with you."

"Fine don't mind my privacy will you."

"Sorry, Look Gerry's hopping mad about something out there. We need to get this briefing done."

"Fine." Said Janice starting to pull on her fire proof underwear. I normally don't wear anything under this lot, but since your here I'll have to."

"I'll turn my back while you strip off if you want. Just listen to what I'm telling you." Dave turned his back, and started to read off the list of requirements and test patterns for the remainder of the day. Janice undressed fully and pulled on the special Long Johns and Tee shirt top.

"Ok Dave I'm covered now." Janice said, whilst she sat down to put on the fire proof socks. Together they went over the plan.

"I thought we would do more running today." Janice said surprised at the changes.

"We need to save the cars for tomorrow. That's what's getting at Gerry. John has had to allow the TV cameras in for a run tomorrow morning. it's something to do with the money." Dave explained, he wasn't fully sure himself, Gerry hadn't given a full briefing.

After they had run through the requirements Dave left the trailer, Janice followed after pulling on her overalls. Stepping outside she bumped into Vanessa who was about to enter the trailer. "It's like Oxford Street in here." Janice complained.

"Don't worry it'll get worse." Vanessa warned. "You had better get used to being caught in the buff if I were you love."

"I suppose your right. Time's money now."

"Here," said Vanessa passing over a new set of overalls. "I want you to wear these tomorrow." The new overalls had the Microsoft logo across the chest and back.

"Why, what's happening tomorrow." Janice asked puzzled. "We need to put on a good show for Microsoft, they and others have been given some bad impressions of us. If you want to make it in the Fl world then tomorrow is the start of your PR apprenticeship. If we fail then you will also fail."

"Thanks for the pep talk Vanessa." Janice replied not very encouraged by her words. "Are there any problems with Westfield."

"No, none technically, but if the money doesn't come in then yes, we're all out of a job." Vanessa explained simply.

Janice left the new overalls in the trailer and ran through the garage to the car.

"Right Gerry I'm ready."

"Took your bloody time Janice. Hair not quite right." Gerry snapped back.

Then he said "Sorry. I didn't mean to snap. We actually have plenty of time today. Dave explained everything didn't he."

"Yes, five steady laps to get the feel of the car, then a further fifteen in this car, then straight out in the second car, and repeat."

"Yes I want to set a base line after the first five laps, then we can check that base line against the second car. Both have been set-up the same." Gerry added.

Janice pulled on her helmet and climbed into the car. This was the first time she had sat in an Fl car ready for a test. Her pulse rate was climbing, she suddenly went very dry in the mouth.

Dave as busy connecting her helmet communications line to the car, and her emergency air supply. He then reached down and started to fasten the safety harness. There were two straps that came over her shoulders, two that came over her thighs, and one that came through her crotch. The driver cannot fasten the harness themselves, they would never be able to get it tight enough. The braking G force alone would send them crashing into the front of the cockpit. With braking G's of around 6G and similar cornering forces a Formula one car isn't a toy. The car would be able to accelerate for standstill to one hundred miles an hour and back to standstill in under six seconds. They wouldn't be trying that today though, all that power through the gearbox would surely break it immediately. That was one of the areas that would be under test. The only real test of the drive train was under driving conditions.

Once Dave was happy with the straps he passed the steering wheel to Janice for her to click into position. Once done she could then speak to the outside world. Sitting in the car, with all the team working around her, Janice felt slightly out of control. Events were starting to unfold quicker than her mind could take then in at that time. She knew however that once the engine started she would be the one in charge. The radio crackled in her ear, bringing her back to reality.

"Ready for start up." Dave's voice said to her.

"Yes." Came the response. Janice put her right arm up with her index finger in the air. This was the recognised signal to start the engine. Gerry had the lap top computer plugged into the side of the car ready. Eric was at the back of the car had already engaged the air driven starter into the back of the gearbox. Once he saw Janice's finger in the air he depressed the button on the starter. It whirred loudly in his hands, the engine coughed a couple of times and then caught. The engine revs went up to five thousand revs per minute and held steady. Eric quickly removed the starter and cleared away from the back of the car. He could already feel the heat from the twin exhaust pipes, they exited on the top of the engine cover just in front of the rear wing. About face height for the mechanic using the starter. Bloody designers, no consideration for the working classes, Eric mumbled to himself.

Once Gerry was happy he unplugged the Laptop from the car. The engine revs dipped slightly then resettled to an even beat.

Janice thumbed the button on her wheel to speak. "Ok lets go."

The mechanics lowered the car to the ground, Janice then pressed the clutch disengage button on the wheel and selected first gear. She started to increase the throttle opening to bring the revs up to seven thousand which was the minimum to allow the car to pull away. As the revs were reaching the correct level she was about to release the button on her wheel when the car suddenly lurched forward, it seemed to jump about three feet, before the engine stalled.

"Bloody women drivers." Eric said moving forward.

"Less of it." Dave said smartly to Eric.

"Janice what happened." Dave then said into the coms set.

"Don't know, I was about to release the button when the clutch suddenly engaged."

"OK, don't worry. Gerry check the programming for the clutch release." Dave said. It was Dave's responsibility to ensure that the test's were carried out. Gerry was know one of the team and was taking orders from Dave.

Gerry plugged the computer in and accessed the required part of the programming. After a couple of minutes reading through the lines of coded instructions, he said. "Found it, there's an error in the release line, it was set to release the clutch automatically, once six thousand revs had been reached. I'll take that line out now, it's not needed." It only took Gerry a couple of minutes to make the correction and re-down load the program. Once complete Gerry gave his thumbs up to Dave.

"Ready Janice." Dave asked

"Yes." She replied, she again put her hand up. Eric engaged the starter and the procedure commenced again.

This time the engine fired immediately, Janice engaged first gear, increased the revs and released the button. The car moved, the rear wheels spun on the wet slippy surface before gripping generating a cloud of smoke, which consisted of a mixture of rubber and atomised water from the roads surface. The car moved away down the pit lane

On exiting the pit lane she was immediately adjacent to the first corner of the Donington circuit. She took a wide line around that corner looking for some grip. She was used to driving this circuit in her F3 car, but was amazed at the lack of grip that was being generated by the Westfield. Although the tyres were cold, and the slight delay in the pits wouldn't help. She took the first lap very steadily. The last thing she wanted to do was throw the car into one of the traps around the edge of the track on her first lap.

After a couple of laps she could feel the car responding better to her commands. Her own confidence was increasing. She radioed "Dave." "Yes." Replied Dave.

"I'll make it ten steady then fifteen quicker OK."

"Understood, yes OK."

In the pits Gerry was watching the telemetry screens, so far the engine temperature had remained well down. In the test room by this time the temp even with the new pistons would have been pushing the upper limits. All other systems were running well. The Telemetry results came in once per lap each time the car past the pits. On board the car there is a storage device that collects all the data in real-time, it is this compiled data that is burst transmitted. The computers in the garage collect that data and interpret it into a series of graphs. Each laps graph for a particular set of data can be overlaid over either previous laps, or another cars.

Janice by the eighth lap was beginning to get the feel of the car underneath her, even though the engine management had been de-tuned, she was starting to appreciate the power that would be available to her in full mode. At the end of the ninth lap she radioed, "Dave."

"Yes." Responded Dave. The radio talk was kept short. This was due to a number of reasons. The first being the noise factor, long messages could become confusing if words were lost. The second was that the engineer in the pits had no real idea of the work load the driver was under at any particular time. He may interrupt with a long or complex message at the wrong time, causing the driver throw the car of the island. That is the term used by many drivers for the track.

"Starting the quick laps now."

"Understood." Dave replied. It was also a general convention for all communications to the driver to be addressed through the race engineer for that driver. This again was to prevent confusion, and the driver and engineer were a team. They built up a working relationship together, a third party interfering could break that relationship, or trust. The driver must have total trust in his or her engineer.

As Janice circulated the track Dave paced up and down in front of the monitors. The mechanics at the test session sat out of the way, all could hear the conversations through their head sets, but wouldn't interfere. It was cold a boring at the back of the garage, most of them had been stood on the pit wall for a while when the car had first started running, but due to the miserable conditions they had moved back indoors. "Happy with things so far Gerry. Dave asked.

"Yes, look the engine temp is perfect so far."

"Why is that. We had better cooling in the test house surely."

"I don't think it is just down to air flow over the radiators, air flow over the engine casings must also help. Carbon fibre casings are a new area none of us really know what effect they have on heat dispersion."

"True. Look the lap times are coming in good now."

Janice had put her foot down so to speak, her lap times had improved. She was now lapping the circuit faster than she had ever done so in her F3 car with plenty more to come. All wasn't easy though, the Westfield was very unstable going through the section called the Craner curves. This had the effect of slowing her on the approach to the Old hair pin. The car settled down then through Copse and onto the back straight, but again became unstable into Goddards before coming back onto the start and finish straight. She continued on with the lap, then part way through the Craner Curves complex she felt the car become even more unstable from the rear.

At the same time that Janice started to increase her pace, one of the rear wishbones on the suspension started to flex under the strain that of the increase in pressure. As the laps continued the movement in the wishbone increased. This movement in the wishbone caused the rear wheel on that side of the car to change its geometry in relation to the car and tracks surface, causing the car to be unstable.

"Dave." Janice radioed

"Yes."

"It's a bitch through the, AHH SHIT...." The radio went silent. Also the track went silent as the sound of the engine stopped immediately. The instability of the car caused Janice to wander of line for the final phase of the Craner curves, she automatically corrected the error, but the increased load on the rear suspension arm caused it to fail suddenly. This allowed that corner of the car to drop to the tracks surface, causing an immediate and fast spin.

"Janice." Dave shouted into his mike. No response. The track had taken on an eerie atmosphere, it had changed from a place of noise to silence in an instant. Dave looked around the world seemed to have changed into slow motion.

The mechanics were already running to their rescue truck, but to Dave it looked as if they were trying to move through thick treacle. Then the world suddenly speeded back up, and noise returned, this time the sounds of people running and the raised voices of urgency.

"Old Hair pin," Gerry said to them, running to jump onto the back of the truck. John and Vanessa were standing on the pit wall. John said "I *can* see what looks like tyre smoke just past the exit of the hair pin."

As the truck approached the corner Eric pointed to a wheel laying on the infield. There were marks on the tracks surface that had come from carbon fibre rubbing on the surface. They could see the car just past the exit of the corner parked alongside the protective tyre wall, or what was left of the tyre wall. The tyres were scattered all around the car. Dave was still trying to raise Janice on the radio while they were driving to the scene.

As they approached the car Dave could just see Janice moving around in the cockpit. Then with relief he saw the steering wheel come flying out and her arms trying to wrench herself out.

"Janice are you OK." he asked as he arrived at the car.

"Yes." She said muffled by her helmet. "The radios dead."

"Were you knocked unconscious." Dave enquired while the rest of the team started to extract the car from the piles of tyres surrounding it.

"No, just as I was speaking to you the rear snapped away from me, and I ended up buried in old wet stinking tyres. I couldn't get rid of them at first." She was wet through, with all the rain that had come down recently the tyres had filled up. On impact they had flown around the car, and over the cockpit kindly depositing their contents over her. Dave radioed back to John. "Janice is fine, the car lost a rear wheel. From the track it looks like it came off before impact."

"Thanks Dave." John replied "I'm driving up to collect you and Janice." John was just exiting the pit road when the call had come through.

"Thank God for that." Vanessa said.

"These things happen. We build the cars strong to take these knocks. I'm worried though, why the wheel came away. Maybe we curtail the rest of the test today."

"You still have to run tomorrow though John." Vanessa said to him worried about the press.

"Yes I know, but if there is a problem with the car I couldn't risk sending Janice out to perform knowing it could fail. That would be criminal."

"True, but it did run fine up to her pushing harder."

"We'll see." Join said as he pulled up onto the grass. He ran across to the car after greeting Janice.

The car wasn't baldly damaged apart from the right hand rear wheel missing. It looked as if one of the suspension struts had broken, this had over loaded the other and resulted in the whole lot being torn away from the car. Whilst the damage to the car was slight it looked

decidedly second hand.

"Take Janice and Dave back to the pits Vee." John shouted "I'll stay here with the lads while they recover the car."

Vanessa did as she was asked. On the way back round Janice said. "For a couple of laps the car was *a* real bitch through the Craner Curves, it didn't matter what line I took. Just as I radioed it let go. I radioed because I could feel it getting worse. I was going to ask if you could check the telemetry for the suspension readings."

"We'll have a look once we check you out. You've taken quite a knock."

"I'm fine Dave, I just need to shower and change out of this suit, I'm soaked." Janice was also starting to shake. Dave wasn't sure whether it was just cold from the water or the fact she was shocked from the impact. Normally racing drivers put such incidents out of their minds. They are all a bread apart and don't seem to suffer from the same emotions as the normal driver.

Once Janice had showered she was back to normal, she had changed into the new suit Vanessa had handed to her just before the start of the last test. Dave was busy looking over the rear suspension of the second car when she walked up to him. "Will I be taking this out later."

"Not sure yet Janice. We need to have a good look at the other car. Its taking some time to recover."

Vanessa was standing on the pit wall, "It looks as if they are bringing it back now." She shouted back to them.

Out at the scene of the incident Gerry had decided not to wait for a truck to arrive with a lift on the back, but to tow the car in. they had, had to man handle the car out of the tyre wall and back to the track surface. He was worried about damaging the underside of the chassis any more. As it was the rear diffuser looked to be damaged beyond the point of repair. The replacement cost of that would be £5000. They would also have to remove the undertray, if that was damaged it also would be a cost of £5000. Any incident in Fl is expensive. It was because the undertray was damaged that Gerry decided that a tow would be Ok. If a mechanic sat in the cockpit and one sat across the nose of the car, then because of the rigidity in the car the floor pan on the damaged corner would not touch the track surface any more. Eric had brought over the wheel assembly that was laying in the infield and deposited that on the back of the truck

John instructed two of the mechanics to go back to the incident point on the track and walk along the circuit looking for any particles of carbon fibre. They couldn't afford to suffer any further damage caused by foreign objects. This was usually classed as FOD, and the track walk called FODing. This was an essential, but could be a very boring job. Luckily for the two men selected it was only a small area of track to Fod.

Chapter 23

Gerry spent the next couple of hours inspecting the damaged components that had caused the crash. On one of the suspension arms he thought he could detect an area of weakness. He checked that same area on the second car. After a further half an hour of being bent over looking closely at both arms on the second car and the remaining arm on the crashed car, he groaned as he straightened his back. "John look at this." John came over to the work bench where Gerry had placed the broken components from the rear suspension. "This is the arm that I think broke first. It then stressed the others beyond their limits, causing failure" Gerry pointed to the area of breakage.

"It looks like a small cut mark." John said after looking at the arm very closely.

"Yes it looks as if it was sabotaged." Gerry said.

"Why would someone do that." Asked Janice.

"To slow us down again." John replied. "Is the other car Ok Gerry."

"I cannot find any signs of tampering on it, but unless I totally strip and check every item I cannot guarantee it." Gerry said with an air of despondency.

"How was the sabotaged." John asked

"It would only take a simple cut with a sharp knife to create a stress raiser. Given a short amount of time that would weaken the arm." "And you can't see anything on the other arms."

"No."

"Janice, how do you feel about driving the other car. It's your call." John said.

"Lets try it." She said. Her words were strong, but she did have some doubts in her mind.

"Dave." John said as he turned. "Get number two warmed up." John didn't want to waste any time. The quicker he got Janice behind the wheel the less time she would have to dwell on her decision.

As the noise of the second cars engine burst into life, all attention turned towards it. The mechanics busied themselves around the car, allowing it to rev. This performed a number of tasks. Mainly it was used to ensure that there were no fluid leaks from any of the components. It also ensured that all the fluids were heated through before they were put under the stress of running.

Once the engine had been shut down Janice climbed into the cockpit. She would for safety sake never climb into the car whilst the engine was running. Once she had been strapped into position, the engine restarted and all the checks completed she exited the pit road, and through Redgate the first corner. She again took the car on a number of steady laps. "Dave." She radioed

"Yes." Came the reply through the static from the radio. "This chassis feels totally different, has it been changed." "No." Dave replied. Although he knew that to be untrue. The rear diffuser was slightly different on the car. He didn't want to pass that information on to her just yet.

"Ok, starting fast laps."

"Understood."

It was clear from the pits that Janice felt at home in that chassis from her second lap onwards. The crash had been erased from her mind, she seemed to have full confidence in the cars ability to respond to her commands. As she increased the power her lap times started to fall. They were still well outside the times that an Fl car would normally produce due to the restriction from the management system, but they were quicker than the times from the morning session. After the required number of laps Dave radioed. "Box next lap."

"Understood, Box." Replied Janice. Box was the terminology for the pit. The word box came over the radio clearer than pit, it caused less confusion. She had enjoyed the session, whilst the lap times would not have got her anywhere near the qualification level for a typical Fl grid, for a first day test session it had gone well. It was a pity about the problems that morning, but that was all in the game. As she drove down the pit road one of the mechanics stood to wave her out, so that they could wheel he backwards into the garage. She swung the car across the pit road and killed the engine. The car immediately went quiet, all the vibrations she had been feeling through her bottom ceased. John and Vanessa were stood on the pit wall, they looked pleased with that session also. They were talking about something together looking in her direction.

When Janice removed her helmet, her hair was wet through with sweat. Even though she had only driven a few laps, and the weather cool and wet, the exertion and heat generated was quite phenomenal. If she were to get the drive for next season Janice realised that she would have to work hard on her fitness level. She could feel the muscles in her neck beginning to ache with the exertion of trying to stop her head being thrown around due to the forces generated by braking and changing direction. She headed for the trailer to shower and change.

"Where's Janice." Gerry asked Dave. "I need her for the debrief."

"Don't know." Dave replied "Probably gone to the trailer, I'll look."

Dave headed off in the direction of the trailer.

"Bloody women." Gerry retorted.

"Doesn't look like he's calmed down much." John remarked to Vanessa, as they came over from the pit wall following their conversation.

"What did you think to her driving Gerry." John asked.

"She settled down well following the incident this morning. It must have taken some nerve to climb into the other car when we didn't really know what the true cause was."

"We were just discussing what to do about the drives for next season."

"I would wait." Gerry said. "Her fitness could be a problem, and the fact that I wanted to do the debrief now. Not wait for an hour while she makes herself look presentable again."

"Did you tell her Gerry." Vanessa asked.

"No, but it's normal practice."

"I didn't know that." Vanessa replied.

"But your not a driver." Gerry responded.

"True, but she may not have done that in her last team."

"That could be why they aren't leading the championship." Said Gerry storming away to the trailer.

Dave was stood outside the door. "Where is she then." Gerry shouted.

"The showers running." Dave replied.

"So." Gerry said opening the trailer door.

"So, the shower only has a small curtain to stop the water coming out. I thought I'd let her have some privacy."

"Ball's." Gerry said stepping inside the trailer. "Janice, it's debrief time."

"Can't I have any peace." She retorted.

"No we need the information from you know whilst its fresh in your mind, and not tainted with considered thoughts."

"Fine, Dave pass me the towel will you, I left it on the seat."

As Dave passed the towel to Janice he couldn't help see her naked form through the clear curtain "We'll have to re-arrange this trailer for you Janice." He said as she stepped out with the towel wrapped around her.

"Yes, I would like to be able to change in private. It might be Ok for you guys to flash your pricks at each other. I like to keep myself to myself"

"Right." Gerry said "lets get on."

The session took a good hour to run through. Longer than the actual driving. Gerry was unnaturally hard on Janice. Dave at times found it embarrassing to be sat there. It was like an interrogation. He also felt sorry for Janice, Gerry hadn't allowed her to dress, she was still sat with the damp towel wrapped around her. It wasn't too warm in the trailer either. He could see that Janice was shivering mildly. Finally Gerry let up, he either had run out of steam or was satisfied with the information gleamed from his driver.

"I'll make a brew next door while you get dressed Janice." Dave said getting up and pulling Gerry with him

Janice was fuming, she had just finished getting dressed when Vanessa knocked on the door and came in. "Fucking hell." Janice shouted. "I've just had to sit here with only a fucking towel to cover me while that bastard grilled me alive."

"Hey, hey calm down Janice. I only came into say John and I were impressed with your driving today."

"Well you can fucking keep it."

"Janice don't be like that. Look Gerry isn't normally like that. It's just that he doesn't agree with the TV being here tomorrow, and he likes to do the de-brief as soon as you get out of the car."

"He never said that to me."

"No, look he's not really a people person, he's an engineer. The car comes first before the feelings of those around him. Once you accept that you'll get on fine."

"But it took longer to de-brief than drive."

"I think he only did that to make a point."

Janice sighed. "Dave has made me a hot drink next door, come lets talk there. I can warm up then."

"You go Janice. I'll talk to Gerry, and John. We need to sort this out. John wants' you to continue. We may well be in a position to offer you one of the seats for next year." Vanessa realised she was sticking her neck out with that statement, John and her had only discussed the possibility. John had agreed with Gerry it was too soon. Vanessa only said it to try and calm matters down. She couldn't afford the team to lose it's only driver at this early stage. That would set torrents running through the funding program again.

As Janice left the trailer she was still seething at Gerry's attitude to her.

The next morning the weather hadn't changed. In fact it was actual rain that was coming down, and not just a constant drizzle. The mechanics had been working over night to repair the crashed car. It wasn't the teams intention to run the chassis that day, but John had wanted it repaired and on view for the camera's. Janice had arrived early, and Gerry seemed to be in a much more amiable mood. He had spent the night going over the test data taken from the car's telemetry. He had the down loaded the data from the telemetry computers into his own lap top. This computer allowed him to simulate design changes for the suspension settings, aerodynamic changes, and weight movements. He had found that by moving the centre of gravity around the car he could affect the balance positively or negatively for different corner combinations. This effect isn't new it is an art to ensure the centre of gravity is placed in compromised position to ensure the car is almost balanced for all the corners on the circuit. What John was working on was an adjustment that would allow the centre of gravity to be moved electronically from the pits throughout the lap and the race. This would use the telemetry programs that Ian was working on in Seattle. He had also found some minor changes to the suspension that would further enhance the cars high speed cornering balance. His mood had changed because he now felt that yesterday hadn't been wasted.

About an hour before the test session was due to start, the press started to arrive. Vanessa met them all and gave each member a presentation pack. The pack contained all the relevant information about the team and its goals for the coming season. She gave them a conducted tour of the trailers and the garage including close ups of the cars. Some of the more important camera men were allowed to film part of the drivers and engineers briefing session. This had been rehearsed prior to the start of the session. Vanessa didn't want any signs of confusion. Janice had been asked to describe the cars responses to the changes in the tracks surface from her point of view.

Once the film crews were happy with the incidental shots, the car's engine was started for warming up. Once the engine was warmed and shut down Janice walked out in her new overalls and took her place in the cockpit. She looked like a film star, make up and all. Once she was fastened into the car and the engine re-started she took to the track. Dave had again reminded her that she would have more power available to her in this session.

The car had a different behavior today. It was as if the car knew of the importance, and relished in the increase in its power. It was almost as if she were having to hold the car back, and not her trying to squeeze as much as possible from it. They were running the car on full wet tyres today due to the conditions. It took two laps for them to get up to temperature. At the end of the second lap Janice radioed that she would now start her quicker laps. She was filly enjoying the sensations being fed back to her from the car. Gerry stood in the pits was keeping a close eye on the telemetry screens. At the end of every lap the cars onboard computer fed the information to him. He could see the lap times starting to fall. By the third lap Janice was lapping quicker than her fastest from the previous day. He felt was pleased with the results. Before the session had started he had moved the ballast weight in the car ten centimeters towards the nose of the car. From the strain gauges on the suspension he could detect the improvements in balance.

After a further ten laps had been completed he called Dave over. He was worried about the hydraulic oil temperature. It had suddenly started to rise.

"Janice BOX." Dave radioed immediately on seeing the graph.
John looked at Dave questioningly. "Why bring her in." John hadn't

seen the telemetry at that time.

"This." Said Dave pointing to the screen. "She'll loose the gearbox if she doesn't come in now."

"Dave." He heard crackling in his head set.

"Yes Janice."

"Box."

"Yes Box this lap."

"Understood."

Twenty seconds later they heard Janice slow the car as she approached the pit lane.

"Janice stay in the car when you pull up."

"Understood."

This wasn't the normal procedure, but Dave wanted to talk to Janice and explain why she had come in early. They could talk with more privacy over the radio than if she had jumped out of the car asking questions.

The film crews were happy with the results. Vanessa had done an excellent PR job on them. She had avoided telling the crews how many laps would be completed. Following Janice's early abort she talked to the reporters telling them that it was a rap for the day, and that any questions would be answered once they had returned to base in Wakefield.

The piece that went out that evening on all the news networks showed the team to be in an extremely strong position for the next season. The result of which was a call from Bill Gates himself. He agreed to release the next installment of his funding package, and he didn't understand why his people had been taken off the Westfield project, he would see to it instantly that work continued.

Once the film crews had departed the circuit the real work could begin, but first Gerry needed to understand why the hydraulic oil temperature had risen so quickly. When he overlaid the graph from the previous test he could see a definite change in pattern. The hydraulic oil is used to move cylinders to change gear. If the temperature rises too much then pressure is lost by leakage around the seals, the result of that will be for the car to jammed in one gear. End of race.

It took them most of the afternoon to sort the problem out. The car had been losing a small amount of oil with each gear change. This reduced the amount available in the tank. Therefore the oil was being worked harder, which increased its temperature. They found one of the actuating cylinders seals to be at fault. Once changed and the tank topped up the system worked again. "It just goes to show, in a million dollar car it only takes a one dollar part to make it fail. 'Gerry said to Dave as they prepared to send the car out for its final test.

Janice was well into the last test run of the day. The car was running beautifully. As she moved through the section called the Craner Curves where the track sweeps left and right in a series of bends it felt as if it was floating on a cushion of air. She could feel the vibration of the engine through the seat, and a small amount of kick back through the steering wheel, but that was all. It was difficult for her to comprehend the actual speed the car was travelling at. Whilst the track is surrounded by crash barriers, at that point they are positioned well away from the edge of the track. Therefore the sensation of speed that is generated by peripheral vision is lost. Under acceleration even on restricted power, the scenery seemed to come towards her in a series of leaps. Her eyes would focus on an object some distance in front, and in a blink of the eye the whole scene had changed the object would be much closer, but there didn't seem to be a stage in between. She was now at a position driving the car where she didn't need to put conscious thought into the driving process. The driving was done by reflex action. Her thoughts were on giving feed back to Dave. She found that for most of the lap she was talking on the radio, giving precise information back to the pits. Very much like a test pilot in a new jet fighter.

During this phase of testing, the lap times were secondary to the need for data from the car, although the laps must be quick. Later in the year much closer to the start of the next season Westfield would start the true performance testing phase. Handling and reliability were the prime reason for the tests.

Janice was disappointed when she heard the call to box over the radio. "Understood, box this lap." She replied.

Chapter 24

The weekend following Westfield's first track test, the Austrian Grand Prix was run. Even though the McLaren cars ran better, more in keeping with the form shown earlier in the season. Ron Dennis decided that in order to clarify the traction control debate he must lodge the protest he had planned at the British Grand Prix. This he did, the FIA forced Ferrari to give the FIA scrutineers access to the engine management programs.

At the next Grand Prix in Germany the FIA announced that in their opinion Ferrari were not doing anything illegal, and that they couldn't detect any traction controls. At that Grand Prix the Ferrari team struggled, in practice they couldn't control wheel spin on the stadium section of the circuit. The consequence was they started well down the grid. From then on the race would be an uphill struggle.

Over the following weeks the cars were driven more than a thousand miles each. All of that track testing fell on the shoulders of Janice. During this time she was still competing in the British Formula Three championship. She had test sessions to complete for her F3 team as well as Westfield, but she took it all. In fact the Fl testing helped in her own championship battle. She had managed to improve her standing in the championship over James Haden.

Ian arrived back from Seattle after a six week stay with a new telemetry unit. This unit could give a constant feed back to the display screens in the pits in real time. It also made it possible for the Engineers to adjust up to four features on the car whilst in motion. These features could either be electronic parameters for the engine management, or they could be small servo driven to make small adjustments to suspension settings and wing heights.

Gerry discussed his theory of moving the ballast weight to effect the centre of gravity. Whilst Ian agreed that this was indeed possible he had reservations about how the driver would react. There was also the problem to overcome of what would trigger the signal. It could be a program that was particular to each circuit, or it could be done manually by an operator sat at the monitor. Both had problems. Ian did agree to write a simple program for the circuit they would try the system out on. Again as in all tests the driver wouldn't be told of the change. Gerry didn't want impressions, and if a driver knew that there was a difference between two chassis then they could make an assumption of what the change would give, and possibly give false information back. The other problem was that with current test program, which was concentrating on the reliability of the package, they would have to wait for the performance test phase. This wasn't due until November. The other problem would was that these tests would have to be done in warmer climates. Therefore they would be away from base. John was arranging to book the Paul Ricard circuit for the first test. He was also negotiating to get a session at Barcelona. The problem was that circuit was also used by many of the current teams, it was proving to be difficult to find a suitable slot.

In Turin Michali and Stefan were released from jail. The prosecuting magistrate following a lengthy investigation found that they were only guilty of tampering with the evidence at the scene of a crime. Which also included the taking of a car without the owner's consent.

Whilst these crimes would have to be answered in a court of law, he could not find reason for their detention any longer. The Magistrate required bail of Two Million Lire each. This was posted by Mr. Bettoni, they released into his custody.

During this period Alfons had been busy trying to locate the money for Mr. Bettoni, he had followed Vanessa around the country on her many visits to current and potential sponsors. At no time had been able to discover the identity of the mysterious woman seen with Vanessa whilst she had been in Italy. The reason for this was partially due to John taking three weeks out on holiday in the Maldives.

Whilst in the Maldives John had kept in touch daily with events back at base. During this time he had noticed changes in Fran, she seemed to more relaxed with her own femininity. She spent most of the day sun bathing and swimming nude. On their last visit to the Islands she had swum nude but never sun bathed. The nightly love making sessions were also less reserved, she tended to lead and be far more experimental. John was well aware of her relationship with Vanessa, part of him did feel uncomfortable with it, but in the main he realised that the changes in Fran were for the better.

On their return to the UK Vanessa had arranged for an interview and photo shoot for a number of magazines. The idea behind it was to further promote Johns standing in the celebrity world. Vanessa had felt that Whilst John was known within the closed world of Motor Racing he didn't have the charismatic aura of many of the current Fl team principles.

One of the shoots was on home life, a picture of John and Fran was included in an article describing the daily life of a Team Principle. This article was picked up by Alfons, reading through the article he skipped over the photo, then he thought he recognised the picture of the woman. He went to his collection of photographs stored on his PC, taken on his many stakeouts, he located the set he had taken from the bushes in Vanessa's garden one morning earlier in the year. The set showed the naked form of Vanessa in her kitchen with another person approaching and cupping Vanessa's breast. One of the pictures showed Fran's face clearly. There was no doubt about it. The mystery woman was Fran Bennet, the wife of Westfield's team principle.

He called Mr. Bettoni. "I've found the identity of the woman." He said.

"At last, you're slipping Galli."

"She's so low key you wouldn't believe it. But I have some information about her, she's having some sort of relationship with the Plat woman."

"Evidence."

"Yes, I've got a number of pictures of her in a compromising position with miss Plat."

"Good, use them to try to recover the cash from Miss Plat or whoever."

"Fine." Alfons said breaking the connection.

In Italy Bettoni thought, this could be a break. Westfield could take over from Ferrari now Lorenzo is out of the game. I need another importer.

Alfons decided that the money must be with Westfield, he had found no evidence at all in Vanessa's house or any of her accounts. Therefore he decided that he would make contact with Fran Bennet.

Two days later Fran was opening her mail, she opened an A4 sized envelope and pulled out two sheets of paper, one had a simple message printed on it. 'We want the money returning. Do not contact the Police. I will be in touch.' That was all, she picked up the second sheet, it was a computer printed photograph, it clearly showed her face behind Vanessa's and her hand cupping one of Vanessa's naked breasts. She remembered some months ago, the morning after the first time her and Vee had slept together. She had followed Vee into her kitchen, seeing Vee standing naked she couldn't resist fondling her. The picture must have been taken then. The realisation hit that somebody had been outside at the time. Shocked she didn't know what to do, as far as she was aware John didn't know about her and Vee, frightened her first response was to tear the documents and burn them. She then phoned Vanessa. "Help me Vee." She screamed.

"Fran, what's wrong." Vanessa said on answering the phone. Fran's tone frightened her. Something terrible must have happened.
"Vee I think I'm being blackmailed by the people we took the money from."
"How." Vanessa replied more relaxed, at least this could be dealt with.
"I've had a picture sent to me of you and me together. They want the money returning, I think they'll send a copy to John if I don't give them it."
Vanessa thought for a minute, then she said. "Don't worry darling, John is aware of us. I told him before we went to Europe."
"You did what." Fran said shocked again. "He never said anything."
"No, but I don't think he minds." Vanessa thought about telling Fran the circumstances behind her telling him, but thought better of it. Fran had enough to worry about right know. "What instructions have they given you."
"None, all the note said was that they want the money returning, they have also told me not to contact the Police."
"Ok, don't do anything, they'll be getting in touch again, we'll

decide then what the response should be."

"Yes, by the way where is the money."

"What's left is in your spare bedroom. I left it at the back of the wardrobe when I stayed over on our return. Do you want me to come over."

"No I'll be fine, should I tell John"

"Yes I think he should be told."

"Ok. Bye Vanessa." Fran press the end button on her phone, and re-dialed Johns office. She told John about the letter, and the money. She also discussed the conversation she had, had with Vee. John was comforting and asked "Do you want me to come back home."

"No I'm fine now. Its the next letter that frightens me." Fran replied.

"Don't worry about that, we can tell them to take a running jump. I am well aware of you and Vee."

"Yes but what will they do then."

"Don't know, just wait."

"Fine." Fran said reservedly. "See you later then."

"Yes Bye." As John put the phone down he looked concerned. The problem wasn't the current attempt at blackmail, but what could happen when the blackmailer realised that it had failed.

Chapter 25

Two days later another letter arrived for Fran. It was of the same shape and the same Font had been used to print her name and address. She passed the letter to John. He opened it carefully, inside was one single sheet of paper. It simply instructed Fran to make contact with an e-mail address via the Internet Failure to comply by the end of the week would result in the photographs being sent to her husband. John simply sent an e-mail to the address, telling the blackmailer to swivel.

Nothing else was heard from the person over the next fortnight. Fran had relaxed again, she had almost forgotten about the incident. The photographs never materialised either.

Following the death of Gianni Lorenzo, the Ferrari management investigated his practices. The more digging they did the more they became aware of the unsavory side of his character. They went to great lengths to distance themselves away from his associates. The very first move was to dismiss Mr. Bettoni as a security consultant. They also issued statements through the press of the investigations, and follow-ups as and when further revelations were discovered. The FIA also started investigations into the dealings of the Ferrari man, and the current management. Due to Ferrari's immediate reactions to their own findings, the FIA's investigation decided not to take any further action. They did however through Ferrari uncovered the records of the meetings between Ferrari, Renault, BMW, and Honda in Paris.

It was clear from those meetings that the group were involved in a conspiracy to hold back new teams from joining the ranks of Fl teams. The FIA formed a working group to investigate each of the companies involved. To determine at what involvement the companies or individuals of those companies had in the conspiracy, and to recommend to the FIA what action should be taken. What was clear, but with no evidence to link it to the group, Conoco had failed in its bid to enter for the following years season. Lack of funding had been the stated reason given by the company. Their bid would be taken over by BAR who had purchased the Tyrell team at the start of the current season, funding wasn't a problem for them, they had a large tobacco sponsor backing them up.

The dismissal of Mr. Bettoni by Ferrari, ceased Ferrari's bid to recover the lost money. However Bettoni, bitter from the dismissal and in need of money to support his life style would continue the recovery program. How had yet to be decided, thankfully to him due to Ferrari now not being involved he could use more forceful tactics. Off greater concern was how Bettoni could get Westfield to fulfill his obligations to the Union Corse Failure wasn't an option if Bettoni wanted to survive.

By coincidence Vee decided that they must move the money out of the Bennett's house into safer keeping. They hadn't yet decided what should be done with it. One option was to return it. However Ferrari didn't seem to be interested in it. With the current investigations underway for them to accept it back then they would be admitting guilt. Fran decided to put the case into their safety deposit box at the local Bank.

The testing program was now starting to approach the more difficult phase of performance tests. During the reliability test phase the cars had suffered a number of failures. Some were expected, where in house made components either failed on test, or following the session had shown signs of near failure. More concerning to Westfield was the high incidence of bought in failures. The items ranged from seals, bearings, instruments and electronic components.

The problem was that whilst many of the items were low in cost, each and every one of them represented an immediate failure. Every item had been supplied with certificates of conformity. When they failed they cost the team hours in rebuilding the assembly where they were housed, any shelf stock of the item or the assembly had to be checked. Westfield were forced into setting up lengthy and costly goods inward inspection procedures.

When batches of items were found not to comply with the specification ordered by Westfield, and the items returned to the supplier, in every case the supplier returned the goods to Westfield stating that they were not from them, and were in fact counterfeit. This left Gerry believing that somehow they were being randomly targeted, and their deliveries were being substituted. To get around the problem Gerry had to create a separate company which he used to order and receive the goods for Westfield. He simply used his home address. Once the orders started coming through the inspectors found no failures. Test orders for Westfield from the same supplier failed. There was his proof, however he couldn't tell who or how the items were being picked up.

The current Grand Prix season had know finished with final a twist. The McLaren team coming out victors over Ferrari. The weather in the UK would prevent further performance testing. To counter this John had booked the Paul Ricard circuit in Southern France.

It was also crunch time as far as the driver line up was concerned for the next season. During the testing in the UK they had been able to get a good grounding of Janice's ability. She had shown a strength of character, had been able to shrug off incidents, and could handle the car. Her fitness level had improved over the period as well. John was happy to go along with Vanessa's recommendation to sign her as a driver for the next season. That was easy, the problem was who to sign for the second seat.

The list of available drivers had diminished, but James Haden Janice's main rival from the F3 series still was without a drive for the next season. A number of F3 teams were discussing drives, it was also rumored that another Fl team were talking to him about a test driving seat, but not a full drive. The main problem was could James and Janice get on together in the team. They had both clashed during the last season both on and off the track. Their personal rivalry had been blown up in the motoring press to similar level to the bitter rivalry that had been reported a few years ago between Schumacher and Hill. The reality was somewhat less than the all out war, but did exist. The problem was Haden's belief that women were not racing drivers, and that Janice had taken his seat in the Westfield.

"Vanessa do you really think that our approach to Haden will soften his resolve." Gerry asked, in a meeting arranged by John to discuss the lineup.

"Yes I do, I know we cannot change his belief's, but at least giving him the drive will prove that she didn't take his drive."

"But my impression is that he won't be able to work with her." Gerry replied, "What do you think John."

"I have a more open mind on him than you. Rivalry between team mates is rife. In fact that helps development of the cars. The person any driver wants to beat is the driver of the same car design, that proves who is the better driver. They will strive to develop the car with their own engineers to enhance its performance."

"That's all well and good, but we need to ensure that the

development is done to the teams benefit." Gerry replied

"I agree, that's your job to ensure that engineers talk." John then added. "The other problem is that there really isn't another driver out there who is available, or who we can afford that fits into our criteria."

Gerry retorted "So why have the bloody discussion then."

"It has to be a collective decision." Vanessa said.

"But it's made." Gerry said getting up to leave. "I've got work to do if you two haven't." He didn't slam the door behind him, but it was very close to.

"What's eating him these days." Vanessa asked.

For a couple of weeks Gerry had been acting strange. He would lose his temper at the slightest incident. Once Dave called a wrong test parameter to Janice whilst driving. The mistake wasn't serious, in fact it had helped them to understand another problem, but Gerry had laid into Dave with aggression.

"Not sure, some rime back he mentioned he was seeing a woman, he never expanded on it, even though I have asked a few times." "Gerry and a woman." Vanessa asked surprised.

"Yes, but I don't know if that's it or what."

"Ok John are you going to approach Haden's manager or do you want me to."

"You see to it Vee, just don't offer him more than Janice."

"Fine, see you later."

It took Vanessa three weeks of intense negotiations to secure a contract with Haden. The problem wasn't with the driver, but his manager. He had wanted to demonstrate to Haden that he could wring a better deal out of Westfield than Haden could have done himself. Even though in the end James Haden's contract was basically the same as the one Janice had signed herself some weeks ago. The man had argued over some of the smaller conditions of the contract, rather than the monetary side. John had made it quite clear to them that there wasn't any more to be had. James had been ready to sign, his other offers hadn't materialised. John thought that this could have been down to the manager. At the first chance he got he would advice Haden to change, he found this guy to be destructive in negotiations.

Due to the protracted negotiations there was very little time left before the scheduled tests in France. The day James arrived at the factory the transporters were being loaded with all the equipment. To make his own point John hadn't allowed Haden into the workshop areas until he had signed the contract. The cars had been stripped ready for the over land journey. One of the mechanics did a quick seat fitting, unfortunately James didn't have his suit with him. He ended up wearing a pair of overalls, whilst this gave an impression it wouldn't give *a* true form. They would have to hope that it would be satisfactory for the tests. A new one would have to be taken at a later date.

The transporters would take two full days to arrive at the test circuit. However due to the transport laws in France, heavy Goods cannot travel over weekends, therefore the transporters would have to arrive at the track by the Friday night and park up. Each transporter had two drivers, this would allow them to drive round the clock. As well as the four transporter drivers the team would be taking a further sixteen people for the three day test session. This would include the two drivers, John, Vanessa, Gerry and Ian. The two race engineers for the cars and eight Mechanics. Whilst this seems to be a lot, for a race
there would be around thirty in the team. The bill for the three days testing would amount to around one hundred thousand dollars. It was therefore imperative that they came away with a meaningful set of data. The teams budget would allow only one further fly away test before the start of the season in Australia. John had also asked Fran to join the team in France. This was for two reasons, one that she could help to prepare food for the team during the day, the second was that John was still worried about the failed attempt at blackmail. Gerry had considered asking John if Anne could have come along to help with the food, but when John had announced Fran would be joining them he forgot the idea.

The romance between Gerry and Anne had blossomed, Gerry had got to the stage of asking Anne to marry him a few weeks ago. Whilst she was pleased at the request, she had asked him if they could wait a while longer. Anne had been a spinster for so long now, the thought of sharing her life fully with someone else was frightening, she just needed the time to adjust. This had upset Gerry for a while, he couldn't understand her delay. He was now starting to come around, and understand the reasons.

Alfons had been watching the Bennett's house for a few days. At no time had it been left unattended, until early one morning both occupants left. They were both on theft way to the airport to catch a flight to Marseille for the three days of testing. Alfons saw his chance had arrived.

He had been surprised by the response from the Bennett's e-mail. Whilst he wasn't one hundred percent sure that it had been sent by John Bennet, if it had been Mrs. Bennet then she was certainly playing a strong bluff. Maybe she did have balls after all. He had discussed the response with Bettoni, he had suggested a cooling off. They would play a wait and see game. He had told Alfons to enter the Bennet's house on the off chance that the money was still there, or to see if there were any other clues around.

After twenty minutes of searching Alfons was sure that the money was no longer there.

On returning to his office he reported the facts to Bettoni. It was clear that the Bennet's had left the UK for the forth coming test in France. Bettoni decided that he would go to France himself. He had friends who were members of the *Union Corse.* This was a group similar to the Italian Mafia that organised crime throughout France. Between them they would watch the group at the Paul Ricard circuit an opportunity may well arise. The money was now not the important issue. He needed Westfield to fill the gap with his loss of a friendly face at Ferrari.

Chapter 26

The first day of testing was drawing to a close, and things had not gone well.

The mechanics had had an early start preparing the two cars. The transporter drivers had set up the garages over the weekend. The cars had been unloaded, but they required re-assembly.

In the first session Janice had gone out quickly and set a base line for the cars, she had taken on the role of number one tester due to Haden's inexperience with the cars. Haden had been five seconds off the base line set by Janice on his best lap. One of his problems was his seat, the quick job had been a waste of time. He complained that he was moving around in the seat, and couldn't get feel for the car. His engineer Russell rigged up some padding with foam and tank tape. This made the seat tight but would at least hold him in position. His lap times did improve but were still disappointing

Towards the end of the second morning session Russell told James to Box that lap, unfortunately Haden didn't respond to the call until he was passed the pit entrance, part way down the start and finish straight Haden felt the revs starting to fall away, the engine felt as if it was being strangled. He had been told to slow down and return to the pits. Haden hadn't slowed sufficiently, when smoke started to billow out of the exhaust's, the pit crew heard a pop and then silence. The engine had exploded. The engine had let go on the entry to the first corner, leaving *a* trail of oil around the racing line. This delayed Janice's next test until the stricken car could be recovered and then the track cleaned.

Gerry had taken Haden to one side on his return to the pits. A bollicking wasn't the right word, Gerry had vented his spleen on the young man. An engine change wasn't in the test program, and would delay them further. Due to Haden's poor response to the car they were already well behind schedule.

By the end of the day Janice and Dave had managed to get their test program back on schedule. She had improved her lap times over the base line set in the morning by a further three seconds per lap. In the world of Formula one this was an order of magnitude. Haden had improved his times but was further behind Janice he was now six seconds behind.

If that represented a typical grid, and Janice was on pole with that time then Haden would not have qualified. He would have to be within one hundred and seven percent of the quickest time. He now faced an uphill battle to establish himself in the team, plus his confidence had been badly dented.

That evening whilst a meeting between Gerry and John was in progress discussing the day's events, Janice tried to pass on some tips to James. Unfortunately he was is an even blacker mood than he had been earlier in the day, when Gerry had torn into him for delaying in coming into the pits. The engine blow up had cost the team two hours in the

engine change. The two hours would be difficult enough to catch back with a driver who was performing well, but James was well of the mark. To compound the cost the team had also lost an engine block in the blow up. If he had pulled into the pits, or slowed down and cruised round then they may at least have salvaged a block.

"Not an impressive start for Mr. Haden." Gerry said to John and Vanessa.
"No, I agree but remember it is early days. If you look at his lap times compared to the early lap times that Janice put in at Donington then he is on track." John replied.

"Janice only had half the power then, he has full use. She would listen to Dave. Mr. Haden seems to feel he has something to prove." Gerry Replied.

"Only to himself." Vanessa added.

"It may be, but its cost us an engine." Gerry replied feeling as though he was being ganged up against.

"Well you made sure he knew that earlier didn't you Gerry." John said. "Well look lets move on, where are we with the testing." John continued wanting to move the discussion away from the problems with Mr. Haden.

Vanessa butted in, "Look this is going to be technical, so if you don't mind I'll take Fran into Marseille."

"Oh, err yes fine." John said.

"Good, h'm if you don't mind we'll stay there over night, there's some good night spots around the water front area. You'll not need either of us tomorrow will you." Vanessa added.

"I suppose not, one of the lads can provide the eats." John said resignedly.

With that Vanessa left the two men to go over the day in detail. She picked up Fran and both of them headed for the port of Marseille.

Once through the city they quickly found a pleasant Hotel on the water front. It was conveniently positioned for the other night spots of the district. Both of them were blissfully unaware that they had been tailed since leaving the racing circuit. In fact they had had five different members of the Union Corse following in succession. The local leader was a man by the name of Pierre Label, he was in control of all the smuggling, gambling, drugs and protection rackets, along with controlling the sex trade in the area. He had over a hundred men and women working for him in the various disciplines of his business. Each one of them could trace their ancestry back to their routes on the Island of Corsica. It was on that Island that the Union had formed.

Label called Bettoni once word had reached him that the woman were now in Marseille. This was a stroke of luck for Label, the port was his base, he could call upon any one of his business arms to assist.

"Great." Said Bettoni when Label's call came through. "Just maintain a watch tonight."

"What then Bettoni." Label asked.

"I think an early morning raid on their hotel rooms. Is kidnapping in the Union Corse's line."

"Anything is in our line my friend." Label replied.

"Good we meet at five in the morning outside their hotel. Goodbye." Bettoni said replacing the phone. Now he would get his own back. The money wasn't the only repayment he wanted from the Westfield team.

John Bennet took Both Janice and James out that evening, he felt he needed to build a relationship between the two drivers. Due to the problems that had been encountered in signing James Haden, he had not had sufficient time in the car to develop trust and confidence. Janice had covered almost two thousand miles so far. She now knew all of the cars qwerks. They managed to find a small restaurant close to the circuit where he hoped they could discuss the situation. John was well aware that Janice had already tried to help James.

Whilst John was away from the track Gerry and a small team of mechanics where busy working on Janice's car. They were busy installing the movable ballast system. Due to the increase in weight the amount of ballast had to be reduced from eight kilograms to six. This would reduce the amount of movable mass, and therefore reduce the amount of variation felt by the driver. Gerry had built the new parameters into his computer model. The results were still encouraging.

One of the problems that Ian had to contend with was communications. They had not yet received the final telemetry system from Hitachi. The new system did not need line of sight to establish links with the car. The system would find the nearest communications satellite and bounce the signal from the pits to the satellite and back to the car, even if the car was next to the transmitter. The speed in the early days was the problem, but with the latest technology in signal speed boosters it only took a couple of nanoseconds for the transmissions to take place. Unfortunately the system had been developed, but the first user units were still under construction. This meant that Ian had to find a suitable position high up that would allow visibility all around the circuit. His problem was that so far during the first day of running he had been unable to find anywhere that covered more than fifty percent of the track. Height was the major problem. He could get around it by mounting a dish on a helicopter, but cost was a major issue. Gerry required the test to be run over a half an hour's worth of track time. They couldn't afford the expense for something that wasn't a certainty.

It was Eric who provided the solution. "Why not use a balloon." He asked. Ian looked at him with astonishment. Then said "Yes we could mount a dish on smallish balloon, and tether it above the pits."

"What type were you thinking of Eric." Gerry asked.

"I don't know boss, your the brains. But don't weather people use them."

"That's right Eric, Ian try the local weather station Provence has one somewhere, see if they will lend us one."

"Great he has the idea I have to find one and put it in action." Ian said jokingly. He was pleased that a simple solution had been found.

It had been some weeks since Vee and Fran had actually had the chance to sleep together. Vee's work at West field had meant that she had had to travel around Europe meeting sponsors and journalists. Therefore both were secretly looking forward to the chance to enjoy each other's bodies once again.

Following their meal they walked quietly around the water front area of Marseille soaking up the atmosphere Like many of the worlds water front area's it had developed its own unique atmosphere. The area had also been transformed away from its industrial and workman like routes into a cosmopolitan district of Bars, Restaurants and Shops. Eventually they retired to their hotel bedroom.

John hadn't made the progress he would have liked. Some progress had been made, but the underlying problem was that Haden didn't feel that women should be in Formula One. He resented the fact that Janice had beaten him in the Formula Three championship, and that she had been given the test driver's seat with Westfield ahead of him. He was convinced that if he had been given that seat then his ability in the car would have been ahead of where Janice currently was.

John decided by the end of the evening that all he could do was monitor Haden's progress, ensure that he didn't do anything detrimental to the team, and make his decision early in the new season.

He took James to one side on returning to the circuit, and made sure that James understood the position. That he still had a drive, but he must demonstrate his ability to learn and improve, both himself and the car.

Chapter 27.

Early the following morning Pierre Label and two of his men were gathered outside the small Hotel where Fran and Vanessa had stayed. Bettoni arrived shortly after. The time was five AM. They made their way down a small alleyway to the rear of the Hotel, where the kitchen door was located. At that time of the morning the alley and the kitchen were still deserted. The door presented no problem to Jean-Paul a burley Corsican. They quietly made their way through to rear stairs. These lead from the kitchen area to all floors of the Hotel. They were normally used by room service waiters and cleaners.

Fran and Vee were on the second floor of the hotel. In rooms adjacent to each other, but without connecting a door. The four men split into two groups of two. Label took Jean-Paul whilst Bettoni took the other man Jacques. As quietly as possible they opened the doors of the two rooms simultaneously. Bettoni had taken the room that was booked to Fran. He and Jacques made their way silently to the bed.

In the other room Label and Jean-Paul were doing much the same. Both the rooms were in darkness, Bettoni reached down to turn on the bedside light, whilst Jacques was ready to pounce on its occupant. As the light came on they saw the bed was empty. It had not been slept in that night.

In the room that was booked to Vee, Label turned on the light. To Jean-Paul's surprise there were two forms in the bed. He pulled the bed cover back to reveal the naked bodies of the two sleeping women. The sudden movement of the bedding being removed and the light coming on roused both of them. Jean-Paul leapt to grab Fran and cover her mouth to prevent her from screaming. Vee woke immediately, she always had the ability to come around to fully in an instant, she sized up the situation, and leaped towards Label who was just moving away from the light switch. With her forward momentum she managed to land a couple of well aimed punches on his jaw and nose. The punch that landed on his nose shattered the bone and cartilage, with blood splattering out over his face. The force, and the shock of the blows pushed him backward towards the wall. Vanessa then kicked out at him with her feet, at her second attempt she managed to disable Label with a well aimed blow to his crotch. Label felt as if his balls were about to explode with the force of the blow. He sank to his knees in agony. Not yet finished with Label Vanessa gave him a heavy round house punch to his jaw, this snapped his head round, and rendered him unconscious. The force of that blow spread Labels blood over the wall and across Vanessa.

She then turned to try to assist Fran who was taken unaware by the attack of Jean-Paul, and was struggling under his weight. Vanessa climbed onto his back to try to wrestle him away. This she hopped would give more room for her to use her skills.

As she struggled with him Bettoni and Jacques arrived at the rooms door. It was quite a sight to see the naked body of Fran struggling and kicking on the bed to try to throw Jean-Paul off, Vanessa with blood splattered over her naked body attempting to pull him off Fran. Jacques leapt in to rescue Jean-Paul, he managed to get a glancing back heal to his crotch, for his efforts. It wasn't hard enough though to cause him to let go. Between himself and Bettoni they managed to overpower Vanessa. They pulled her to the floor. Once there they pulled her arms up behind her and bound her wrists. Jacques then bound her ankles, and pulling the remainder of the cord up and through the binding round her wrists they managed to disable her. To finish the job she was then gagged.

The fight had left Fran by this time. She had never stood a chance, they only bound her wrists, and gagged her to stop her screaming. Bettoni quickly roused Label by throwing a bowl of cold water over him. He stood very, carefully, seeing Vanessa trussed up on the floor he viciously kicked her in her crotch. The blow hit her on her pubic bone causing her to scream with the pain. The gag managed to suppress the noise. "Enough Label." Bettoni said. "Jean-Paul, Jacques carry the vicious bitch between you. You." He said pointing to Fran "This way." He grabbed Fran and lead her out if the room into the corridor still naked.

Jean-Paul and Jacques carried the still struggling, naked, blood splattered Vanessa, with Label taking up the rear uncomfortably, they left the Hotel by the same route taken to gain access.

Outside Fran was pushed into the back of a waiting Renault Cargo van, and Vanessa was unceremoniously dumped onto the bare wooded floor. It was still only ten past five in the morning.

It was seven AM before there was any sign of life at the circuit. There was an embargo in force that prevented any noise before ten AM. This left the team plenty of time to prepare for the days test sessions.

By eight all the mechanics were at work on the cars, whilst the engines couldn't be run there was still plenty of work to be carried out. Both cars needed to be safety checked. This entailed a check of all the safety systems within the cars, all nut's and screws had to be spanner checked, and the braking and steering systems checked out. Each phase had to be signed off by the number one mechanic responsible for that car.

The drivers were busy going through the requirements for the days testing with their own Engineers and Gerry, basically a base line would have to be set. This would be done with the car in the configuration from the previous thy. Then the plan called for a series of changes to be made to the cars set up. Each of the changes were designed to complement each other. However if one change proved to be unsuccessful then they would need to back track to the previous set up and re-establish the base. The plan also called for both cars to be set up the same, Gerry would use the average data from both cars over the timed runs to determine the level of improvement. At this stage he felt it would be detrimental to the overall task of car improvement if he allowed the drivers to dictate preferences. That would come later once both of the drivers were far more competent.

Of course there were variations from the previous day. The track temperature would be different, the atmospheric conditions will have changed. This was the reason they took base line laps at the start of each session. If fact the conditions would change throughout the day also. The settings that gave the best performance in a morning may well prove to be totally wrong for the mid afternoon session. It is all a matter of compromise. However Gerry's plan was to gather as much information as possible from the tests. He could then feed the results along with the track and atmospheric information into his computer model. This could then be used to predict the necessary aerodynamic, and the engine management settings for an expected outcome. This information would then be automatically down loaded to the car, allowing certain adjustments to be carried out even during the race.

At Ten AM the cars were allowed to start. The mechanics again went through the warm up procedure, before allowing the drivers to climb into the cars. It was a tight squeeze to get into the cars, the drivers had to stand on their seats and then slide their bodies down into the cockpit, twisting their shoulders at an angle so that they could fit underneath the impact absorption material that surrounded the cockpit rim The material was there to give the drivers heads protection against side impacts. Once inside the drivers engineers could then fasten the seat belts, and the engines restarted.

Janice left the pits first, she would do one lap to warm the tyres of her car, and then put in two or three quicker laps to establish the base line for the following test runs. James was held back for thirty seconds before he was allowed out onto the track. This was to allow a gap between the two cars. In no way did Gerry want the two drivers racing against each other.

Chapter 28

The white Renault Traffic Van was now approaching the small mountain town of Moustiers Ste-Marie. In the back still unclothed and bound was Fran and Vanessa. The ride at first whilst frightening and uncomfortable from being bound, was in the main smooth due to much of the route being on Autoroutes, but as the van had started to climb into the mountains they had been bounced around more. For Fran she could sit on the floor, she had only overbalanced a couple of times. Vanessa however had had *a* bad ride, the way she was trussed up she couldn't sit. On each corner as the van was thrown around she would slide around on the rough wooden flooring. Her hips and back were red and bleeding from the abrasive nature of the wood.

All the way Jacques who was also in the back of the van had been leering lecherously at the two naked women. Vanessa whilst uncomfortable due to being defenseless wasn't too bothered about her nakedness. However for Fran it was different, she was trying her best to hide herself from his gaze, but each time the van moved she would have to move to steady herself, this exposed her sexual area to his piercing eyes.

Once through the town the van pulled off onto a rough farm track. This bounced the women around even more. Vanessa was close to crying with pain at each movement of the van. At the end of the track the van stopped at last. They were outside an old farm cottage, Jean-Paul opened the rear doors, the women both felt the cold blast of the mountain an. Jean-Paul indicated for Fran to jump down and go into the cottage, he and Jacques grabbed Vanessa and dragged her across the floor of the van, scrapping more skin from her sore body. At first she thought they were just going to allow her to fall to the ground and drag inside, but Jacques took pity on her and undid her ankle bindings. She was then pulled to her feet and pushed roughly into the cottage. Due to the lack of feeling in her legs she immediately stumbled. She was roughly half lifted half dragged inside.

They were both led to a small back room where they were pushed inside. The door slammed behind them, and they heard a key turn in the lock. Fran looked scared to death as she looked at Vanessa. Vanessa indicated for Fran to stand back to back. Vanessa then started to work at Fran's bindings. It took her awhile, and Vanessa could feel her fingers going into cramp, but she managed to undo the not allowing the cord to drop free. Fran quickly removed the gag from her mouth. She was about to speak when Vanessa gesticulated for her to remove the bindings around her wrists. Fran managed to undo the bindings quicker than Vanessa had done, but she could see what she was doing. Once undone Vanessa removed her own gag, and said quietly. "Shh, don't worry Fran, we'll I'm sure everything will be fine."

"Vanessa I'm sacred that that lecher will attack me again."
"We'll be safe, they want us as hostages, they'll try to get John to pay a ransom for us. For that they'll have to show that we're safe." "But it won't stop them from molesting us."

"I know it will be difficult for you, but don't worry " Vanessa said finally. She had been looking around the room whilst she had been talking. On the floor there was a double mattress, it was covered by a rough woolen blanket. In the corner of the room there was a small sink and toilet, there was no screen to separate it from the room, but at least it wasn't a bucket. She walked over to it, on the way she had picked up the blanket and passed it to Fran. "Here put this over your shoulders." The mere fact that Fran could cover up her nakedness helped to calm her. She felt less vulnerable, sitting down onto the mattress she pulled her knees up to her chin, and pulled the blanket fully round herself.

When Vanessa tried the tap cold water flowed from it. On the side of the sink there was a dirty looking cloth, she wrung it out, and gingerly dabbed the damp cloth onto her wounds, in an attempt to clean some of the dirt from them. Once she had finished she tried the flush on the toilet, it also worked. "Sorry Fran but I must wee." Vanessa said.

Just then the door burst open, Jacques and Jean-Paul entered the room. "See I told you." Jacques said pointing to Fran. "She's just dying for it." As he approached her he started to pull the zip on his trousers down.

"Leave her alone." Vanessa shouted as she leaped from the toilet.

"The bitch is loose." Jean-Paul warned as Vanessa moved forward.

"What the Fuck are you doing." Came a shout from outside the door. Jean-Paul looked behind him as Bettoni entered the room, his entry stopped Vanessa in her tracks. "You're fucking animals can't keep their filthy dicks in their trousers." Vanessa said.

Bettoni said "If either of you dare touch either of these women, then I'll cut your balls off myself. Understand. Now get out." Both of the men moved back out of the room. Then Bettoni said "Her put these on, I'm sorry about those two, the sight of two pretty women has gone to their brains. Unfortunately they aren't the brightest, and they keep their brains between their legs." Vanessa came forward and picked up the cloths that had been brought in. "I'm sorry they aren't up to your usual standard, but its all I could find." Bettoni added. Vanessa inspected the clothes, Jeans and shirts, she passed a set down to Fran. "Here Fran slip these on love." She said tenderly. Then as she started to pull on the shirt she had kept back she said to Bettoni. "Why have you taken us?"

"Quite simple my dear, you have something that doesn't belong to you, and I want it back with interest."

"So what happens now?" Vanessa asked.

"I am surprised that you asked such a question, with your background."

"Meaning?"

"Do I have to spell it out. I've done my research on you, and all is not what it seems. You act the innocent female, but we both know that this is only an act." Bettoni said straight to Vanessa. Then he added. "Right I'll leave you both here. Someone will bring you food and water. I'm afraid you will be here for some time, don't worry about the animals, they won't touch you. So long as you behave. Any trouble from you and I won't be able to control them. By the way miss Plat don't ask for any favors from Label, you managed to crush one of his balls with that kick."

Once Bettoni had left Vanessa sat on the mattress next to Fran. Fran leant over and started to ay on her shoulder. "Don't worry all will be well you'll see." Vanessa said to her. Whilst she said that Vanessa was thinking to herself 'how the hell did he find out.'

Back at the track Ian had arrived carrying a large box. Inside was the weather balloon he had managed to get from the weather station. "When do you want to by this out." He asked Gerry.

"This afternoons run should be fine."

"Ok I'll set things up." Ian said as he went out of the back door of the pits.

John was stood on the pit wall watching his cars circulate the track. Each time they came onto the pit straight and accelerated towards the first corner, the noise increased in intensity. It was so load that without his headphones on it would hurt. As it was he could feel the noise hitting his chest and reverberating through his body.

Once the cars had completed their allotted number of laps for the morning session they pulled into the pits. Immediately the silence that descended over the track was in itself painful. As they came to their garages the mechanics responsible for that car descended upon it, they lovingly wheel the car backwards undercover, so that they could tend to the beast as if it were a prized race horse. The two drivers jumped out and immediately went into the de-brief area of the trailer parked behind the pits.

In this session James had made a big improvement over his performance yesterday. He was still slower than Janice, but was know within a second of her lap times. He found with that performance improvement his confidence in the car had improved, and his ability to describe the handling of the car in the de-brief was better. He could also relate his feelings of how the car behaved to the words of description that Janice used. She had the ability to describe in words just how the car reacted to the tracks surface. These she would add to the graphical printout of the suspension movements. The idea was then to be able to build up a more detailed picture of how to further improve the cars set-up.

In the other trailer John had set up an office, in there he had phone fax and e-mail links back to his office in Wakefield. He had just finished giving a briefing session to Bill Gates on the cars performance.

Chapter 29

Vanessa was still cradling Fran in her arms when the voice of Jean-Paul was heard. "Both of you stay back away from the door." The door was then unlocked, and he entered carrying a tray with two plates of pasta, and some water. He put the tray down just inside the door and left the room, locking the door behind him Vanessa got up and brought the tray over. "Here Fran, eat this, once you've got some warm food inside you'll feel better."

In the Garage Eric had been checking Janice's car, he found that the oil level had reduced following the morning run. It wasn't unusual for a formula one engine to use some oil during a run, but he was concerned about the amount that had been consumed. As he filled the tank he called over to Gerry. "Anything unusual with any of the engine readouts from this engine."

"No why? Gerry asked.

"It's used a couple of litres of oil." He said, then. "Shit." As the tank over flowed. Some of the oil had spilt onto the garage floor. He walked over to a bench at the back of the garage to get some paper towels to clean up the spillage when Janice walked up to her car. Before Eric could shout a warning she stepped onto the oil and slipped. As she went down she screamed in pain. "Bloody hell." She retorted "My knee popped." Gerry came over to inspect the damage. As he touched her knee she screamed in agony again. "Dave call the medics over, quickly." Gerry called.

Whenever teams conducted tests they were obliged to have a team of Paramedics at the circuit at all times. It was the teams responsibility to pay the area authority for the service. They must also ensure that there is a Helicopter available if required. This need not be at the circuit, but can be called upon in the unfortunate event of an accident.

The medics arrived in the garage quickly, and diagnosed a ligament strain, nothing too serious, but it would prevent Janice from driving that day.

Gerry said to James. "You'll have to drive Janice's car this test."

"Why?" James asked.

"We're trying some changes, they've only been put on her car so far. All you need to do is drive as per normal, set the afternoon base, then leave it up to us."

"Ok fine you're the boss, but you'll have to change the pedals and steering wheel."

"Yes I know, the lads will see to that. Go get ready, ten minutes and you're out."

The mechanics set to work on the car making the changes. Janice was helped to a chair out of the way at the back of the garage. She was upset that she would have to sit out the rest of the day, but knew it was for the best. There was no way she could drive that day.

When James came back in carrying his helmet she said. "Look after her for me wont you."

"I'll do my best." He said as he climbed in.

Whilst James was out setting the base laps for the test session Ian had climbed onto the roof of the Garages and was playing with the weather balloon. He had attached a small dish to the bottom of the balloon, and then let the balloon's tether out until it was about one hundred and fifty feet above the roof. This was the height that he and Gerry had calculated would give them the required spread to cover the circuit. Once back in the garage he sent a test signal to the car, he got a response immediately. "Ready Gerry." He said.

James was abiding by the normal procedure, once he had completed five laps he came into the pits, he was surprised when Gerry sent him straight back out with no adjustments.

"Continue on." Dave radioed to James.

"Wasn't the base correct?" Asked James over the radio. "It is fine, we want you to put fifteen more laps in." "Understood." James replied. He then started to push the car harder. Ian switched on the balance shift program, they knew it had started to work because James radioed back after the second full lap. "The car feels different." He said

"How James." Gerry asked, this was a break in protocol, normally all communications would go through Dave.

"The balance seems to have improved in both quick and slow corners." He said. As James got used to the car Gerry could see the improvement in the lap times. On his last lap he was half a second quicker than his quickest of the day. The following lap he again improved his times. Janice sitting at the back of the garage watched *in* amazement at the times coming in. by the time James had completed a ten laps he was lapping a second faster than her fastest time.

"I knew this car was better than mine." James radioed back, he was enjoying the feeling and responses the car was giving him.

Whilst the test was running John was back at work in the trailer, he had a number of e-mails to reply to, he was also putting the finishing touches to the next planned test session booking This one would not be *a* closed test, as this one was, but would be shared by a number of the other UK based teams and would take place at Barcelona in Spain.

As James was lapping he was talking constantly on the radio back to the pits. His excitement with the improvement was clear to all, the talk however was all technical feedback of how the car felt and responded.

As he approached the twelfth lap his times started to slip, he radioed. "The car isn't as precise on turning in as before."

Dave checked the readouts and replied. "Can't see anything wrong here, continue for a few more laps."

"Ok understood." James answered.

Ian set to work on the computer, he had a theory that possibly the balance program needed to be modified. As the laps went by the frantically typed on the key board, he was attempting to allow his program to learn, in learning the program would re-adjust the cars balance lap by lap, in accordance with the reducing fuel load.

Unseen by anyone a small hair line crack had appeared where the pinion gear was attached to the steering column inside the steering rack. As the car cornered this caused the crack to expand, giving the vagueness in cornering that James could feel. With each corner it got worse. The car was approaching the final corner before entering the pit straight. At this point on the circuit James was past the pit entry point and would have to complete a further lap to come in. "I'll come in this lap it's getting worse." He said. He was about to add another comment when the shaft sheared. James lost all control over the direction of the car. "Shit no steering. "He Radioed. "I'm applying the brakes."

As he did the forces from the braking pulled the car immediately to the left. James automatically turned the wheel to correct, but since it was no longer connected to his front wheels the response had no effect. The car hit the barrier hard on the left front. The impact occurred with the car still travelling at over one hundred and twenty miles an hour. The front wing and nose disintegrated sending shards of carbon fibre high into the air. As the left front wheel hit the barrier it too was smashed off. The wheel flying back into the cockpit area narrowly missing James's helmet. The car then ricocheted across the track, this time impacting heavily onto the right side. This time with no nose cone left to absorb the impact James's body took an even greater pounding. His brain smashed into the inner face of his skull rendering James unconscious immediately. Also his other organs were thrown forward into his chest wall and rib cage. The car lost both wheels and suspension on the right side. The twisting impact sheared the engine mounting points ripping the entire rear of the car off. As it slid down the pit wall a brief fire ball irrupted, but thankfully was immediately extinguished by what was left of the onboard systems.

The mechanics could only watch in horror as the physical forces fried to convert half a million pounds worth of racing car and driver to a mass of fibre and pulp. The car had only just stopped moving when the Paramedics started to move. As the car came to a rest they all feared that the car had been totally destroyed.

John sitting in the trailer heard the engine noise cease suddenly. He knew that this could only mean one of two things. Either the engine had blown or the car had crashed. He jumped up and to run to the track side. As he left the trailer his PC beeped as an e-mail came in.

It only took a few seconds for the mechanics to reach the wreckage. Whist the car was now not recognisable for what it had been, it had no wheels, rear end including the engine, this was laying in the centre of the track, the cockpit and drivers area was still intact. James was sitting with his head slumped forward still strapped in the car. There was no sign of life from the driver. With a knife one of the mechanics cut through his helmet strapping, with two holding James's neck one very carefully removed the helmet. This allowed the Paramedics to get to James. It was obvious that he wasn't breathing, his teeth were clenched together, it took one of them to force his mouth open whilst the other inserted a tube into his airway. As the tube went in they all heard a gasp as James's automatic breathing response forced air into his lungs.

Gerry looked back and saw John running out of the front of the garage. "John call the Helicopter in." this stopped John in his tracks. He returned to the garage to make the call.

By the time the Helicopter arrived at the circuit they had managed to extract James from what was left of the car. The medics weren't happy with his responses, they had introduced intravenous fluids to try to help stabilise him for the journey to hospital in Marseille.

All this time Janice had remained seated in the garage, she was shocked by what had happened, what made it worse was that it should have been her, that had been her car.

John and Gerry looked on as the mechanics started the grim task of collecting all the broken parts of the car. "Make sure you don't do any further damage guys." Gerry called out. "I need to try to piece the thing back together." The task that would now befall onto to Gerry was to fully investigate the reason why the accident had occurred. It had been so devastating that they couldn't risk sing the other car until the full reason had been found.

This test session was over. Not only had they lost a driver, just how bad he was nobody could tell at this stage, but it looked bad. They had lost one car completely, and their other driver was injured. John looked devastated. This could signal the end of the battle before it had fully commenced. Where the hell was Fran and Vanessa he thought to himself. He needed Vanessa to be back at work, she would have to deal with the press, and with James's relatives. Better ring them quick he thought to himself. No first make a list, he decided. John found a chair at the back of the garage away from Janice who still looked shocked, and started to list who he must contact. Fist place went to James's father, second he must ring Bernie Ecclestone. He demanded that all the Formula one teams reported incidents to him personally. The list then went down all the sponsors. This would take some time, John left the garage for his office.

Anton was getting worried, he had dispatched Vanessa to Marseille yesterday to follow up some information he had received regarding a tie up between Bettoni and the Union Corse. If the link up had taken place then the whole investigation could would have to be stepped up. So far they had managed to keep everything under wraps. The problem was that the French authorities had so far refused to co-operate in the task. The inclusion of the Union Corse would mean they would have to be involved. This further worried him, unfortunately whenever the French had been involved in the past in such investigations things had turned sour. He suspected the section had been infiltrated.

The problem was that Vanessa had contacted him when they had arrived in Marseille, but he not heard anything since then. He had asked one of his operatives to check the hotel out earlier that afternoon. The report when it came back didn't ease his worries. The hotel didn't have a record of either Miss Plat or a Mrs. Bennet registered. They had simply disappeared.

Chapter 30.

It took John an hour to complete all the calls, the call to James's parents had been harrowing, at this time he didn't know whether James would survive the journey to Marseille or not. His call to Bernie had been quick, Bernie told John he would send Sid Watkins out to the hospital immediately. Professor Watkins was the medical advisor to the HA, he was also Professor of Neurosurgery at the London Hospital. His skills had been put to good use by the sport over the years. Bernie assured John that James would receive the best treatment, and that he was sure all would be well.

Unknown to John following his call to Bernie, he had contacted James parents and made arrangements to fly them out to be with James, in his private jet.

It was only after John had finished all his calls that he turned to his PC, when the screen saver cleared John saw that he had a message waiting. Just as he was about to call up the message his mobile phone bleeped at him. "Bennet." He answered.

"Ah Mr. Bennet." A distinctly foreign voice said.

"Yes who is this ?" John asked. Not many people had his mobile number.

"Please let me introduce myself, I am Anton Abonovicz a Police Inspector with the Italian Police based in Genoa."

"Ok Inspector, how can I help you." John asked suddenly worried, he still hadn't heard from Fran or Vanessa.

"Please don't take this the wrong way, but have you heard from your wife or Miss Plat today ?" He asked.

John was now very concerned, "No I haven't. Why do you ask?" John asked hurriedly.

"You haven't heard anything from them, r anybody else."

"No I said not." John retorted. "Please tell me what this is about."

"Please don't worry, I just need to speak to Miss Plat when she returns." Anton said calmly trying to bring the situation under control. "Look let me give you my number, please ask her to call me when she returns." Anton gave his personal number to John, he knew Vanessa would have to number to hand, but he felt disturbed that they hadn't shown yet, therefore if someone else contacted John then he hopped he would give him a call back himself. Then he added, "Please call me if she hasn't returned by the morning." He then broke the connection.

The call had disturbed John even more, he left the trailer to find Gerry.

Bettoni was sat in the farm house waiting. So far no response had come back to his PC that the message had been read.

"Its been fucking ages." Label said to Bettoni. "It would have been better using the fucking phone." Label wasn't confidant that this new technology gear would work. "Are you sure it can't be traced back to us here." He added.

"No chance, the call has been routed through a number of service providers, that prevents the trace." Bettoni told him. "Just be patient. He may not be at his terminal."

"What if it's not on." Label asked.

"No problem, as soon as he turns it on the mail will come up."

Fran was settling down. Vanessa had been right the food and drink had helped. "What's going to happen." She asked.

"Don't know yet Fran., but one thing's for sure, we'll be here for some time."

"Why ?, what do they want ?" Fran asked.

"The money I guess for one thing." Vanessa said.

"Fine I'll tell them where it is, they can have it." Fran replied cheering up.

"Trouble is, I know don't think that, that's all they want."

"Why ?"

"Just something that was said earlier."

"What ?"

"By your full of fucking questions aren't you." Vanessa replied, then she said "Sorry, I didn't mean to snap. Look I'm not quite what you think."

"What do you mean."

"I'm not the PR Director of Westfield. Well I am, but I'm not I work for Special Branch on international crime." Vanessa said pausing for a while.

"Go on." Fran said. "You don't think John is involved in anything illegal do you."

"No not at all, I've been using Westfield as a front to conduct an investigation into crime's using motor sport to transfer diamonds into Europe."

"So what's that got to do with these pricks." Fran said pointing towards the door.

"Gianni was the link between Ferrari and one of the men behind the shipments."

"But he's dead."

"Yes, true but the man I want is Bettoni. Look Gianni worked for Ferrari, he brought in Bettoni to supposedly look after the security for them. In fact he was a drug dealer. He used the Ferrari transportation to move the goods around the world. Gianni in fact was being manipulated by Bettoni, not only that but he was also responsible for a number of espionage crimes against other teams, although I wasn't that bothered by those. It did give me an opening." Vanessa explained.

Fran was suddenly worried again. "That means that we're not going to get out of this." She almost screamed at Vanessa.

John found Gerry looking closely at one of the parts from the wreck, Janice was stood uncomfortably by his side.

"Ah John, look at this." Gerry said holding the end of the steering column.

"Sorry never mind that Gerry, Fran and Vee haven't returned from their trip yet, and I've just had a weird call from an Italian Police Inspector asking for Vee."

"So." Said Gerry puzzled.

"It was almost as if the inspector knew that they hadn't returned, but was hoping he was wrong." John said.

"Sorry John, but what do you want me to do, or did I miss something."

"No, no Gerry, it's just me. I think I must be reading too much into not hearing from them. You don't suppose that they heard about James and have gone to the hospital do you." John added hopefully.

"Could have, can't see how, but it is possible." Gerry said.

"Anyway, look the crash was caused by a fault with the column. The pinion has sheared off, and the crash didn't do it. The column had an old crack in it. I'm have the column removed from the other car to check it out. We may need to remake the whole batch."

"Good, good." John said absently. "Have you got the number for the hospital." He then asked.

Gerry looked at him, and then thought John's worried to hell, and not about the cars. "No I haven't, it will be on the permit for the track though." Then he turned to Janice. "Take John back to the trailer and find the permit will you."

"Come on John, lets sort this out." Janice said.

The news from the hospital was mixed, Janice had enquired after James first. She had been told that he had arrived in an acute state, still unconscious, but had stabilised. He was now in intensive care, he had had a scan, this had shown a swelling to his brain. He was luckily he didn't have any further injuries, and was now in intensive care where they had sedated him, but had not introduced mechanical life support. At this time he was able to breath for himself. The plan was to keep him sedated to allow the swelling to reduce, they would only then allow him to recover back to full consciousness. As to whether they had seen Fran or Vanessa they didn't think anybody of those names had been to the hospital so far. They did tell Janice that a Professor Watkins had spoken to them and was at this time en-route to the hospital.

It was only after Janice had given John the news that he turned to his PC, he remembered there was an e-mail waiting for him. He cleared the screen saver and called up the message. His heart almost stopped when he saw the message.

Janice was sitting at the desk next to John as he moved the mouse to retrieve the e-mail, she saw him suddenly pail. "John what's the matter." She said worried. John didn't reply, he just sat looking at the screen. When Janice lent over John she saw the message herself. It was simple and very much to the point. *'We have someone close to you, if you wish to see them returned unharmed DO NOT CONTACT THE POLICE. Do not attempt to contact us. Someone will call you in two days time at your home number. If you are not there one of my two captives will cease to exist.'* Janice on reading the message picked up the intercom system and called Gerry.

"What's wrong Janice." He asked.

"Please come to Johns Trailer now Gerry it's urgent." She put the radio down, and gently got John to move away from the screen, onto one of the settee's along one of the sides of his office. She then set to, to make a coffee for him.

As soon as the message had been retrieved by John a computer about one hundred miles away beeped. "He's got the message." Bettoni said to Label.

When Gerry arrived a couple of minutes later she just pointed to the screen and said. "Read that." Gerry did as he was asked.

"Shit." He said simply. Then looking at the desk top he saw the pad alongside the key board. The pad had a number and the name of the Police Inspector on it. "I'm going to ring this guy." He said.

"NO.." Shouted John. "They said no Police."

"I know." Gerry said. "But this guy is Italian you said. We are in France, I'm not ringing the French lot." He quickly dialed the number before John could stop him. Janice just sat at his side trying to comfort him as much as possible. Poor man she thought, what a day he's seen one of his cars destroyed, one of his drivers almost killed, maybe unable to drive again, and know his wife and colleague taken captive, but why should they be taken.

"Hello, is that Inspector Abonovicz." Gerry said when the call was answered.

"Yes. Who's this."

"I'm Gerry Watts, part of the Westfield team. You called my boss earlier regarding Vanessa Plat."

"Yes." Anton replied guardedly

"Look we have had a message from someone who is claiming that they have her and Fran Bennet captive."

"Right, thanks, err where are you know."

"At the Paul Ricard circuit in France."

"I'll be with you in an hour. Stay put and don't call anybody else over this. OK."

"Fine. I suppose." Gerry replied suddenly puzzled by the man's response. How can he do anything, if he's Italian then he won't have any responsibility in France.

It took Anton about an hour and a half to fly by helicopter from Genoa to Paul Ricard On landing he headed straight for the paddock area at the back of the pits. Gerry was stood outside Johns trailer waiting for him "Hi you must be Inspector Abonovicz, I'm Gerry Watts. Johns inside, I'm afraid he's not taking this well."

"Understandable, lets go inside." Anton said pointing to one of the doors. "This one ?" he asked.

"Yes go through to the front, that's where the office is."

Once inside Anton introduced himself to Janice and John. Gerry showed him the message on the computer.

"Right quite simple isn't it." Anton said. "No return e-mail address either. Not that that would have helped us to trace them." He added.

"So what do we do know." Gerry asked.

"You do as instructed. Pack up and go home." Anton told them. "This case is over to me now."

"How can it be. You're Italian." Gerry said.

"No Polish actually. I only work in Italy." Anton corrected. "I work for an international Police organisation. We can operate across a number of borders without too much interference." Anton didn't feel it wise to add that the only European country they had problems with was France.

"We have another problem, one of our drivers crashed today. He's in Marseille *in* a critical state we need to keep in touch with his progress as well." Gerry added.

"I don't mean to sound unsympathetic, but you can do that from England. It will be best for you to comply with that message. If these people are who I think they are they will get nasty."

"Why have they taken them." Gerry asked. "It sounds as if you know them."

"Who can say at this stage, money probably." Anton said.

There was knock at the door, Janice opened it, and one of the mechanics came in. "We're packed boss." He said. "Have Ito get the transporters on their way ?"

"Not just yet." Gerry said. "We have another problem. We'll all be leaving tonight. Get the guys packing this trailer up ready for moving out. We just need to arrange flights home for everyone." Gerry added.

Its time to call the boss, Anton thought to himself. The base for his investigations was in the European buildings in Brussels. His call went straight through to a small set of offices tucked away in the basement of the building. Not many of the thousands of office staff or members of the parliament knew of its existence.

"Problems chief" Anton said "Vanessa and another woman have been taken. The other woman is the wife of the Westfield Grand Prix team owner."

"Any demands so far ?" Anton's boss asked.

"No, only that they will be called in two days time, back at home. I would say that Label is involved know for certain

"I want this mess tidying quickly Anton. Can you do it without French help."

"Yes boss ." Anton broke the connection. Anton knew it wasn't a can you statement, it was a will do statement. He needed to make a number of calls, at this time Anton had four other operatives in and around the South of France, they would have to drop their own investigations and concentrate on finding where they had taken the women. He wanted them found before the next call.

Whilst Anton was busy calling his team together Vanessa and Fran were trying to settle down to their first night in captivity. So far whilst they had been held at the farm house they had been treated respectfully. That was following the first attempt at sex by Jean-Paul and Jacques earlier. It seemed that Bettoni and Label had control over the men under their command.

Chapter 31.

It was well past midnight when the Anton's small team had its first break through. They had spent all their time since they had been called together going through their long list of informers in and around the Marseille area. Anton wanted them to concentrate on the Hotel where the women had according to the register had never stayed, but they had found a witness to say that he had seen the women entering the Hotel the previous evening.

They had pulled in one of the cleaning staff, she had told the detective that she had been instructed to be late into work that morning. When she had started work, two of the rooms, rooms she knew to be occupied, had already been cleaned. On arriving she had seen a van parked at the rear of the building, it was a van she had seen around before, and suspected it belonged to some of the more unsavory characters that frequented the adjoining district. A couple of case were being thrown into the rear of the van.

"OK." Said Anton to one of his men. "I want a list of all the property outside of Marseille that is either owned by or has connections to the Union Corse."

"Not in Marseille." The detective questioned.

"No, I don't think they would risk holding them in the city. It would be too easy for one of them to make someone aware of their presence." The detective left to conduct his search. To the other man in the room Anton said "You know this Label better than most, where do you think he would go ?"

"*I* would head out into Provence. There are plenty of small villages and deserted properties out there. I'll bet the Corse have a number of small bolt holes in the hills."

"Yes true, that could make things difficult. However we do know that they have Internet access."

"You only need a phone line for that. Once you've subscribed to a provider you can move the terminal around. That won't help us trace them. A phone call would have been easier to trace."

After *a* short while the detective assigned to finding the

properties linked to Label came back into the room. "Most his property is in Marseille." He said "However, there are five addresses listed outside the area. Most are on the coast towards Nice, one is in the hills close to a place called Moustiers Ste-Marie."

"What do you think." Anton asked the detective called Pinon.
"That could be the place." He said.
"Right you get up there and keep watch, call in once you've arrived, we'll keep digging here."
Pinon left the room quickly. It would take until the early hours of the morning to find the place.

Once through the small town of Moustiers Ste-Marie Pinon found a place of cover to leave his car, he then set off on foot over one of the adjoining hills. From the look of his map that hill would bring him to the back of the farm buildings. He would then need to find a good place of cover, where he could sit out the day light hours and keep a careful watch on the movements.

Once in cover he called back into Anton. "I'm here, the place is in use. Most of the building is pretty run down, but the main building has some lights on, and there is some smoke coming from the chimney. What's morel can see it has a phone line to the building with a new branch to a room at the rear. I think we've hit pay dirt." He reported.
"Good." Said Anton. "Stay put, report back in mid morning."

By this time John had arrived home, Gerry had called Anne on the way, to get her to make sure the heating was on at the house, he also asked her to stay with him and John. Gerry had promised Anne that he would explain his reasons when they arrived.
Later in the evening the phone rang. Anne answered "Yes."
"This is Anton, is John there." The caller asked.
"Just a minute." Anne held down the secrecy button on the phone. "Gen-y there's a man called Anton asking for John."
"Here I'll take it." Gerry said taking the handset away from Anne "Hello Anton, this is Gerry Watts."
"I don't want to sound too optimistic at this stage Gerry, but I think we have found the place where they are being held."
"Bloody hell, that was quick." Gerry responded. "When will you

get them out."

"That might be the hard part. They have them in a farm house tucked out in the hills. We don't know where in the house as yet, nor do we have any idea of how many men there are in the building. I have a man keeping watch. I'll send more up in the morning, that way we will be able to get a better picture of the numbers involved."

"That's bloody marvelous news Anton."

"Look don't start thinking this will be all over by tomorrow, it won't, we may have to watch the place for days."

"Yes OK Anton I've got that, but at least you've made progress. John is resting at the moment, I won't say anything until later."

"Good, I wouldn't get his hopes up just yet Gerry, I'll ring tomorrow with a further update."

"Best if you ask for me Anton, I'm worried about John. The test session didn't go well. We have a driver in intensive care in Marseille right know as well. The future of Westfield is in the balance, with all this it could have tipped the balance for him."

"OK I understand, bye." Anton broke the connection.

Anne looked at Gerry smiling. "That sounded like good news." "It could be, they think they have found where the girls are, but getting them out might take a lot longer. We will just have to wait."

"Oh I see. Look I'll just nip home, I'll bring some things over I'll stay here in the spare room."

"Good idea, we'll both stay tonight, then tomorrow I'll need to go to the factory, the cars will be back by then. I'll get the lads started off loading and stripping them down. I'll be back by mid day, hopefully before those bastards call."

Following the call Anton directed two more of his men to join Pinon at the farm. He called Pinon back to brief him on the increase in numbers, and what he wanted from them.

He then settled back to wait, as he relaxed he thought, 'distance is going to be the problem. The question was why did they insist on sending Bennet all the way back to England. Surly it would have been better for both parties to have been in France. Unless they had some other motive.'

He put his feet up and listen to some music. Anton always found it better to think his way through problems with music playing, whenever he was away from home he always ensured he had a supply of his favorite CD's to hand.

Quietly sipping a brandy he thought, 'Yes that must be it there must be another motive for them.' He thought long and hard but it wouldn't come to him. He was tired, so he turned in for the night.

He was staying in an apartment on the outskirts of Marseille. It was one of many such apartments scattered around Europe, that were reserved for the sole use of the special investigation teams if they so wished. Vanessa never used them, she preferred to stay *in* Hotels. They normally fitted her cover better than using the apartments.

Chapter 32

Gerry left John's house early, he wanted to make sure that he could be back before mid day. Not only did he want the test cars removing and the one remaining car stripping. The other was beyond salvage, it could be dumped, they may be lucky and find a few sensors that still functioned, but he wanted all the rest of the steering assemblies stripped and checked. He would have to send the columns away for x-ray inspection, that would be the only way he could risk using them.

Janice had called him the previous evening, she had been concerned that Westfield didn't have a representative at the Hospital in Marseille with James, she had had his permission to fly back out today to be with him. Gerry after considering the request had agreed, the only stipulation was that she had to call him every day. This she agreed to, and had repacked ready for the early morning flight back out.

John woke about mid morning, following a shower he felt a new man, two things occupied his mind, one was to achieve the freedom of his wife and Vanessa, the second was to ensure that his cars did reach the starting grid for the next season. Leaving his bedroom he bumped into Anne coming out of the guest room.

"Anne, what are you doing here." John asked.

"Gerry asked me to stay with you. He's gone to the factory to off load the cars. I'm very sorry about your wife John." She said slightly embarrassed to in her boss's home without his knowledge.

"Oh so your here to nurse maid me are you." John said without feeling.

"No not at all, if you don't want me here I'll leave."
"No, sorry if I snapped Anne, I'd welcome the company." "Gerry said he'd be back around midday." Anne said turning to go down stairs. "Do you want breakfast or anything." She added. "Yes that would be nice thanks." John said as he followed. Promptly at eleven am the phone rang, John picked it up before Anne could get to the phone *in* the kitchen. "John Bennet." He said.

"Ah Mr. Bennet." The voice said on the other end. "I am speaking on behalf of the party that is holding your two friends."

"You mean my Wife and colleague." John corrected. "What

ever." The male voice replied. "This call is only to establish you are where we want you."

"I want to speak t." John started to say, but was cut off immediately by the caller.

"Shut the fuck up and listen." The caller snapped. "You will only speak to answer my questions. As I was saying we will call again tomorrow with further instructions. Until then stay put." The caller then broke the connection. The call had lasted a total of twenty seconds only. Even if a trace had been put onto the call it would have come up blank.

"Was that ?" Anne asked looking at John.

"Yes it was the kidnappers. They are only test me. No demands as such yet. We have to stay put." John answered.

"Call Gerry now John please." Anne told him.

"I'm not used to being told what to do by a secretary, but I suppose your right." John picked up the phone and dialed Gerry's mobile number. Once Gerry had answered John quickly filled him in on the call. Gerry was annoyed with himself that he had missed the call, but was pleased that John was back with them. Gerry told John that he had agreed to Janice going back out to be with James, John was in agreement also. He thought that it would help to cement working relations between the two. Providing James came out of the coma fit and well.

With nothing else to do John set of for the factory leaving Anne to mind the phone at his home.

Whilst John was driving in Gerry phoned Anton. He told them of the conversation John had had with the man Anton thanked Gerry and told him to expect more of the same. He felt that the group would string John out for a few days before the demand would come. That way they would be softening John up, and he would more than likely give in to them.

Following the Call Anton called Pinon. "Who left the building this morning ?" he asked.

"Only Bettoni this morning." Pinon reported.

"Has he returned yet ?"

"No. Wait a second." Pinon said. "Label has just come out of the building, he is walking to his car." Then a few seconds later. "He's leaving for the village now."

"Have you any idea yet how many of them are in the house ?"

"No I've only seen Bettoni and Label outside so far." "Ok keep watching."

Well I'll bet there are at least four of them there. Two will remain inside whilst Bettoni and Label will do the running around. It looks as if Bettoni is the one doing the calling. It would make sense his English is better than Label's, Anton thought to himself. He again settled down to wait. Anton had considered leaving France for England to be with Bennet, but had decided that for now it would be best to stay put.

Life was starting to settle down in the house, Fran and Vanessa had become resolved to their fait of being held for some time. The easiest way for them would be to become subversive, so long as the demands were acceptable. "God I could do with a shower." Fran said to Vanessa

"Yes, and a change of clothes would be nice. Wait a little and I'll see if I can talk one of them into giving a little." Vanessa said.

John sat down to discuss the test session with Gerry once he arrived at the office.

"Well all in all, it was a good session really." Gerry said.

"You mean it only cost us one car and one driver, it could have been worse."

"No not at all, I mean the results we obtained before the crash were excellent. The engines ran much better than I dared to hope. So far no gearbox problems have manifested, and the new telemetry system worked."

"Yes I suppose your right. Where would we have been placed if that had been a Grand Prix on lap times ?"

"Janice's best would have been around twelve to fifteen I think. James on day one would not have qualified. Even if Janice had been on pole James was more than seven percent slower than her. On day two James's best would have been around Sixth to Eighth."

"That good, yes it was a good session. Remind me Gerry what caused the crash."

"I'm not one hundred percent sure yet, but it looks like the steering column had a fault, it appears as if the pinion gear sheared off the end of the shaft."

"What caused it ?"

"Simple design error, the shaft and pinion gear had been machined from a single piece of titanium. It looks as if there's a stress raiser in the corner where the shaft's diameter increase's to the diameter of the pinion."

"Solution ?"

"Simple re-make the shaft and pinions from two pieces and join the pinion to the shaft with a glue."

"Glue ? are you sure, we've had one failure due to design I can't accept another."

"Trust me John, I'm a designer." Gerry replied smiling.

When Janice arrived at the Hospital in Marseille she sought out James's parents and Professor Watkins. She found them sitting talking in one of the relatives rooms close to the intensive care ward where James was.

"Hi I'm Janice Higgins, team mate of James." She said "How's he doing." She added to the Professor.

"At the moment he's still under sedation. He's coping with it well, there hasn't been any further deterioration in his condition."

Janice turned to James's mother and said "I'm sorry, it should have been me in that bed. He was driving my car, I slipped in the garage on some oil and couldn't drive. So he had to use my car, it had some special gear on board that hadn't been installed in his. I feel responsible for the accident."

James's mother looked at Janice. "If you think that I could accept that *as* an apology young lady then your wrong. Yes *I* would agree that it should be you in that bed. Although I would agree with James that you took his seat anyway, and I suppose that that would then have still put him in the bed, because the car that crashed would still have been his, and therefore he would still have been driving the dam thing."

"Look I'm sorry you feel that way, and I understand your feelings, but let me make one thing clear I didn't steal his seat. *I* took the seat because *I* was deemed to be more worthy of it at that time. We were and still are in competition with each other." Janice replied back to her, she now understood where James got his ideas from. All through this his father had stood back not taking much notice of the two women.

"Look you two." He said as he turned, "Bickering between you won't help James. This young lady hasn't come here to argue with us, she has come because she like us feels for our boy in there." He pointed to the inert figure laying in the bed through the glass partition. Then he said to the Professor. "Carry on please, you were telling us the next phase."

"Yes Mr. Haden, they will scan his brain later today, if the swelling has continued to reduce then they will start to reduce the level of sedation he is under. This will slowly, and I cannot stress the word enough, slowly bring him back to consciousness." Sid Watkins said to them.

Since his arrival Sid Watkins had been talking to the doctors treating James, firstly about the condition of the driver when he arrived, and secondly about the treatment and prognosis of his condition. In a way he was pleased the learn that there were no other apparent injuries to the man. The safety measures taken at the circuit, even though it wasn't being used for Grand Prix racing, only practice, and the measures taken on the cars had worked. The problem had been something that his committee was still working on, and that was the G force experienced by the driver in high speed impacts. The man's body had been well protected and restrained within the shell of the car, but his organs had no protection against the sudden reduction in speed from the second impact. It was this that had caused the bruising of his brain and subsequent swelling. At least everyone was confident that he would make a full recovery, whether that would mean he would be back racing in time for the start of the next season or ever was still unknown.

Chapter 33.

The following day at 11 am Johns phone rang again. "Bennet." John answered.

"You will attend the Barcelona test session in December." "Pardon." John said.

"You fucking heard." The voice shouted back. "If you fail you will be a widower." The line was then broken.

Gerry looked at John who was stood with a puzzled look on his face. "Was that them again." Gerry asked.

"Yes." John replied "They are demanding we attend the Barcelona test. Or they will kill Fran. The problem is will we have any cars to run."

"Simply yes John. I will ensure that we have two cars available. You make sure the bookings are still in place, and we have a driver. Call Janice make sure she's back here by next Monday." Gerry got up and said "I'm going to the factory I've a car to build." Then he said as an afterthought, call Anton and let him know, I've been keeping him informed." With that Gerry left.

Anton took the call from John, afterwards he thought this is getting nasty they are threatening too early into the game, and they didn't mentioned Vanessa this time. He called Pinon who had just left the farm, and was sitting outside a local café in Moustiers Ste-Marie, he had left one of the other detectives on watch. They were taking turns in shifts at the farm. "Do you have any idea of the numbers involved yet." He asked.

"Sorry Anton no. we've only seen Bettoni and Label so far."

"Ok." He hung up. He felt that this was going to be long drawn out job. He couldn't authorise a raid on the building. First he didn't have a layout, second he had no idea how many guards he was dealing with. Also he mustn't forget the original investigation. Whilst the line on Ferrari, or more to the point Gianni Lorenzo had finished with his death. Could Bettoni who he suspected of orchestrating the deals be now trying to line up Westfield. If that was the case then as sorry as he was for the Bennet's he would have to allow the thing to be brought to a head.

Later that evening Vanessa saw her chance. Jean-Paul had just brought them their evening meal. Instead of just quickly putting the tray down and leaving, he lingered just long enough for Vanessa to *say* in a sweet voice. "We could use a shower Jean-Paul, I would be most grateful if you would let us have one after dinner." She smiled at him as he turned towards her. At first she thought the tone of her voice had perhaps been too seductive for him, and that he would try to once again force himself upon her or Fran. Fran was sitting on the bed watching she also became concerned. Then Jean-Paul said in his guttural French. "I will see if it can be arranged." He left and locked the door behind him.

"Well that might have worked." Vanessa said smiling at Fran.
"It could have got you raped as well Vee."
"No he wouldn't dare. Bettoni scares him."
They had just finished their meal when the door opened again. Jean-Paul stood in the doorway. "You can shower now, one at a time and I will watch."

Fran looked disgusted at Vee. "I can't shower with that creep watching me." She said

Then Jean-Paul said in halting English. "Strip here if you want shower."

"I'll go first Fran, I'm desperate to feel clean." With that Vee took of her jeans and tee shirt. She followed Jean-Paul out of the room. He took her to a small combined shower and toilet just down the corridor for the room they were being held in. Vee for once didn't feel comfortable being naked, but the excursion allowed her to see a bit more of the building where they were. Jean-Paul held the door open for Vee in order to pass him she had to squeeze past him, as she passed she could smell his odor, it was disgusting. Once in the room she quickly showered, all the time he stood in the doorway leering at her. The water felt good on her skin, there was a simple bar of soap in the shower, it was good enough to produce some lather, which was quickly washed away. Somehow the water refreshed her, as she dried herself she didn't feel his eyes upon her body in quite the same light. Once dried she was escorted back to the room. "It's not that bad Fran." She said as she entered the room. "Just strip and get under the shower you'll soon forget your being watched." Fran didn't feel reassured by the words, but she did need to clean up. She undressed and without a word followed him out of the room. Jean-Paul went through the same procedure as with Vanessa. At no time did he try to force himself upon the women, even though the thought had crossed his mind. He did enjoy the feeling of power he had over them.

When Fran returned Vanessa was relived, she hadn't been sure about Jean-Paul with Fran, they had tried to force themselves upon her earlier. The reason for them singling out was that, Fran was older, and she did have larger breasts than Vanessa. She was also more submissive than Vanessa. "Thank you Jean-Paul." Vanessa said when he returned. "I hope you enjoyed it as much as I did." She smiled. "We could also do with some more cloths, and some women's things." Jean-Paul didn't say anything he just nodded as he left the room. "Well ?" Asked Vanessa.

"The water was good, but I still feel dirty, he watched every move,... ugh." Fran shuddered.

"Get used to it love, I think we're here for a long time, best just humor them.

It was still three weeks before the test session at Barcelona, the guys at Westfield were being driven hard by John. They were aware that Fran was missing, but the didn't know about the demands being levied by the kidnappers. Gerry wanted two running cars to be available for the test even though they would only have a single driver again. The problems facing the team wasn't just that one of the cars had been destroyed, spare chassis were already part complete. They would be hard pushed, but it was possible. The problem was that following Paul Ricard they were down to one engine. That unit was up to its mileage limit and needed a rebuild. All the Grand Prix engines had a seven hundred mile limit. That is to say that once the unit has covered that mileage it must be stripped and re-built. If not failure will occur in a devastating way.

All the Westfield units were bar-coded, the code had to be entered into the computer to enable the unit to be started, following each run data was down loaded from the cars onboard computer and transmitted to Westfield's main computer in Wakefield, this logged every hour and mile run against each engine. At the start of the Paul Ricard test Westfield only had three units available. Two were destroyed at the test. The first on day one when James failed to stop when told. The second in the crash. The unit in James's car did have some mileage left, but only one hundred, that wasn't enough to justify taking the car all the way the Barcelona and back. The team would have to work day and night building two from scratch and re-building the third. They would then have to continue to build at least another six units plus a third car. This would give the team three cars to take to each race, with three engines each.

By the time Janice arrived back from Marseille James had started to recover consciousness. Sid Watkins was pleased so far with his recovery, he had spoken to Bernie Ecclestone about rehabilitation. It was clear that first he needed to be brought back to England. Sid had suggested that he be transferred to the London Hospital where he worked, he could oversee the return flight if it was done within the next day. James seemed to be strong enough to stand the flight. The problem was that if he was to regain his career as a racing driver Sid didn't want him around James's mother. From what he had seen over the past week she would inhibit any recovery. He had suggested that Bernie should talk to Westfield about sending James to Willi Dungel in Austria. He specialised in such rehab. He did realise that cost would come into play, he had no way of knowing what the funding or budget constraints there was at Westfield.

The transfer of James back to London went to plan. Once installed in the London, Sid Watkins could continue to monitor his progress closely. It also helped that friends and family could visit. For someone recovering it is important that they are kept active. Periods of no activity allow the mind to wander, and if not checked in someone as active as James was, then depression can quickly take over. It was critical for James that this wasn't allowed.

After a week in the London they started to introduce some gentle physiotherapy. He had been immobile for two weeks, and it is amazing how quickly the body adapts to that state. It seems to forget even how to walk, the first stages were to get him standing. This was to allow him to regain his sense of balance, from that first session, it was clear that James was a fighter, he pushed every session to his limit and beyond on occasions.

Once the Rehab at the London had started Bernie called Sid to tell him that he had spoken to Westfield, and whilst Bennet agreed that

James needed the best treatment available, they would struggle to fit the cost of Willi Dungel into their budget at this point. Bernie had therefore agreed to pay the bills, and that Westfield would repay the cost over the coming season. No doubt, Sid thought, with interest of fifty percent
knowing his friend Bernie. He therefore made the arrangements to send James to the Austrian clinic in a week's time.

Anton had been considering the problem of the hostages, and had come to the conclusion that for the sake of his investigation he would allow them to continue to be held. One worry was that since the last message where they demanded Westfield attend the Barcelona test no other word had been heard. He had spoken to John Bennet on a number of occasions since, and he seemed to be coping well with strain. But know he needed to speak openly with John, this could only be done face to face, he therefore made arrangements to visit him at his Westfield headquarters. In fact that had been to only place he had been able to contact him. He seemed to be spending twenty four hours a day there.

For the last two weeks John had worked like a demon, he had not gone home at all during that period. What sleep he managed get, he took by using the settee in his office. Gerry had made arrangements with British Telecom to have any calls to Johns house re-routed to his office, just in case the kidnappers tried to contact John. None had come through though since the last one.

The cars were making progress, new steering columns and assemblies had been constructed, Gerry had taken the opportunity to complete a re-design of the whole assembly, and not just the column. This would allow the team to alter the steering lock quicker than on the old design. The steering lock needed to be adjusted for certain circuits, Monaco being one of them where the corners were tighter than most.

The problems wasn't with the chassis's, in fact the team responsible for the chassis build had completed all three by this time, and had started the layup procedure for a forth tub.

The problems lay in the engine build section. All the metallic components had been completed, most of these items had been subcontracted out to small engineering companies around West

Yorkshire. The problem was to do with the carbon fibre engine and gearbox casing's. Up to date the team hadn't experienced any difficulty with pressure integrity, but the last batches had all failed to hold the required pressure without showing a leakage, it was only small, point zero nine millibars per minute of leakage, but it was enough to scrap the cases and have to re-lay up further batches.

It had been Dave Brian who was now Janice's race engineer who had produced the first set of casings. The responsibility for the last set had been Chris Watts, Gerry's brother who had produced the last lot. Dave had watched Chris lay-up the first of the replacement blocks, and had noticed that whilst Chris was as meticulous as he was in the procedure, he did change one action in the process. It was that small change that had caused the problems. Once shown, the next block out of the chamber passed the tests. Chris was back on track, and the team were back in with a chance.

When Anton Abonovicz arrived at Westfield's headquarters, he found John resting in his office, even though it was midday. John had been up most of the night assisting with an engine build

"Good to see you John." He started. "I needed to speak to you face to face, because firstly I feel I needed to explain a few facts, and secondly we need to agree a course of action."

"Fine." John said wearily. *"I* would like Gerry to sit in as well, he's up to speed on everything. Coffee while we wait ?" John said walking over to the desk. "Anne will you find Gerry and ask him to come in please." He said into his intercom.

Gerry arrived *a* few minutes later, and poured himself a coffee before sitting down next to John, and opposite Anton.

"Ok Anton fire away." John said.

"First let me explain who I am, and who I represent. I work out of Genoa, but I don't work for the Italian Police. I am a special investigator for a Brussels based organisation, reporting to the European Parliament on international crime. We have been recently investigating crime, or should I say a form of crime that falls into the smuggling category for some time. In fact we narrowed it down to one man in particular, a Mr. Bettoni."

"So if you know who why haven't you arrested him ?" Gerry asked.

"Gerry knowing is one thing, proving in a court is another. Investigation is finding, and then providing sufficient evidence to successfully prosecute. If I allowed him to go to court without that evidence, and he wasn't found guilty in trial, then it would make my job to incriminate him impossible. So, last year Bettoni managed to recruit Gianni Lorenzo, who you both know worked for Ferrari. He made it look as if it was he that had recruited Bettoni as an advisor to Ferrari. Through Lorenzo they started a small operation in bringing contraband into Europe, using the Ferrari transporters."

"Contraband, you mean drugs?" John asked.

"No, drugs can be found far too easily by customs, and these days in order to make the shipment worth while the amount has to be high. A transporter whilst big cannot carry sufficient. No the contraband is Diamonds. Anyway things went wrong for Bettoni, as you know Lorenzo was killed earlier this year. Unfortunately for Bettoni, Lorenzo also had a small sideline in industrial espionage. It was through this that he managed to get himself killed, by one of the men he bought information off. That was where Fran became involved."

"You say Fran, what about Vanessa?" John asked I notice at no point have you mentioned her."

"OK, Vanessa works for me." Anton said.

"What, she works for Westfield." Gerry said quickly.

"No, she is a special services investigator seconded to work for me. Working for Westfield is a cover. Because Bettoni had hit upon using the Grand Prix circus to move Diamonds produced in Russia and other smaller third world countries into Europe, either to Amsterdam or London. Then I needed to have someone on the inside. The problem was that all the established teams wouldn't take on an outsider. Your team had a more open view, you came along just at the right time. Vanessa took up office, and she did a good job for you, without knowledge of the Grand Prix game. It would have also enabled her to gather evidence over the next year, sufficient to incriminate those involved. Unfortunately for me she also came across Lorenzo's sideline, and took it upon herself to follow that up. Her cover is now blown as far as this investigation is concerned, yes she is still captive, and will still have use's."

John and Gerry looked at each other shocked by what they had heard so far. "I never knew." John said.

"That was the idea." Anton replied. "Right what do we do. First let me tell you I know where they are right know. In fact the building where your wife is being held is under surveillance. I believe that there are four men guarding them."

"So why don't you storm the place and release the girls ?" John said hopefully.

"No, problem is I don't know where in the building they are being held. We can only watch the place from a distance. The risk would be too high. Vanessa is one thing, she can look after herself. Your wife is far more vulnerable. No I think the best plan is to let things continue." John was about to interrupt with a protest, when Anton put his hand up and continued. "No wait hear me out John please. They want you to go the Barcelona. That in my mind is because they or one of them will be there. I don't believe they will bring your wife along." Anton said in order to stop John building his expectations. "They will make contact with you, and try to recruit you to take over from Lorenzo. Barcelona is within the Union, so I think that will only be a test. It will be the Australian Grand Prix where the main shipment will be brought back from."

"Question." Gerry said. "Why not just sell them in Australia ?" "The sale of Diamonds worldwide is controlled by the DeBeers organisation. There are two major sale's one in Amsterdam and one in London. The amount of stones for sale at any one time is strictly controlled. This control keeps the price high. Therefore you could say DeBeers are price fixing, this could be true. But there are other more unofficial sales outside the DeBeers sale house's. These tend to be low grade stones. By bringing in specially selected stones produced outside DeBeers, and selling them within the confines of DeBeers pricing, then this allows the importer to gain a much higher price for his shipment."

"What would jibe worth ?" John asked.

"Well a typical shipment would bring in about Ten million Dollars. That would represent a profit of about five million."

"Shit that's the sort of fund raising we could do with." Gerry said gleefully.

"True, but not legally." Anton replied.

"So let me get this straight." John Said "You want us to wait until Australia, next March before we stand a chance of releasing

Fran." "Yes. As things currently stand" Anton said simply.

Chapter 34.

As the last transporter was nearing completion for packing before the long journey to Barcelona, the final nail went into the last packing crate containing the last engine. The team had successfully completed the re-build program. It would take four days for the transporters to make the long journey to Barcelona in Spain. The convoy would consist of two car transporters and the control vehicle, with six drivers. The longest part of the journey however would be by ferry across the Bay of Biscay to northern Spain. The rest of the team would follow in three days. They would fly direct to Barcelona and then drive to the circuit.

The news from Austria on James was mixed, he had made progress, but was finding the work hard. Willi Dungel was well known throughout the racing world for being a hard task master. The program of exercises was designed to build up James's fitness and stamina, to a level beyond that, that he had prior to the accident.

During the recovery phase Janice had spoken to James almost every day. She had not however seen or spoken to his mother since the meeting in Marseille. Janice could now well understand why James had been the way he was. It seemed that away from the track at least the two of them could be on a more friendly term.

Once the transporters had left the factory John could once again relax. He went home for the first time in weeks, but he found the house had changed. It didn't feel like home, he knew Anne had kept popping in to make sure all was well, and to dust for him, but it just felt empty. It was as if it's spirit had left with Fran. For the first time in weeks he missed her.

In France the two women had settled down to life in captivity. Time passed slowly, but Vanessa had managed to get some comforts out of their captives. She wouldn't tell Fran what the cost had been, but on occasions her shower's had taken longer than normal, and Vanessa seemed to be more subdued following those occasions. Fran could well guess what the cost was, she had to admire Vanessa her spirit, for she knew that there would be no way those men would touch her.

They had some drawing materials, the only stipulation was that at no time must they thaw their captives. Periodically they would both be removed from their room together, and it would be checked. They were also given paper to allow them to write. Both found this to be difficult however. Shower time hadn't altered, the only change was that on some occasions it would be Jean-Paul and on other Jacques would take his turn.

Then one day the door opened and Jacques said to Fran. "Your to come with me." She stood to follow when Vanessa said. "Why."

"You keep your nose out."

Come, now." He said, and roughly grabbed Fran to ensure she left the room with him.

She was taken down the corridor, and past the shower room. A door opened at the end of the corridor, suddenly she felt frightened. They've had enough of Vee they want me now, she thought. Jean-Paul stood leering at her in the doorway, as she got within arm's length he grabbed her and pulled into the room.

It was a sifting room, obviously the room where they spent most of their time judging by the state. The only comforting part about the room was the roaring fire in the grate, it seemed to give the whole room a calming atmosphere.

Suddenly a voice from a person unseen by Fran said. "Mrs. Bennet, I hope these two have seen to your needs." She looked round and saw Bettoni standing close to the door she had just entered the room by.

"No." She said, suddenly feeling brave. "I'm not with my husband. When will we be released ?"

"Well that all depends my dear." He said. "But first I would like you to pass a message onto your husband. You will sit in that chair." He pointed to an armchair by the fire. "You will then look at that video camera, and tell him you are well, and that we are looking after you. You can also add just how much you miss him. I will then be taking that tape with me on a little excursion."

"And if I don't ?"

"Well then, Jean-Paul will bring your friend in here, and well, you won't like what he will do to her, while you watch, and I film of course. I think that would have a similar effect on your husband." He said menacingly. Then he asked. "What's it to be, you do realise that it will make Jean-Paul's day don't you if you won't co-operate."

"I'll do it." She said moving to the chair.

In all it only took a few minutes to make the tape.

Once complete she was escorted back to the room. "What happened ?" Vanessa asked once they were on their own again.

"They filmed me talking as if to John." She replied. "The problem was if I didn't do what they wanted they threatened to film you being assaulted by Jean-Paul."

"Yes I've been afraid of that, all they really want me for is to get at you. I'm of no other value to them."

"*Is* it because of what you told me before."

"Yes, in fact as far *as* they're concerned I would be better out of the way."

The Westfield group arrived at the Barcelona circuit the day before the test session was scheduled to commence. John first had to go to the race control building to sign in on behalf of his team. There he was allocated a garage space, and given a rundown of all the regulations that would govern the test. Since this was an organised session, and not a private test, as the team had been used to so far, they had to abide by the circuit managers rules. All of these were also the rules laid down by the FIA.

The cars were allocated test times when they would be allowed out onto the circuit. They were allowed to run as many laps as they wished during those times. Unlike before there would be other cars running during their allocated time, therefore Janice would have her first taste of driving a Formula One car with other cars of a different design using the same road. Providing all went well this would help the team to gauge their cars and drivers performance against what was to be the future competition. Some of the other transporters had already arrived, these included, Jordan, Arrows, and McLaren, others were expected to attend later.

It was late into the afternoon when the Westfield convoy arrived, a spectacular sight it was for the guys stood waiting. The giant vehicles all with their sky blue and cloud effect liveries, driving down the access road to rear of the pits in a cloud of dust. They were late in arriving, this had been caused by a puncture on the second transporter, after they had left the ferry at Santander. For the next four hours the mechanics were busy off loading all the equipment, and preparing the garage space. Once completed they were allowed the night off to relax before the work started in earnest the following morning.

John was sat in his hotel room watching CNN news when his mobile phone rang. "Bennet." he answered.

"It's been a long time Bennet." The voice came back. "I want to you to drive to El Masnou along the coast towards the French Border. In a View area just before the town you will see a Winnibago RV stop along side it. Be there in forty minutes." The caller then broke the connection. John sat listening to the call tone for a few seconds before he dialed Anton's number. "He's been in touch." John said once Anton had answered.

"What instructions ?"

"I've to drive to El Masnou go to a trailer and wait further instructions. I need to be there in forty minutes."

"You'd better get moving then." Anton said. "Call me later with the results."

John made the journey in just under the time stipulated, standing outside the trailer there was a lone figure. In his hand he had a small radio transceiver. Unknown seen by John he had passed an accomplice of the figure standing by the trailer a few miles down the road. He had positioned himself to ensure that John had travelled alone, and that he hadn't been followed.

As john pulled up the figure walked forward. "Nice to see you Mr. Bennet." John immediately recognised the voice to be that of Bettoni. His facial expression was a natural extension of his inner feelings, concern for the well being of his wife, but also the hatred for the man who was the cause of all his and her torment.

"Can't say the same myself." John answered angrily.

"Now, please don't lets fall out, I have a little proposition for you, but first I would like you to come inside, and watch a short video. I'm sure it will interest you."

John got out of his car and followed Bettoni inside the trailer. He knew it was a risk, but didn't have any option if he wanted to see Fran again. He had half hoped that they would have Fran inside the trailer, but he now knew they had only brought a video along.

He watched the tape with sadness, at the end even though John was well known for not being emotional, he did have tears in his eyes. Bettoni knew then that John would go along with anything he proposed.

"It's a moving thing, isn't it seeing someone you've missed for a long time on a film." Bettoni said to John.

"You bastard." John replied as his anger boiled over. John knew this was a mistake, he had fallen head long into the trap Bettoni had set, but he just couldn't help himself.

"Ok Bennet, lets get to business. I have a little test for you, fail to comply and you won't see her again, not even to bury her." Bettoni said menacingly. "I have a little shipment I want you to take back to England for me. It's not very big, I'm sure you will be able to hide it somewhere in one of your transporters. Once in England I want you to take it to this address in London." Bettoni handed over a slip of paper it had an address in Holborn written on it.

"First." John said, "When will I see my wife."

"When I'm satisfied that you will do the work without question." John then knew that it would be sometime before she would be released, even after completing this task he was sure there would be others. "When will I get the D,," John just stopped himself saying diamonds, and quickly recovered, "drugs ?" He asked.

"Who said the package will contain drugs." Bettoni asked quizzically.

"Well that's what bastards like you want to import isn't it." John replied trying to keep up the pretence.

"Not at all, whilst I would agree that some of my associates deal in them, I personally don't, the package will contain diamonds."

Again John could feel his anger rising, he didn't know whether it was because of Bettoni's high handed way of dismissing the drugs aspect. That the crime he was being asked to perform wasn't really a crime because it wasn't related to drugs. Or that it was just the fact that Bettoni had actually won, and John would carry out the duty for him. "Just fucking tell when." John replied. That wasn't really the question he had wanted to ask or they way he had wanted to ask it.

"Now, now Bennet, I'm the one in control, NOT YOU." Bettoni retorted back. "You will take delivery of the item tomorrow afternoon, one hour before the end of the test session. It will be delivered to you personally."

"What if we don't make it through customs, what will happen to Fran ?" John asked.

"You will make it through, I'm relying on your ingenuity to ensure that the items will be delivered."

"See you tomorrow." John said testing Bettoni.

"No I'm afraid not, someone else will give you the package."

Shit thought John, I'm sure Anton wanted to catch Bettoni in the act. This isn't good. Unfortunately for John he didn't have any choice at this stage. He just turned at left the trailer for his car. Unfortunately the look of disappointment flashed across Johns face, the change in his expression was only slight, and only lasted a moment, but it was enough. Bettoni had been studying Johns face throughout the meeting, he saw the change and then just as quickly he saw John catch himself. It was really the fact that John had realised that his expression had changed, that caused Bettoni for once to feel that he may not be completely in control.

On the drive back to the circuit he telephoned Anton, John had been right about Anton not being pleased about the drop off. He *also* expressed his own concerns about the possible outcomes of this test, there was no chance of Fran being released. In fact Anton had a worry that she wouldn't be released following the Australian Grand Prix either.

Chapter 35.

Anton arrived in Moustiers Ste-Marie late that night, he had called Pinon to ensure all the team would be available for a briefing. Anton felt that the time was now approaching for them to step up the level of surveillance, and to plan how to release the captives.

The change had come about really because Bettoni was ensuring that he would be keeping a low profile, and therefore could only be linked by association. That link would not be strong enough to incriminate him.

"Do you have any idea yet how many we are dealing with." Anton asked Pinon.

"As far as I can tell, four," Pinon replied, "there's Bettoni and Label of course, and we think that there are two of Label's men in there doing the guarding. We also think we have found where they are being kept. Let me draw you the layout as we see it." Pinon took out a piece of paper from the cars glove box, and sketched a rough schematic of the single storey house. "This is the room where they are kept," he said pointing to the room at the rear of the building. "This is the front room, you can see the smoke rising from its chimney know," he said pointing down the hill towards the farm. "We have occasionally seen movements down this corridor." He pointed to the access passage from the back room to the front room. "Here is a bathroom, we have seen the girls being moved from where they are locked up to here, never both together always singly with one of the guards."

"Very good," Anton said. "At the moment we know Bettoni is still in Spain, do you know where Label is ?"

"No, but I don't think he's in the farm." Pinon said.

"So tonight could be a good time to stage a rescue." Anton said to them.

"Well yes, if that's what you want." then one of the men said

"Shh, look there's a car approaching the farm."

They all watched the car's approach in silence. When it stopped in the yard to the front of the building they saw Label and Bettoni get out, along with a third person, none of those watching knew who he was.

"Shit," Anton said "That's fucked it for tonight. Still let's plan for Friday, that'll be when Bennet will be delivering the diamonds. Pinon arrange the watches until then, We'll meet on Thursday to finalise the plans." With that Anton got into his car and drove back to Marseille. He would wait for Bennet's call to confirm the arrival of the package.

The following morning practice was well underway. Unfortunately the Westfield team were having problems. Some were car related, but some were driver. Janice had had trouble getting into the groove since the start of testing yesterday. Dave thought the accident that had happened to James last month was still playing on her mind, and it was this that subconsciously was preventing her from reaching the full potential of the car. However that was yesterday, today the car was also misbehaving, she was driving the new number one car today. As with all new cars it was giving a number of minor errors, but in this sport these minor errors caused major problems on the track. At the moment the car was lapping some three seconds of the current pace. The pace today had been set Damon Hill in the Jordan They were still using last year's car at this stage, but no doubt had a number of items on board that were destined to be run on the new chassis. "Call her in for Christ's sake Dave." Gerry called out. "There's no point in her just circulating at that bloody pace."

"Janice, Box." Called Dave.
"Understood." Came the reply. Even with the distortion from the radio her voice sounded relieved to be coming in. whether that relief was from frustration at not being able to get the car running correctly, or just be coming of the track Dave didn't know. When he had more time he would sit down with Janice to discuss her problems. For now though the problems were more electro-mechanical in nature.

Shortly after he heard the pit lane warning klaxon sound. This was to warn those working in the pit lane that a car had entered and to beware. Dave looked down the pit lane and saw the unmistakable shape of the Westfield approaching. The mechanics were already on their way out of the garage to meet the car, and the wheel it back inside.

"Gerry, do you want to warm up number two, or shall we concentrate our efforts on this bugger." Dave asked.

"Stay on this, we know number two runs OK, we need to sort out all the bugs from this pig." Gerry replied over the radio "Ian where the hell are you." Gerry then said into his headset.

"Sorry boss," Came the reply "I'm on the crapper, must have picked up the Spanish shits."

"Put the porno book down and get out here." Gerry said back. The rest of the mechanics who had headsets on laughed. It was true though Ian was suffering, he had eaten on the water front the previous evening, and more than likely had eaten a bad oyster or something.

When he walked into the garage, looking almost white, he got a resounding cheer from the guys who were crowding around the car. "Can't even have a crap in private these days." He said tapping his head set. The mechanics had already plugged in the computer and were busy down loading all the run data.

Whilst Gerry and Dave were analysing that data, Ian would be able to run a full diagnostics on the cars systems.

It was well into the afternoon session before the team managed to get the car back out onto the track. They had managed to trace a couple of Gearbox sensors that were giving erroneous signals back to the main computer. Because the computer didn't understand what it was being told by those sensors, and they conflicted with signals from other sensors, the computer momentarily shut itself down, this caused a major miss fire, and in consequence a loss of power. Once the tyres were and brakes were up to temperature, and the technicians studying the telemetry were happy Dave gave the signal to Janice to put her foot down. "Hit it Janice." He said.

"Sorry." Came back the response. Hit it wasn't a normal request under the radio protocol. "Sorry Janice, clear for test four." Dave replied.

"Understood." Came her reply. Dave just turned to Gerry and shrugged his shoulders, as if to say 'bloody women.'

Janice realised that her performance hadn't been up to scratch so far over the last two days. She had been driving well within her own capabilities. One of the reasons was that this was a new chassis, although yesterday she had run the second car, and the performance hadn't been that much better. The other reason was that this was her first time behind the wheel since before James's accident at Paul-Ricard. She not only felt stale, but had also lost some of her confidence. This afternoons test would be her last chance before Australia, and therefore must improve.

    The car felt much better underneath her this time. She could feel the results of her inputs to the controls coming back through her bottom and spine, as the laps continued her confidence grew. By the time she had completed five laps at the quicker pace she had improved by two and a half seconds per lap. "This is better." Dave said to Gerry who had moved to his side on the pit wall. "Yes, much, but look at Hill." Gerry warned." The Jordan piloted by Hill had again set the fastest time of the session so far. "He's improved by a further point two of a second." His time had been set by running a warm-up lap, then a quick all out lap, then an in lap. This was the normal procedure all the drivers adopted at a Grand Prix.

    The qualification period was held on the Saturday afternoon for one hour. There the drivers would be allowed a maximum of twelve laps, and up to four sets of tyres. Therefore they would normally run four, three lap sessions. With the second of the three laps being the fastest. To

qualify for the grid you either had to post the fastest time of the session, or be within one hundred and seven percent of the fastest time In order for Janice to qualify she would have to be able to put in her fastest lap immediately, and not as it was know after she had completed five or six laps continually.

    Whilst the cars were running John had moved to the entrance to the circuit, well away from any officials concerned with the circuit. he looked at his watch, only a few more minutes to wait, he thought to himself. As the allotted time approached he heard the sound of a large motor cycle approaching the spot where he was standing.

    The rider could see John standing by the road side, he slowed his approach, and reached inside his black leather jacket.

    John saw the man's hand go into the jacket, and pull out a medium sized pouch. The motor cycle was slowing quite considerably by know and was very close, but John couldn't see the face of the rider. He had a full face helmet, similar to the type worn by the Formula one drivers. The visor was black which made it totally impossible for any on-looker to identify the face of the person behind it. The rider didn't stop the motor cycle, as he went passed John he simply tossed the pouch to him. Once he had thrown the pouch the rider opened the throttle of the bike, and with a howl the bike shot away from the scene and was quickly out of sight, but not hearing.

John caught the pouch simply, as he did he instinctively looked around to see if anybody else was around. The coast was completely clear. He estimated that the pouch weighed about one kilogram, and felt like a small bean bag. He loosened the draw string and peaked inside. There he saw a mass of gem stones all uncut, he assumed they were the diamonds. He had never actually seen any uncut diamonds before in his life. They had the appearance of irregular shaped pieces of glass that had been ground around in the ocean for some time. For a while he stood looking at the gems, it was amazing, he thought, the value and the trouble some people would go to for these bits of natural material, and to the problems that this bag had caused him and Fran so far.

He pulled the draw string tight to close the bag, and set off for the pits area. Once reaching the pit wall him signaled for Gerry to come over and join him. Together they walked through the garage and into one of the trailers. Once inside Gerry turned and made sure the door was secure, they didn't want any of the mechanics wandering in whilst they completed the next phase of their operation.

Gerry pulled down a spare seat base they had brought with them for this purpose. He also removed a large plastic bag, which was used to contain the foam used to made the inner seat shells whilst it was expanding. John had retrieved the two chemicals used to make the foam. Then he opened the pouch and poured the diamonds into the plastic bag. Gerry laid the bag into the seat outer shell, and spread the diamonds around the base. "Right who's arse is it to be ?" Gerry asked.

"Well I suppose it's mine that on the line, so it may as well be my imprint." John replied as he sat down into the shell. "Shit this bloody things hurt." He said as he put his full weight on the stones.

"Wont for long." Gerry said as he poured the two chemicals into the top of the bag. Once the containers were empty, he sealed the top of the bag. Within minutes of the liquids coming into contact of each other the chemical reaction started. As with any reaction products are given of, in this case one was heat, the other was a transformation off the liquids into a solid foam mass. The pressure generated lifted John of the stone, so that there was about an inch of foam between John's bottom and the seat outer shell. It took about ten minutes for the reaction to stop, once stopped John could stand up.

Gerry lifted the bag out of the shell and inspected the base. "Great," he said, "no sign of the stones anywhere."

"Won't they show up on anything " John asked.

"Yes, x-ray will detect something in the seat, but who's going to x-ray a seat shell." Gerry replied.

"Are you sure they can be got out again."

"I'm not that bothered really, that's their problem. But diamonds are the hardest thing known to man, apart from Eric's skull that is," joked Gerry, "all they'll have to do is grind the foam up to reveal the stones."

"Great get it stowed away, I want to set of back tonight. this has to be in London on Friday."

Chapter 36.

It was Friday Afternoon, the teams journey home had gone without a hitch. The diamonds molded into the seat base had passed a cursory view by the customs at the Plymouth Ferry terminal.

John at this time was driving into the London district of Holborn, an area once famous for its cabinet and instrument makers, he was looking for the address given to him by Bettoni. John had passed the address onto the Anton, who had informed his associates in London. They in turn had set up a surveillance team, in a building opposite Unknown to John there was also one of Anton's men following, he ensured he kept a suitable distance away, not because John would suspect that he may be followed, but to allow him to see if any of Bettoni's men were on lookout.

As John approached the door of the drop off address all eyes in the room were poised ready. One man had his finger lightly resting on the shutter release button on his camera. The door opened to John's knock, at the same time the camera mans finger pressed the shutter release, and the camera's auto wind powered up, he took eight shots in the next eight seconds.

Stood on the inside of the door was Bettoni. "Good to see you Bennet." He said, "come in quickly." He continued looking outside quickly. This gave the men watching a clear view. One of them picked up his mobile phone and pressed one of the memory buttons.

A mile away from the Farm outside Moustiers Ste-Marie Anton's phone softly burbled. "Yes," he said softly.

"Bettoni is here," the man on watch said. "Bennet has just delivered the package."

"Good, it's go for tonight." Anton replied, and pressed the end button to break the transmission.

"We're on tonight." The man said to his two other companions in the room in Holborn.

Whist the short discussion had been going on John had been led by Bettoni into a room at the back of the building on the ground floor. There was a single barred window looking out onto a rubbish strewn back yard. The small yard no bigger than fifteen feet square was surrounded by a seven foot brick wall. The wall was broken only by a single gate. The gate was made of heavy mild steel sheeting and securely locked by a heavy chain and pad lock. The top of the gate was protected by razor wire, this continued up and along the top of the wall. Protecting the yard from both intruders and prying eyes.

"This is what you want." John said holding the seat base out.
"Very good Bennet." Bettoni said looking at the molding. "But where are the diamonds."

"In the base." John said digging one of his fingers into the foam. He fucked out one of the diamonds. "See its soft, it'll grind back to powder easily, you came then recover your precious diamonds."

"Excellent, this is the reason I wanted to use a team like yourselves. Your all very resourceful." Bettoni said smiling, "now sit down and watch this." He said inserting another video into a player.

John watched horrified at the scene on the screen. He could see his wife being forced to watch whilst two of Bettoni's men systematically raped Vanessa.

The video had been made two days ago, following John's contact with Bettoni. That evening, along with the man Anton had seen arriving at the farm, they had taken both Fran and Vanessa out of their room, and once again took them into the larger front room of the farm. Whilst Jean-Paul had held Vanessa, Fran had been roughly pushed onto a wooden chair. She had then been roughly bound with her hands behind here to the chair. Bettoni took up a position immediately behind Fran, and menacingly said to her. "This is to be a lesson to both you and your husband." On Bettoni's signal the man started the video camera, and Jacques ripped the tee shirt away from Vee's body. Whilst Jean-Paul still held onto Vanessa, who was starting to put up a slight struggle, he roughly pulled her jeans down, stripping her naked.

He then removed his own trousers and with a grin forced Vanessa to the floor, where he forcefully entered her protesting body. Whilst he did his deed, Jean-Paul readied himself for action. He took over by forcing Vee onto her hands and knees and entered her body.

"Stop this." Fran shouted, struggling to free herself from her bounds. She couldn't watch as the two captors continued to force themselves into Vee's body. "Watch." Bettoni said as Fran looked away. The word from Bettoni was a signal for the two men to intensify the attack. They forced Vee onto her side, and whilst one entered Vee's sex and pumped away at her the other forced his penis into her anus, and pounded away. As he entered her Vee let out a piercing scream of pain. "That's the price for not watching." Bettoni said to Fran. After about ten minutes, which had seemed like an eternity the punishment stopped. Vee had passed out from the pain and defilement of the attack on her person. Bettoni said half to Fran, and half to the camera. "That is a lesson, if you fail to co-operate then Mrs. Bennet will be next."

Following the attack they had carried the naked and unconscious body of Vee back to the room. Fran had been pushed along behind. They had dumped the battered and bleeding body onto the mattress. Once the door had been locked Fran busied herself tending to Vee. She tried to wash away the sickly secretions that had been left by the two animals. Fran was worried about the amount of blood that Vee was losing from her anus, but all she could do was to wash the affected areas.

"You bastard." John said as the video finished. "You set of complete bastards."

"That as I said is a lesson to you Bennet. If I don't get your co-operation, then I cannot guarantee the safety of that pretty wife of yours." Bettoni replied. He then said a few minutes later, once his words had, had chance to sink in "Now you will go to Australia, once there someone will make contact with you. They will pass you a number of packages, far more than we gave you as a test. You will then on your return bring then to another address. The address will be given to you with the packages. Only then will we consider releasing your wife."

At that John was shown to the door, he left the building, and in shock drove away from the area. As he started to drive up the MI back to his Wakefield base his mobile phone rang. "Bennet." He said towards the roof mounted microphone.

"John can you talk." It was Anton.

"Yes I'm alone." John replied.

"I know you delivered the package, what did he say."

John sobbed as he described the meeting, he could hardly find the words to describe the scenes he had been forced to witness. When he had finished Anton said. "Don't worry, this has gone on long enough, I'll be in touch tomorrow." At that Anton broke the connection.

In France Anton called his troops together to go through the forth coming nights activities. To help bolster his men's aggression he told briefly them on the rape of Vanessa. All the men at the scene had at sometime been on a team with Vanessa, and all were fond of her. He planned to strike the farm house and the address in London simultaneously at three am the following morning, once the plan had been gone through, and each member of the team was comfortable with their own part, and where they would be striking he shut down the surveillance operation. Whilst keeping watch on the building would be useful, he decided that it was more important for his men to rest, and to prepare themselves mentally for the task ahead.

In London the team leader was also conducting a briefing session. Here the problem was different, they needed to be sure that Bettoni didn't leave the premises before the strike, and so the watch remained on station. The team didn't have the problem of hostages either. Anybody in the building would be identified as hostile.

Just before the strike time Anton moved his men into position. He along with two others would strike through the front of the building, and two others would take out the back door and move through from that direction. Each team carried with them a large steel ram which when handled by two men was capable at one swing of bursting most doors open. They were all armed with submachine pistols, and thunder flash grenades.

As the seconds ticked by each of the men settled down into their own thoughts. Each of them was well aware that if this went wrong, not only would it be their deaths but also they would have signed the death sentence of the two women held hostage. They had already been made well aware of the levels of brutality that these men were capable off. Failure therefore wasn't an option. They each said a silent prayer to their own particular God for the success of the mission, and for their own survival.

Both teams swept forward precisely at the same time, one in France and one in London. At the farm in Moustiers Ste-Marie the front and rear doors to the farm building burst in on the very first swing of the rams. Anton immediately tossed in a grenade. The team at the rear of the building did the same but a second latter. Almost instantly the grenades exploded, it was as if the crash from the doors busting open just increased without a pause. These particular grenades are not designed to inflict death and destruction, they are used to create noise, light and then thick smoke to disorientate the unaware. If however they were to explode right next to any one unfortunate enough to be in close proximity, then the explosion would be enough to injure.

Jean-Paul was asleep at his post next to the rear door of the building when the door bust open, the noise reached through his sleep wrecked brain. As he stirred trying to bring himself back to consciousness there was an ear shattering explosion. His mind registered the start of the noise, and the flash from the grenade. He thankfully never registered another thing. The grenade exploded in mid flight about three inches away from his right ear. The shock wave and the small fragments of shrapnel reduced his skull and brain to a bloody pulp instantly.

Jacques had been sleeping in the front room of the farm. He was awakened by the explosions took and a few seconds to come to his senses, those seconds cost him his life. As he raised himself to a standing position the door to the room burst open, and one of the detectives came tumbling through in a controlled dive, as he somersaulted across the floor the automatic weapons in both hands sprayed a lethal mass of lead around the room. The direction and tumbling effect of his dive had been carefully rehearsed in hours of training exercises to ensure that the spray of bullets would cover the maximum area.

The hail of lead cut Jacques down before he knew what hit him, a number of the bullets struck him in the chest rising to his neck and head. The force of the hail of lead hitting him pushed him in a death dance towards the wall.

Label had also been asleep in the room, he came to his senses far quicker than Jacques, instead of standing groggily as Jacques had, he realised they were under attack and stayed low. One of the bullets hit him in the shoulder, as he crouched down feeling for his weapon. Blood from Jacques sprayed out across his face and hands making his hands slippy. His hand touched his gun which was laying on the floor by the chair he slept in. He tightened his grip on the weapon and started to raise it.

The first detectives roll had finished, with the completion of the roll he also stopped firing. Label turning towards the position of the detectives started to fire. The combination of Jacques blood and his own on his hands meant that he couldn't grip the weapon fully. The recoil from his first firing burst caused the weapon to slip from his hands. The hail of bullets flew over the detectives head by some two feet. Instinctively he turned towards the flash from the discharging weapon and fired a short burst ensuring that the burst covered a sweep right to left. The hail cut across the crouching Label at chest height, whilst none of the bullets was a killing shot, the combination ensured that Label didn't live long enough to pick up his weapon and discharge it again.

The second detective moved through the house to meet up with his colleagues coming in through the rear entrance. Anton meanwhile had gone straight for the room where Fran and Vanessa were been held.

When the initial crash and explosion had occurred Vanessa had immediately realised what was happening. Fran started to wake, but not as fast as Vee, "stay down." Vee said to her. "It looks as if Anton has finally arrived." She couldn't keep the quake out of her voice though. Vanessa realised that if it was Anton then he must be desperate to free them, and she was well aware of what his failure would mean for them. "What ever happens do not get up Fran." Vanessa warned. The noise of the guns discharging in the house was deafening, the noise seemed to reverberate around the room. As Anton opened the door to their room Vanessa could feel Fran tense, as if she was waiting for the hail of lead to hit her frail body.

"Vee, it's Anton," a voice called out.
"Anton, we're here alone." Vanessa called back.
Shortly after the last of the firing the lights came on, before the attack one of the men had disabled the power to the farm. Anton found Fran laid flat on the mattress face down, with Vanessa laying with a blanket to cover her nakedness in a similar position next to her. Since the attack on her they had not replaced the clothing that had been ripped from her body. Not caring that she was naked, and that she was still sore from the punishment she had taken she ran to Anton's open arms. Fran got up more slowly, picking up the blanket as she went, she also went across to Anton, and placed the blanket around Vanessa's shoulders.

Shortly after the reunion Anton received a call from his colleagues in London, they had also mounted a successful raid. Bettoni was the only man in the building, he had managed to loose of a single shot before being gunned down. One of the detectives had been slightly wounded by the bullet as it scrapped past his shoulder. The man following him up had ensured that Bettoni would never come to trial for his crimes. In the cleaning up process they had found both the diamonds and the tape of the containing the filmed rape of Vanessa. This could be useful if Anton was ever brought to task by his superiors to account for the actions he had authorised.

The following morning Anton placed a call to Westfield. "John, good morning, I have someone here who would like to speak to you." He said. He then passed the phone over to Fran.

"John," she croaked "I love you."

"Fran, is it true." He replied, "I love you too." He couldn't say anymore.

"John, it's Anton, We're about to catch a flight to Yeadon. See you in a couple of hours."

Epilogue.

It had been two and a half months since the home coming, John had held Fran in his aims for what seemed like hours. Vanessa had joined in after allowing the couple a few minutes on their own. As soon as they had cleared the airport John took Vanessa to Methley Park Hospital, where he had arranged for a private consultant friend to check Vanessa over following her ordeal Apart from sever bruising to her groin, and a small split in her rectal wall she couldn't find much wrong. However it was too soon after the attack to test for any unwanted extensions to her body. That would have to wait a few more weeks, and it was too late to administer a morning after pill. Given time and the strength of her character she was sure she would make a full recovery.

Over the next few weeks following conversations with John and Anton, Vanessa had decided that it was time for her to settle down, and leave the service. She would continue to work for John at Westfield, whist her work there so far had been more of a sideline, it would prove to be just as exciting as her work for the agency.

It was now only a matter of a days before the start of the 1999 Grand Prix season. James was now fully recovered from his accident, he had returned from Willie Dungel in Austria fitter than he had ever been. Whilst he had not had the opportunity to drive the Westfield since the accident he had been test driving a saloon car. Those test's had gone well, and mentally he hadn't suffered from the ordeal.

Janice had been more than pleased to see James return to the fold. They had secretly fallen in love during his recuperation. She had been out to Austria on a couple of occasions, making sure that Willie Dungel or any of the Westfield people knew of the meetings.

The cars and all the teams equipment had been loaded onto the giant cargo planes for the long journey to Australia. Only the transporter drivers flew with the precious cargo. The rest of the team followed on in slightly more comfort aboard scheduled flights to the far of land.

Since they had landed time had flown by. The first job the mechanics had to do was to paint the garage floors with fresh paint. This strange as it seems is a job that is done before the start of every Grand Prix. It does serve two purposes, one to make the floor look clean and tidy for any visiting guest's. It also ensures that it is clean, dust is one of the enemies of the Grand Prix car. They had to erect all the advertising banners and wall coverings around the garage. All the electronic equipment had to be reassembled and checked, the pit area outside the garage had to be prepared. Instead of painting, they tended to rough the area up. This was to allow the cars more grip. Essential when the car was coming into the area for one of the required pit stops, for stopping and reaccelerating back out onto the circuit. Westfield due the telemetry system also had to ensure that the communications dish and reflector was in place.

Only after all that work could the cars be worked on. The Thursday night saw the mechanics preparing the cars for the free practice the following morning. they would then have to be stripped, checked and re-built again for a further session in the afternoon. The same would also be true on the Saturday. The difference was that on Saturday afternoon it was qualification time.

Qualification started quietly, Westfield being one of the new kids on the block went out early in the session. As with everything else there was a number reasons why they did this. One could say that it was because both the Westfield drivers were new to the circuit, and therefore wanted to get in a banker lap before the big boys came out to play. The truth lay more towards because they were the only cars on the track, the worlds television cameras only had Westfield to put onto their screens. That ensured that Westfield's sponsors whose names were emblazoned across the car got maximum coverage, for when the big boys came out then it would be them that got all the coverage. The risk was that one of the drivers might throw the car of the tarmac and into one of the gravel traps around the edge of the track.

As it was neither did, in fact James managed to put in a lap that in the end would ensure that Westfield got noticed.

By the end of the session both the Westfield cars managed to qualify. James had improved his initial time on his third run out the four he was allowed. He would start from the third row, in grid position six. Janice made a slower start to her campaign and ran for much of the session in twentieth position, but inside the qualification time. Her forth run though was her best. Dave managed to time her exit from the pit so that her flying lap was completed on a clear track, luckily for her the sun was also blotted out by a cloud. This allowed the track surface to cool for just a few minutes, by only four degrees. This combination allowed her to improve her position from twentieth up to tenth. Westfield had managed it. They had built a new team, and qualified for the premier motor racing formula in the world.

Sunday was race day after the session in the morning, called the morning warm up. The cars are prepared for the long race ahead in the afternoon. Half an hour before the start the pit lane is opened. This allows the cars out onto the track. James and Janice left the pit in line astern formation, whilst on the drive around the circuit they weren't allowed to race they could and did drive the cars quickly. This was the only real time the drivers got to test the cars prior to the start.

The following twenty five minutes felt as though they were taking forever. The grid is full of people, most not associated with the teams, but celebrities invited by the organisers or the F1A.

All the drivers during this time struggled to find a quiet area to concentrate their individual thoughts on the race ahead. Some managed to find a spot by the pit wall, others would be quite happy giving interviews to the mass of television crews around the grid.

Janice did her usual, she got her helmet on early and sat in the car strapped in ready. She had more than her fair share of attention around her that afternoon, it was to be expected, she was one of only three females to ever make it to the starting grind of a Grand Prix.

Time ticked down slowly, with five minutes to go the grid cleared of all the on looker's as if by magic. This left the mechanics to remove the tyre warmers and lower the cars to the track surface. With one minute to go John and Gerry wished the two drivers good luck, and left the grid for the pit wall. Gerry however didn't take up his position immediately, instead he disappeared into the garage. Whilst they were leaving the track the mechanics started the cars engines.

The noise of twenty two formula one cars even ticking over on the grid is tremendous. The with a sudden increase in noise the cars leave the grid for the parade lap. They will circulate the track once, and take up their grid position ready for the start. Once all the cars had left the grid, the mechanics from all the teams quickly left the track and took up their safe positions in the garages alongside the pit lane.

Inside the Westfield Garage along with some guest's Fran stood with Vanessa, and Anne the receptionist. Because this was to be the first Grand Prix ever for the Westfield team John had agreed that all the employees should be at the race. Gerry had asked if Anne could join the other ladies in the garage instead of with the other team members in the stands. Fran had recovered well following her ordeal as a hostage, Vanessa true to form had managed to brush of some off the memories, however the growing lump in her belly would ensure that she would never be able to forget the ordeal fully. She had elected to keep the growing baby, even though she was unsure of who the father was.

As the cars took up their positions ready for the start, Gerry appeared in the garage. Outside the noise level increased as the red starting lights came on in sequence. Gerry went down on one knee in front of Anne and said "Anne will you marry me." This simple question went out over the Westfield radio system, the only two who didn't hear were the drivers, who both were concentrating on the lights. Everyone else in the pits and on the pit wall turned to look in amazement. At that instant the five red lights went out, and with a roar all twenty two cars roared down the track towards the first corner.

The End

Other titles by the Author

The Extinguisher

To Follow Soon

The Extinguisher (Revenge)

Made in the USA
Charleston, SC
03 March 2015